ALEX WAGNER

MURDER
AT THE LIMES

Murder in Antiquity

Under the reign of Emperor Hadrian (117—138 AD), the power of the Roman Empire reaches to the borders of the known world, and even the most remote provinces enjoy unprecedented peace and prosperity.

On the well-fortified northern border of the Empire, the Limes, lies the future metropolis of Vienna—at this point no more than a legionary camp, flanked by two insignificant civilian settlements. The local Celtic-Germanic population and the settled Roman citizens call it by the same name: Vindobona.

But all is not as it should be in this remote corner of the Empire...

I

The Roman soldiers arrived at the third hour after sunrise, a time when I was still chasing innocent dreams in bed on this midsummer day. Instead of gazing into the night-black eyes of Layla, my favorite slave, who usually woke me with tender kisses, I was rudely roused from sleep by Darius, my trade assistant.

"A Tribune of the legion wishes to speak to you, Thanar," he announced, and these words instantly roused me from my sleepiness.

Darius was a capable and clever fellow. When he said *Tribune*, he meant *Tribune*. Not an ordinary legionary or one of the numerous administrative officials of the legionary camp who occasionally bought goods from me, but one of the highest-ranking officers in the Roman army.

In one leap I was out of bed, slipped into the tunic and trousers that Darius was already holding out to me, and hurried into the atrium.

The sight that met me there put me on high alert. It was Tribune Titus Granius Marcellus who was waiting for me, a young Roman knight who had taken office in the legionary camp of Vindobona only a few weeks ago. Like many other sons of Roman nobles, he was probably seeking to earn his first political laurels as an officer in the frontier legions. This was common practice. The young knights usually stayed for two or three years and then turned to higher tasks in Rome or in the provincial administration.

I had not yet met Marcellus in person, but of course in our sleepy corner of the province, people eagerly gossiped about every new addition to the highest ranks of the legion, and so I had already heard quite a bit about the young Tribune. As it seemed, he was not one of those spoiled knights' sons who thought to spend their time in Vindobona merely indulging in idleness, but rather took his position very seriously. Allegedly, he even interfered in matters that did not necessarily fall within his jurisdiction. It meant something when a man earned such a reputation within a scant few weeks.

What alarmed me most when I entered my atrium was not just how animatedly Marcellus was chatting with my slave Layla. Nothing unusual about that. Every man wanted to chat with Layla, and more than that if she'd let them. Layla was a rare beauty and a smart and educated conversationalist to boot. She was from Nubia, the fabled kingdom south of Egypt. With her black eyes and hair and skin as dark as ebony, she looked like a daughter of the night goddess.

Tribune Marcellus might be Layla's age, not much more than twenty, and he was a decidedly good-looking man. You had to give him that much. As he spoke, his eyes wandered tirelessly over Layla's face and over her slender, tall figure. I couldn't deny that it gave me a twinge of jealousy.

However, what the Tribune had just said to Layla when I joined them was even more alarming than his obvious enthusiasm for my favorite slave. "When did your master return home last night?" I heard him ask, in a pleasant chit-chat tone, but certainly not to make casual conversation.

I did not wait to see how Layla would answer this question but rather joined the conversation myself. My activities last night were a highly sensitive matter. Why was the Tribune interested in my whereabouts, of all things? Had I been watched? Or even betrayed?

Out of the corner of my eye, I could make out a good dozen heavily armed legionaries in front of the open gate of my house. Not the usual entourage when a Roman officer wanted to pay a mere courtesy visit to a Germanic neighbor. Apart from that, I was nowhere near significant enough to warrant a Tribune's visit. As far as that was concerned, I was under no illusions.

My brother—and our father before him—happened to be the local chieftain of the area that lay north of the Danubius River, thus directly bordering the Roman Empire. Everyone in Vindobona knew that, but it was equally well known that I was considered the black sheep of the family; a disgrace, if my brother had his way. I was certainly not worthy of a visit from a Roman noble. What, by all the gods, was going on here?

I put on the friendliest smile I could muster. "Welcome to my humble home, Tribune Marcellus. To what do I owe the honor of your visit?"

Marcellus returned my greeting and praised the elegance of my estate with an expansive hand gesture that included Layla. At the same time, he scrutinized me just as thoroughly as he had just done with my slave. However, without the charismatic smile.

I read astonishment in his large, dark eyes. Obviously, neither my home nor I myself came close to what he had expected from a trip to the Barbaricum, the land of the savages.

As far as my house was concerned, I had taken as my model the Villae Rusticae, the Roman country estates that had, over the last decades, literally sprang up everywhere south of the Danubius, and I had also been inspired by one or the other architectural feature that I had come across on my trade trips. My home had a Roman atrium for example, decorated with slender columns and a marble water basin, with bronze statues and murals, and an elaborate floor mosaic, on which the Tribune and I were facing each other at that very moment.

In my brother's eyes, this was treason against our people, and I was a pathetic bootlicker, courting the favor of the Romans. Our mortal enemies, in his eyes.

This was an attitude I could not share. I had no particular liking for the Romans, per se. I simply admired their achievements, their tight military organization, the comforts of their culture, and their houses, airy and bright in summer and comfortably heated in winter.

Moreover, I myself probably did not match the typical image of the wild barbarian from the north. Undoubtably Tribune Marcellus—like so many of his compatriots—had this prejudice in the back of his mind when thinking of Germanic people. Even in our enlightened times, when we were no longer the feared enemy but rather neighbors and business partners of the Romans, maintaining the best diplomatic and economic relations, this image of my people persisted as if it had been carved in stone.

The gods had blessed me with that hunky physique that was generally attributed to us barbarians, so that I towered over the Tribune in height, although Marcellus was quite tall for a Roman. And his shoulders were as broad as mine. Moreover, he was more handsome than I was. Why did I notice that? Perhaps because Layla was still standing next to us, silent and immobile, as if she belonged to the decoration of the atrium, while her eyes were incessantly examining the young Roman nobleman.

But apart from my build, I might well have passed for a 'civilized' Roman. I wore my hair short and well-coiffed, and for some months even the kind of beard that Emperor Hadrianus himself had made the latest fashion in the Empire. I did this, too, not because I disdained my own people, but simply because the beard made my otherwise narrow face look a little fuller. At least that was what Layla thought.

Without indulging in further polite chit-chat, the Tribune now started to ask me similar strange questions as he had done with Layla earlier: Where had I spent the previous night and when had I come home?

This was information that I could not give him for the life of me.

I briefly considered claiming that I had just returned this morning from one of my business trips. But what if Layla had already stated something to the contrary? She would never have said anything that would get me into trouble, but I couldn't expect her to lie to a Roman Tribune for my sake either.

So I decided to ask a counter question. Not exactly polite, but still better than talking my head off right away. I put on a reverent smile. "Why is a Tribune of the glorious Legio X Gemina interested in the nocturnal activities of an insignificant barbarian?"

To praise the legion based in Vindobona was never wrong and no mere flattery. Even Iulius Caesar had called the tenth legion, which had now been stationed south of the Danubius for many years to secure the imperial border, his favorite.

Something glowed in the Tribune's dark eyes, although his expression otherwise remained unmoved.

Eternal optimist that I was, I interpreted it as a success of my flattery, perhaps even as a spark of recognition for my boldness. Besides, Marcellus had probably come to the conclusion that he would not have an easy time with me. Whatever he actually intended with his visit to my house. And with his strange questions.

"We recovered a dead man in your harbor this morning, Thanar," the Tribune said bluntly, while I was still basking in the glow of my supposed success.

II

Layla let out a sharp cry. More a sound of astonishment than of fear, I was sure, because my beautiful Nubian was generally not prone to fearfulness.

The Tribune smiled mildly at her, as if to apologize for the fright he had given her. He showed the very best manners—toward Layla.

Turning to me again, he continued in a harsh tone: "The dead man is Lucius Pompeius Falco, our Primus Pilus. He was found at dawn by a patrol boat. Not ten feet from your landing stage. With a barbarian axe in his chest."

Now it was I who let out a sound of horror. The Primus Pilus was the highest-ranking centurion in the Roman legion, and Falco was considered a living legend in Vindobona. He was in his last year of service and had accumulated military awards and honors like no other in his long career.

A murdered officer. In *my* harbor. Killed with a *barbarian axe*. With one blow, I realized what the Tribune wanted from me. Why he had come to my house with a dozen well-armed legionaries. He was not interested in my secret nocturnal business, he intended to arrest a murderer.

I took a step back and struggled not to let my dismay show. "You don't think I had anything to do with this, do you?" I said to Marcellus, straightening my shoulders.

"Didn't you?" the Tribune asked. His bushy eyebrows arched. "My soldiers found Falco's body at dawn already cold and stiff, despite the warm night. That means he had been dead for several hours at that point. Which brings me back to my question of where you were last night. If you are innocent, surely you can answer me?"

Too bad I couldn't do just that.

"I was here, in my house, working late," I said, staying as close to the truth as possible without revealing potentially dangerous details.

Quickly, I added, "If I wanted to murder your Primus Pilus, I would hardly be so foolish as to do it in my own port. And why, by all the gods, would I seek his life?"

"I heard your brother had a fight with Falco recently," the Tribune replied.

Marcellus was well informed, you had to give him that.

"Just a scuffle at a crossroads," I said, "based on a misunderstanding. As far as I know. As I'm sure you've been told, my brother and I are estranged. So, I would hardly kill a Primus Pilus for the sake of his honor. "

"Many a barbarian likes to settle misunderstandings with his axe, I've been told," Marcellus said. "And as for your code of honor—"

"Any Roman citizen, Celt or other inhabitant of Vindobona can buy a barbarian axe," I interrupted him. "From any armorer on my side and on your side of the Danubius. You know that as well as I do, Tribune."

He pretended to have overheard this objection. "And what did the Primus Pilus want with you last night?" he continued.

"He wasn't with me. If he wanted to come to me, his killer probably stopped him."

"But he has visited you on previous occasions?"

"Once or twice. To make a purchase from me."

Marcellus eyed me skeptically.

I held his gaze. "Falco was not a very popular man, was he?" I said. "For all his martial accomplishments. Or because of them? I would imagine he had plenty of enemies. And not just *outside* the camp walls."

The Tribune gave me a contemptuous look. "He may not have been popular. But respected. Revered and feared by his men! None of them would even raise a hand against him. Let alone murder him. Even more so with an axe. Falco was one of our most glorious fighters."

"And I, a peace-loving merchant, am supposed to have killed this veteran of Legio X? With an axe blow to the chest, if I understand you correctly? So from the front? Without even a scratch to my own body?"

I held out my naked, completely unharmed arms to Marcellus. "Your confidence in my fighting skills honors me, Tribune, but I am not the man you seek!"

For a moment we stared at each other wordlessly.

"Have your men already taken Falco's body away?" I then asked.

The Tribune replied in the negative.

"Then let's go down to the harbor. I want to see it with my own eyes. With your permission," I added in a more conciliatory tone. That was more likely to win over a man like Marcellus.

"All right," he said, adding a casual gesture of his hand.

My house lay just above the riverbank, and so it was only a few steps down to what Marcellus had so generously called my *harbor*. The facility consisted of nothing more than a jetty, a boathouse, and a few sheds where I occasionally stored less valuable goods for a few days.

Almost directly opposite, on the south bank of the Danubius, which was quite steep at this point, the imposing walls of the legionary camp rose a good thirty feet into the sky. An impressive reminder of who was in charge on this river.

The Tribune's men followed us down to the water, and two more legionaries were waiting for us on my landing stage, guarding the body of the Primus Pilus.

No point in even trying to escape. But that was far from my mind anyway. After all, the Tribune had not arrested me on the spot and now even took a step to the side so that I could look at Falco's body myself.

I knelt down next to the dead man and examined him closely, trying to get my thoughts in order. I had to keep a cool head, even if that was difficult in the presence of a man like Marcellus. If I said or did the wrong thing now, it would cost me my head. The Tribune was certainly very keen to atone for the murder of a Roman officer as quickly as possible. Whether I had actually committed the crime was of secondary importance. The main thing was that he had a culprit. And if he wanted to execute me on the spot with his sword, there was hardly anything that could stop him. My brother would have been snubbed by such a deed—at least I hoped so, despite our broken family relations—but not even he would be foolhardy enough to march with his men against Vindobona in order to avenge my death.

I pushed the dark thoughts aside as best I could and turned my attention to the dead officer.

Judging from the large pool of blood in which he lay, Falco had indeed been killed here on my jetty. But why? Was the place just a whim of the goddesses of fate? Had one of the enemies of the Primus Pilus waylaid him in this remote spot, of all places, without caring who owned the harbor? But what brought a Roman soldier here, late at night, to the northern shore of the Danubius? Had he really wanted to pay *me a* visit?

This could not be ruled out. East of the legion camp, a bridge led across the Danubius, and the distance from the legion camp to my house was less than two miles. In addition, of course, one could cross by boat. Unannounced visitors came to my house quite regularly, though not necessarily late at night. Without flattering myself too much, I could probably claim that I was popular in Vindobona. Valued as a business partner above all, even if some of my brother's followers would rather have chopped off their hand than buy from me.

Something bothered me about the way the corpse lay on my jetty. It almost looked as if the glorious warrior had just wanted to rest a while from his latest heroic deed. Nothing indicated a long and hard fight, at the end of which the attacker had finally won the upper hand. There was no splintered wood on the jetty, no trace of blood when you looked a bit further away from the corpse.

And apart from the axe that had split Falco's ribcage, there were no signs of a fight on his body. As if someone had only had to make one single axe blow to defeat him. That was unimaginable.

Something else bothered me. Falco's facial expression. There was an almost peaceful expression in his features. Almost as if he had voluntarily finished with life.

Which was equally inconceivable. Falco had certainly not

driven the axe into his own body. Apart from the fact that a man like him would never have left life in such a dishonorable way.

I had known the Primus Pilus well during his lifetime. He had served in Vindobona for many years. Even in death, he was an impressive warrior, full of toned muscles and covered with scars that he had always proudly displayed like a badge of honor. Truly not a man to be defeated so easily in a duel. In fact, you had to be crazy to mess with him.

And yet his attacker had apparently been his equal. Apart from the fact that he had succeeded in murdering Falco, whoever had driven the axe into the chest of the Primus Pilus must have had amazing muscular strength himself. The sharp blade had entered a good hand's breadth deep into the corpse. And yes, it was the kind of axe many men of my tribe liked to carry.

"Well, Thanar, what do you have to say?" Tribune Marcellus reminded me of his presence. His voice rang in my ears. Accusingly, he pointed at the dead Primus Pilus.

I rose without taking my eyes off the corpse. "He was murdered on this spot, I grant you that, Tribune. But not by me! Do you really think I would have been so foolish as to leave him lying here? What would have stopped me from just throwing the body into the river?"

"You tell me. Maybe you were discovered and only had time to escape?"

"And then I returned to my house, where I lay down peacefully to sleep? To wait until you and your men came for me to crucify me?"

To this Marcellus replied nothing.

"No, Tribune," I continued, "as I see it, there are only two possibilities: either some enemies were lying in wait for Falco here, purely by chance, or someone is trying to frame me. Maybe not even me personally, but my tribe. Hence the barbarian axe."

Was that what this strange murder was about? Did someone want to sow discord between us and the Romans?

For a moment, the thought crept into my mind that my brother might have had a hand in it. No one hated the Romans like he did. To kill an officer of the empire, if the opportunity presented itself to him, and he could hope to get away unpunished... I wouldn't have put such a deed past him. But to deliberately pin the crime on me? Would he go that far? I refused to believe that.

My brother detested me, but it would hardly have done him honor to have me crucified. Or condemned *ad bestias*—to the wild beasts in the amphitheater.

I shook off the thought. "Was Falco robbed?" I turned back to Marcellus.

"No. We found his purse on him. With a few pieces of silver in it."

III

It just didn't make any sense. Everything about this murder was wrong.

Street robbers would hardly have left a well-filled purse behind, apart from the fact that I couldn't imagine how mean bandits would want to take on a veteran of the legion of the likes of Falco. Even if there were two or three of them.

I looked the Tribune straight in the eye. "I will find out who did this," I said with far more conviction than I felt. "I will prove to you that I am innocent!"

Marcellus remained silent for a moment while the legionaries who surrounded us watched him expectantly. They, too, would certainly have preferred to see the death of their Primus Pilus atoned for today rather than tomorrow.

"Who guarantees me that you won't just cowardly run away?" Marcellus asked in an even harsher tone than before. Although I towered over him in height, he gave me the feeling that he was looking down on me. For his young years, he made an impressive leader when he put his mind to it—I had to give him that much.

I pointed with my hand to my house, which was above the embankment. "Do you think I'm going to give up everything I've worked for so easily? My home, my business? You can make inquiries about my character. I have a good reputation in Vindobona."

"I've already done that," Marcellus replied, "and as far as

that goes, I think you speak the truth. Even our camp commander has already made purchases from you, it seems. He specifically praised the quality of your furs and your reasonable prices."

Was there a smile in the dark eyes of the Tribune? Was the man enjoying himself while I was fighting for my life?

"You can trust my word of honor," I said, not letting on the anger that was rising inside me. "I will find the culprit and clear my name!"

Once again, the eyes of the Tribune examined me, so penetratingly, as if they could see through me. And he took what felt like an eternity to do so.

"Very well," he finally said. "I expect your full support, Thanar. The murderer must be caught quickly and punished severely!"

We sealed the agreement with a handshake, then Marcellus signaled his men to march off.

Outwardly I didn't let on anything, but inwardly I thanked the gods with a prayer of relief. I had already seen myself in the sand of the arena, eye to eye with a drooling beast that longed to rip out my guts and above me the screams of the audience, eager to witness my execution. And afterwards, as a corpse, impaled on the Limes Road, left as a feast for the carrion birds to peck my bones bare.

Why did the Tribune let me go? Merely because I was the brother of the local chieftain, estranged or not? Did the friendly neighborly relations with an insignificant Germanic tribe outweigh the life of a Primus Pilus for Marcellus? I doubted it. To wipe out the warriors of my entire clan, a single Roman auxiliary troop would have sufficed.

Did the Tribune trust me to be not simple-minded enough

to leave a murdered man lying so conspicuously in my own harbor? Or had he come to the same conclusion as I myself had? That there was clearly something wrong with this corpse?

When I returned to my house, Layla was already waiting for me in the atrium. She put her dark, slender hand on my arm and asked, "Is everything all right, master?"

"For the moment, yes. The soldiers have left. But I had to vouch that I'll catch the murderer of the Primus Pilus myself, in order to clear myself of any suspicion. And I haven't the faintest idea how to go about it."

"I'm sure you'll succeed," Layla replied, smiling at me with confidence. She generally trusted me with far greater abilities than I really had. In this case even more so.

"Listen, Layla," I began, "when you were alone with the Tribune earlier—did he ask you any other questions? Before I joined you two? He seemed to be chatting with you in an exceedingly animated way."

She did not reply at first but was smiling silently, looking as mysterious as a sphinx. Then she asked in her dark, melodious voice: "Are you worried about your secret business, master? The Tribune didn't seem interested in that, and I didn't mention anything that could harm you."

Her words caught me off guard, as if she had punched me in the pit of my stomach. I had never even hinted to Layla that one or the other of my trade goods might have found its way into my warehouse in a not entirely legal manner.

My dismay wasn't lost on Layla.

"Don't worry," she said quickly, "none of your aides have

divulged anything. They are all loyal to you and would never betray you."

"Then how do you know?" I asked, after briefly feeling tempted to deny everything.

"It's not hard to figure out for someone living under your roof, master. There is this one room in your cellar that only you yourself ever open or close. The door to this room does not look different from all the other cellar doors from the outside, probably in order not to arouse the curiosity of the servants or guests who happen to stray into the basement. You also take care not to display your wealth in public, which is very strange when everyone else tries to impress visitors to their house with their treasures. And then there are your trading partners. You often mention some of them by name when you tell me about your business, but you always meet them under cover of darkness, in places you keep secret from me. And you never invite them into your home, as you are wont to do with your respectable associates. Putting all this together, it seems obvious that some of your business is better kept hidden, isn't it, master?"

Layla put on her mysterious sphinx smile again and made a little bow, as if she had recited nothing more than a few pretty classical verses to me.

I didn't know what to say. Was I really so easy to see through? Or was my favorite slave, whom I had actually bought for the sake of her impressive beauty and because of her gentle nature, smarter than was good for me?

"I think the gods are not irate with you for that business," she continued, as if she had not already amazed me enough. "You don't steal from your own folk and only from people who don't have to go hungry because of it." It was a statement, not a question.

She was right about that, too, but how did she know that now?

"Do you trust so blindly in my nobleness, dear child?" I asked her.

"I know you are a good man, master; the best I have ever served. And your deeds prove it. The goods you store in your secret cellar are always delivered to you coming from the south, and you trade them on to the north. Goods from the Empire that you sell to your people, never the other way around. Moreover, they are always very small goods that must be of great value to make the dangerous venture worthwhile. So probably gems and jewelry. And the people from whom you can steal such things do not suffer from hunger, even if you relieve them of one or the other treasure."

I had to laugh involuntarily and pulled Layla into my arms. "You're the most cunning little spy I've ever met," I whispered in her ear. "If you ever turn on me, I'm doomed!"

"I would never do that, master," she replied in all seriousness. Then she breathed such a tender kiss on my cheek that my heart warmed.

What kind of a man was I? I was able to cope with the fact that I could never compete with a warrior like the Primus Pilus, even if Tribune Marcellus seemed to think so. But just being putty in the hands of this girl, that *did* put a strain on my pride.

Layla had hit the mark in every respect with her analysis, which would have done credit to a Greek logician. Of course, I wasn't a thief myself, but among my business partners—the very ones I never invited into my house, as she had so aptly observed—there was one or two fellows who didn't take the law all too seriously. I could not deny that I knew this, for there was a reason when one was offered goods far below their commercial value.

Last night I had dispatched a shipment with such goods from my secret cellar department and sent it to the far north of Germania, a fact I unfortunately had not been able to present to the Tribune as proof of my innocence.

Sometimes I didn't know myself why I was still taking the considerable risk of these dark dealings at all. Of course, a man had to make a living. And at the beginning of my career, when I had personally rumbled on rickety carts over the roads of the Empire and through the potholes of Germania, I had not been able to be picky about the origin of my goods.

But that was now many years behind me. Now I owned the most modern travel wagons and riverboats and left the grueling journeys largely to my assistants. Perhaps the fact that I was still robbing rich Romans of their treasures—even if not with my own hands—was nothing more than my modest act of rebellion against the omnipotence of the Imperium Romanum. Something my brother would never have believed me capable of.

But could there be any connection between the dark side of my business and the dead Primus Pilus in my harbor? It seemed quite impossible. I always paid my partners fairly and on time, just like my assistants, and not by any stretch of the imagination could I think of an enemy who would leave a corpse on my jetty.

I spent half the morning debating with myself whether I should pay my brother a visit. If he wasn't behind the whole matter himself, then as a tribal leader he might at least have an idea of where I had to look for the murderer of the Primus Pilus. If Falco had indeed been killed by a Germanic, which was by no means certain for me.

I had already had my horse saddled, but in the end I decided against a ride north. My brother's castle was a good day's journey from my house, and I could not even be sure of gaining admittance there. I had hardly visited him since he had succeeded our father as the local chieftain. And he had refused to set foot across my threshold ever since the day I installed a comfortable Roman floor heating system in my house.

No, even if my brother knew about the murder—to get even a single word about it out of him was a hopeless undertaking. If one of his men had killed a Roman officer, he would be the very last man to betray this 'hero' to me.

But the goddesses of fate were well-disposed towards me, because at that moment the saving idea came to me. I remembered that I had an appointment with just the right man tonight, to get to the bottom of the murder in my harbor. Someone who knew Vindobona and its inhabitants like no other. He was always up to date about which families were in disrepute or which upstart had just outranked an old-established citizen in terms of reputation and wealth. Or which man was plotting against his neighbor, even seeking his life. And why.

This inexhaustible source of knowledge was Septimus Moltinus Belius, stinking rich brickmaker, member of the Council of the Hundred of Vindobona's civilian town—and for many years my best friend.

IV

Belius and I had an appointment at a place which every rich man of Vindobona knew and referred to as the *Greek's Villa*.

Vindobona, especially the camp suburb, offered a whole range of amusements: one might visit the public baths, go to the theater, or watch gladiatorial games, executions, and animal fights in the amphitheater. There were taverns, food booths, and dens of vice where one could indulge in forbidden gambling, just like in any other small town of the Empire. The Greek's Villa, however, was something quite special. Not just for a sleepy backwater like Vindobona. Even in Carnuntum, the provincial capital, one could not find a comparable haven of *luxuria*, of culinary delights, indulgence, and sensual pleasure.

Here, the rich and powerful of Vindobona met for stimulating conversations, lucullan meals or simply a good cup of wine. But the main attraction were undoubtedly the girls, without question the most beautiful and graceful in the entire province.

At the Greek's Villa one felt like a guest at a country estate of an old Roman patrician family, except that the Greek didn't even have Roman citizenship, and that one had to pay dearly for visits to his house.

The Greek in question was called Lycortas, but no one except his subordinates ever called him by that name. He was a slave trader by profession, but at some point he must have realized that by renting out his girls—and boys—he not only promoted their sale but could also earn a lucrative side income.

A whole series of secrets surrounded the old man. None of his guests—myself included—would have been able to say when or why he had settled in Vindobona, or where and how he always managed to acquire the most outstanding slaves. There were numerous legends about his wealth, or simply about how old he actually was. With his wrinkled face and hooked nose, Lycortas looked like one of the goblins who lived in the woods. And dense forest did surround the walls of his villa. The old man refused to let the trees be cut, except where they blocked his guests' view over the city of Vindobona. Just as the ancient Celts had settled on the ridges of the hills long before the Romans invaded, so the Greek's Villa towered over the city and the river. From the legionary camp one had to ride about a mile and a half to the southwest to reach it.

I myself would never have had the financial means to be a regular guest here. It was my friend Belius who spent more time at the Greek's than in his own house and who invited me to the villa once or twice a week. Belius was not only one of the richest men in Vindobona but certainly one of the most generous.

In front of the estate's stables, which were within sight of the main house, a few slaves stood gossiping together. Among them I could make out Belius' lantern bearer, his two guards, and the four burly lads whose burden it was to haul their master's considerable corpulence all over Vindobona by carrying chair. Belius never left his house without a proper entourage, as he believed a man of rank and status should.

So my friend had already arrived at the villa.

I left my horse with a servant that came hurrying over and strode through the columns of the portico into the house. For a moment, I expected to see the old Greek's cloaked figure pounce on me as he had done all these years, arms outstretched and a euphoric grin on his face, as if he had been waiting for me all evening. I had to remind myself that the old man was no more. That he would never again greet me in the strangely exaggerated way he had done with all his guests.

For Lycortas, the Greek, was dead. It was only a few weeks ago that he had fallen victim to a bear attack, in the very forest that he had never kept in check. For days, the regulars had talked of nothing but this cruel whim of the goddesses of fate. But at some point they had come to terms with the fact that now the *young* Greek was the landlord and host.

The old man's son had long since passed forty, his name was Philippos, and I had hardly ever laid eyes upon him during his father's lifetime. The few times I had run into him in the villa, I had taken him for one of the slaves who ran the household. He always seemed to try to scurry around the house as invisibly as possible.

Since the old Greek's death, the villa had never been the same, for Philippos had not inherited one iota of his father's business acumen or hospitality. Within a few weeks, the girls were only smiling half as radiantly, the food was still tasty but no longer excellent, and the reception of guests had all but vanished into thin air. Where in the past the old man with his goblin grin came running to meet you as soon as you set foot over the threshold, these days you entered the house practically unseen.

I had already crossed the atrium and was halfway to the summer triclinium, the dining room open to the garden, before I was even noticed. And it was not Philippos, the new master of the house, who greeted me, but Orodes, the chief guard slave, who shouldn't really be in charge of welcoming guests.

I did not mind. Formalities and etiquette had never interested me much, but I didn't dare imagine how my friend Belius would take such a misstep. He cared a lot about impeccable protocol and manners.

Orodes led me to the corner of the triclinium where Belius had his regular seat, and I settled down next to my old friend on the dining sofa. From this spot one had a splendid view over the garden terraces, the nocturnal outline of the legionary camp, and the Danubius shining silvery in the moonlight. Music from a group of girls playing the flute and lyre drifted over to us, mixed with the soft splashing of the fountains. Further to the left, a dancer was gyrating her naked hips, and slaves with overflowing food trays hurried crisscross the room.

I would have liked to speak immediately about my little problem, after Belius had stretched out his golden-ringed hand to me in greeting—but the matter had to wait.

My friend was engrossed in observing another guest, a man unknown to me, who was wearing a garishly colored robe and was about to use the silky long hair of a half-naked youth as a towel for his freshly washed feet. An act of decadence that Belius could not condone and which incited him to a breathless tirade on one of his favorite topics: luxury addiction. If Belius had his way, the entire upper class of Vindobona was addicted to the sweet poison of luxuria, and hopelessly so. He himself, of course, excepted.

"*Parsimonia* and *modestia*, these are the virtues to strive for!" he proclaimed with a theatrically raised index finger. Frugality and modesty...yes, Belius was clearly a master at those. At least that was what he seemed to think. He was my best friend, and I loved him dearly, but his self-assessment was sometimes a little off.

I nodded, impatient to finally get to the murder in my port. But it was not to be, for just at that moment another of Belius' favorite topics thwarted my plans. Or rather, his favorite girl.

Her name was Suavis, and I was absolutely certain that neither frugality nor modesty were part of her vocabulary. She had been born in the Villa, a popular and cheap way with slaveholders to get new slaves, and had the golden blond hair as well as the blue eyes of a northern Germanic. Belius had been obsessed with her for years, even back when her body had more resembled that of a boy. In the meantime, however, Suavis had matured into a true beauty and was certainly the most desired girl in the entire villa.

Clad in nothing but a gauzy face veil and a very low-slung breast band, she was now dancing in front of our sofa, swaying her snow-white, still very girlish body to the sounds of the music. I did not even attempt to start any kind of conversation with my friend.

The way Suavis smiled at Belius suddenly brought back to my mind the morning's events in my atrium. How warmly my Layla had received the Tribune—and the stab of jealousy that it had given me old fool. Layla had surely only been out to appease Marcellus. Perhaps I even had her to thank for the fact that I could still sit here and watch a pleasure girl dance instead of awaiting my execution in the legion camp's dungeon.

At that moment, another girl appeared: Chloe, a dark-haired beauty who settled on my thigh with feline grace. She was clad in a colorful silk robe after the Asian fashion, which exposed more than it concealed. And she exuded a fragrant cloud of nard oil that almost took my breath away.

If the words of Lycortas, the old Greek, were to be trusted, Chloe's family tree stretched back to the legendary Greek hetaerae, the most exquisite prostitutes the world had ever seen. But in her nature, Chloe was more like a playful young predator, always in a good mood and up for any nonsense. She might be the same age as Suavis, but otherwise the two girls couldn't have been more different. The cool beauty from the north, who liked to act aloof and mysterious, and the sensual Greek, who knew how to cheer up even the gloomiest man with her laughter.

Chloe was my favorite in the villa. Or rather, she had been—before the gods had brought Layla to me. Since then, I preferred a good meal, a visit to the bathing grotto or a simple massage to Chloe's amorous arts. Although they really left nothing to be desired. The fire in my loins, which had always unfailingly ignited whenever I had entered the atrium of the villa, now wanted to burn only for Layla. Not even a few cups of Falernian wine could change that. Sometimes I seriously worried that my beautiful Nubian had bewitched me. Since the death of my wife, no woman had cast such a spell over me—and those darkest of times already lay behind me for half an eternity.

Tonight, however, things were even worse for me. Not even the smell of all the delicacies that were served to us was able to please me. There was something strange in the air—something that I had probably brought myself. It was as if the God of the Dead had followed me here. I couldn't get the sight of the Primus Pilus's corpse in my port out of my mind.

I just couldn't hold on any longer, I had to confide in Belius. He was just about to get up and follow Suavis to one of the guest rooms when I brusquely turned to the two girls and asked them to leave us alone. They obeyed without objection and disappeared as suddenly as they had appeared.

Belius, however, looked at me, startled. "What's gotten into you, Thanar? Are you not well?"

V

"No," I said truthfully, and then I told Belius everything that
had happened to me. I rambled on about the Primus Pilus's
corpse in my harbor and about the terrible fact that Tribune
Marcellus wanted to blame me for the murder. Then I wal-
lowed in self-pity about how it was now up to me to find the
real culprit as quickly as possible and that I had no idea how
to achieve this feat. "That's why I need your help, old friend,"
I concluded, looking expectantly at Belius.

"My help? Shall I vouch for you with the Tribune? I am sure
I will find a hearing with him, even if Marcellus is new in
town. My word will carry some weight, I can promise you
that much—but whether it can outweigh a dead Primus
Pilus, I do have my doubts."

"That's very generous of you," I replied, "and I may yet have
to come back to your intercession—but I actually thought
you might have some advice. That you could help me find
the murderer. Don't you know of someone who wanted Falco
dead? Or who wants to bring me to my doom? Do I have enemies in Vindobona that I don't know about?"

Belius' brow furrowed deeply. "As far as the former is concerned," he grumbled, "the question should probably be:
who did *not* want Falco dead? I can name you a good two
dozen men who would have been only too happy to send that
bully to the underworld. Not counting the legionaries of his
cohort. He allegedly treated them like galley slaves. I have

34

rarely met such a savage and ruthless man. Even here in the villa he behaved like the worst rabble. I truly cannot say that his death moves me to tears. Whoever drove that axe into his chest did Vindobona a favor."

"Falco was a guest here?" I asked. I myself had never met the Primus Pilus at the villa, but I also didn't come and go here nearly as frequently as Belius.

"Only once every few months. He probably couldn't afford more from his pay. The rest of the time, he surely tortured the camp whores."

Belius waved to a slave and ordered a cup of violets wine. After taking a hearty sip, he continued, "Now that I think about it, I believe Falco was even here last night. Yes, he was! I saw him just after I'd arrived. It's a wonder I noticed him at all, although for once he didn't make a racket. Otherwise, he always had something to complain about when he graced us with his presence here. Fortunately, that was really not often, otherwise I would have ended up hiring a murderer myself to split this brute's ribcage! Sometimes Falco criticized the food, sometimes a girl did not correspond to his wishes—and always he made his complaints in such a loud voice that one could hear him even in the garden. A few weeks ago, he actually picked a fight with *me*, can you imagine that!"

"You don't say!"

Belius shook his head indignantly. "I was on my way to retire to the bathing grotto with Suavis, and he got in my way like a mugger and claimed the girl for himself. When there is truly no shortage of girls here at the villa! As a Roman officer, he should be entitled to preference, he claimed."

"And how did you react?"

"I let him have his way, of course. What was I supposed to

do? Mess with a brute like that?"

"And last night, he was here too, you say? When did you see him?"

"Shortly after I arrived—must have been half an hour after sunset, I think."

"And how long did he stay?"

"I don't know, my friend. I was here with business partners, and I really wasn't paying attention to him. A guy like that isn't even worth ignoring."

"I agree with you there. It's just that I can't ignore his body in my port, unfortunately. I wonder if he might have picked another fight last night with one of the guests here? Who then reacted less stoically than you?"

Belius scratched his chin. "I think everyone present here would have noticed a fight. But why don't you ask Philippos? Maybe he overheard something. Although, I haven't seen him at all tonight." Belius let his eyes wander around the room, but there was no sign of our host.

I had my doubts as to whether Philippos was aware of anything at all in this house. He clearly seemed overwhelmed with his father's legacy, with the management of the villa.

"I can't imagine, however, that any of the guests here would resort to the axe to settle a dispute with the Primus Pilus," Belius said. "That kind of man simply doesn't socialize at the villa. If someone wants to dispose of an opponent here, they hire the appropriate scoundrel to do it, if you know what I mean. And not necessarily on the same night as the fight. That would be rather stupid. And then have the body dragged to the other bank of the Danubius? What's the point? That doesn't make any sense."

Indeed, it did not, especially since the body had not even

been dragged to my port. The Primus Pilus had died on the spot where he had been found, of that I was sure.

Falco must have made his way across the Danubius for some reason after his visit to the villa yesterday. Across the bridge or by boat—for the villa was less than half a mile from the south bank, and with the current and a few powerful strokes of the oars, it would have been easy to cross to my landing stage. As Primus Pilus, Falco could probably afford to come and go as he pleased in the legionary camp. Perhaps he'd had another appointment that night after he had visited the villa. Or someone had waylaid him on the way back to the camp.

I was moving in circles. So many possibilities; but how was I supposed to know which one was the right one?

At that moment, another thought came to my mind. Had Falco really intended to visit me at night—for the same reason that I always met some of my own business partners only at night? Had the Primus Pilus in some way gotten wind of my secret goods and wanted to secure himself a nice piece at a favorable price? That was a possible explanation, but not a very reassuring one. Quite the contrary. If my dark dealings had actually gotten through to a Roman soldier, my life was no longer worth a sesterce.

Suddenly it seemed almost certain that I would soon end up in the arena, whether as a murderer or a fence of stolen goods. My situation was thoroughly hopeless. Did I seriously expect Belius to hand me the name of Falco's murderer on a pretty silver platter, here and tonight? How naive I was. And how hopelessly inexperienced when it came to hunting down a murderer.

"Anyway, you should pay attention to your safety," Belius

snapped me out of my gloomy thoughts. "How long have I been preaching this to you?"

I nodded absent-mindedly. Belius meant well, of course, but the idea of taking my every step with an entourage, leaving the house only with two powerful slaves at my side—that was just not for me. I didn't want to live that way. I loved to jump into the saddle of my horse when the fancy took me and go wherever I wanted. And Vindobona was not a place where you had to fear for your life. Street robbers and other scoundrels avoided the Limes, the border of the Empire, where thousands of soldiers were stationed. They preferred to stick to the roads of the hinterland.

Only when I made trade trips to distant lands did I resort to well-armed guards. Not so much for my sake, but to protect my valuable cargo.

I had been a peace-loving man for many years. But that did not mean I did not know how to defend myself.

At least I had always assumed that until now. Much like the Primus Pilus, I suppose. Certainly, *he* had never been concerned about his own safety, on the streets of Vindobona—until someone had struck him in the chest with a barbarian axe.

Was it Belius' words of warning that made my way home seem darker than usual?

A narrow forest path led from the villa to the Limes Road. A path that my horse found all by itself. It had already carried me home on this route hundreds of times. I gave the reins to the animal and tried to encourage myself that my situation was not as hopeless as it appeared to me. Unfortunately, without any significant success. All I could think of were the carrion birds that would soon be pecking at my corpse if I failed to solve the murder in my harbor.

Suddenly there was a cracking sound in the undergrowth, just a few steps behind me. Was I already hallucinating in my despair?

But my horse seemed to have heard it, too. It snorted restlessly and fell into a trot. I grabbed the reins that hung limply around the animal's neck, brought my steed to a halt, and listened into the darkness.

Nothing. Not the slightest sound. Which was not a good sign. It meant that the small animals in the immediate vicinity, which usually rustled in the foliage on their nightly paths, had taken flight—from a larger predator.

I had to think of the bear to which the old Greek had fallen victim. But a bear breaking through the undergrowth would have made more noise—and such a beast would have pounced on me long ago.

A pack of wolves on the prowl maybe? Or was it a human lying in wait for me? Just like for the Primus Pilus last night, possibly at the very same spot? Why had this thought not occurred to me right away!

I loosened the reins and spurred my horse until it fell into a gallop. I carried my sax with me as usual, a short, sharp blade, but it wouldn't do me much good against an opponent who was hunting me under the cover of night.

There it was again, the crackling in the undergrowth! Now it actually sounded as if something big was breaking its way through the woods. While my horse rushed forward, I peered over my shoulder into the darkness. The tall trees shrouded the path in almost impenetrable blackness, and yet I felt as if I could make out a shadow. A faceless figure that now stood in the middle of the path. Apparently motionless, as if it just wanted to look at me.

I quickly turned again, pressed my heels into my horse's flanks, whereupon it sped along even faster. It could only be a few hundred feet now to the Limes Road, and from there a scant mile to the legion camp. No one would dare ambush me within sight of the gate guards.

At that moment the arrow hit me. Only when it was already too late did I hear its soft whirring, then it bored into my back with such force that it almost threw me out of the saddle.

The next moment my sight went black. I felt as if my faithful stallion were stumbling under me. Even the trees suddenly swayed and lurched as if they were about to come crashing down on me.

No, it was I who was just hanging in the saddle like a wet sack, unable to hold myself upright. It was only with great difficulty that I was able to cling to my horse's bushy mane.

I'm dead, was all I could think.

VI

I needed help, and I needed it fast. At a frantic gallop, my stallion turned onto the wide Limes Road. Here it was a little brighter, and not far ahead of me the western gate of the legionary camp rose into the night sky. This was my salvation. If I could make it there.

Suddenly the gate seemed infinitely distant and to recede a little further with each gallop of my horse.

Again, my sight went black. I struggled to keep myself in the saddle. There were doctors in the legion camp, one of whom I even knew. Thessalos, a very friendly young fellow.

They won't let you in, it flashed through my mind, while the Limes Road swayed and lurched beneath me like a sinking ship. And then suddenly it felt as if the night itself was falling down on me. Like a heavy dark cloak, it enveloped me, took away my vision, robbed me of my breath.

I managed to hear the faint voice of a soldier asking me to state my business, and I recognized the blurred outline of another who was blocking my way with his spear—then I toppled forward into the mane of my horse.

"I bring news for Tribune Marcellus!" I managed to utter with the last of my strength. It was the only thing I could think of. "Get me to a medicus!"

Then the night swallowed me up.

I awoke many hours later in the Valetudinarium, the hospital of the legionary camp. Outside, the morning was already dawning.

Out of the corner of my eye, I saw a slave hurry out of the room, and a few minutes later he returned with Thessalos at his side. The young medic with whom I had spent many a convivial evening playing dice in the tavern. Now he smiled encouragingly at me, bent over me, and checked my bandages.

I lay on my stomach and was bandaged like an Egyptian mummy. But apart from a slight pulling sensation in my back, I felt no pain. Instead, my head was foggy, as if I had paid homage to the divine Bacchus all night. Thessalos must have administered some kind of concoction to me. But I was alive, thank the Gods!

"Fortuna was with you, old friend," said the medicus, as if he had read my thoughts. "A few minutes later, and I could have done nothing more for you."

I thanked him from the bottom of my heart for saving me while I had to remind myself what had happened to me in the first place.

The archer! Through the fog in my head, I asked Thessalos to show me the arrow he had cut from my body.

The medicus nodded and turned to comply with my request, but at that moment a voice sounded behind him that I remembered all too well. "It was an arrow of the type used by our archers," it announced, and in the next moment Tribune Marcellus was standing next to my bed, examining me with his dark eyes.

"A Roman arrow?" I repeated as I carefully rolled to my side.

"An arrow of the sort that can be made by any fletcher on

42

this side or the other of the Danubius," Marcellus replied. A pinched smile flitted across his youthful features. Then he said, "You bring me news, I hear. Were you able to track down Falco's killer?"

"I...no," I stammered and tried to sit up. But all strength seemed to have left my body. "I just wanted to let you know that I myself was ambushed, certainly by the same villain who killed the Primus Pilus. Here's your proof that I'm innocent! "

The Tribune made no effort to go along with my—admittedly very spotty—logic. "The same villain? Not perhaps rather a man who thirsted to avenge Falco's death?" he ventured. "Someone who wanted to judge the murderer of our Primus Pilus himself because I failed to do so?"

I had not come to this conclusion, but it made considerably more sense than the one I had just presented.

Panic rose up in me. I tried again to straighten up so that I wouldn't have to look up at Marcellus like a sacrificial lamb. Thessalos rushed to my aid and supported me, while the Tribune only appraised me with a cold gaze.

"How did it happen, this assault on you?" he asked as his eyes roamed over my bandaged torso.

That he was at least inclined to listen to my story, I interpreted as a good sign. A glimmer of hope! I told him in detail what had happened to me and also that Falco himself had visited the Greek's Villa the night before. "So his enemy might well have waylaid him in that part of the woods," I pointed out. "When Falco started on his way home. Just as I did tonight."

"An estate near the Limes Road, you say?" Marcellus' eyes narrowed.

I nodded quickly. I was surprised that the Tribune did not know the Greek's Villa yet. Many of Vindobona's officers frequented the place, at least occasionally. I had even met the camp commander there on many an evening.

It also seemed to be a new piece of information for the Tribune that Falco had gone there yesterday. At least I had found out something—even if it was not of much use to me. How and why the Primus Pilus had made his way from the villa to the north bank of the Danubius was still completely in the dark.

"How would it have looked like if I had been killed tonight?" I thought out loud. "Why was I supposed to die?"

"What are you getting at?" asked Marcellus.

"Just trying to figure out what the attacker might have intended. I am convinced that I did not by chance become the victim of some highwayman—on the same day that the body of a Roman soldier was found in my harbor. And I know that nobody wanted to take revenge on me because of Falco's death. Because I did *not* murder him. So I assume that the same assassin was lying in wait for me; the murderer of the Primus Pilus."

"So what?"

"He shot me with a Roman arrow—after killing Falco with a Germanic axe. The death of the Primus Pilus got you involved, Tribune, and my death would certainly have resulted in an act of revenge by my brother. Maybe that's what the murderer is after, maybe he wants to cause trouble between neighbors. Between Romans and Germanics."

"An insurgent?" The Tribune raised his eyebrows. He seemed unconvinced by this theory.

"Well," I relented, "at least with my death the case would

have been solved for you, right? You would have assumed, as you said, that it was an act of revenge, and the real murderer would have gotten away. Maybe that's all he wanted. He speculated that you would arrest me first thing this morning, and because you didn't, he carried out this apparent revenge attack. What do you think?"

"I think that you talk quite a bit, Thanar. And that you seem very desperate to convince me of your innocence."

"Because I am innocent!"

"Or because you're guilty."

The bed beneath me suddenly seemed to rear up. The walls of the hospital came threateningly close to me. But now was not the time for a fainting spell.

I took a new direction. A very dangerous one, but I didn't have a better idea. And I could hardly make my situation much worse.

"Who would want to avenge the Primus Pilus, in your opinion?" I asked Marcellus as I struggled to fight down the dizziness. "One of his men? I have been told that Falco did not have a single friend in the legionary camp. That none of the soldiers under his command shed a tear for him. Quite the contrary."

The Tribune did not reply.

"Besides, if I had actually killed Falco, how did this supposed avenger know about my deed? Did he watch me do it? Then why didn't he rush to the aid of his Primus Pilus, why did *he* survive?"

Once again, I received no answer. The Tribune's features seemed as rigid as those of a marble bust.

His silence unsettled me, but nevertheless I continued, "And if this witness only cowardly observed the deed from a hiding place, why didn't he at least report it to you—instead of taking vigilante action against me? Do you approve of such behavior by your legionaries?"

Making the suggestion that not everything was as it should be in the legion was a highly dangerous undertaking, and I was well aware of that. I could just as easily have erected my own cross, but I just couldn't think of a better way. I had to convince the Tribune of my innocence, no matter what the cost.

The longer I talked, the more firmly the thought settled in my head: Falco's murderer was probably to be found among his own people!

That made sense. After all, it was his legionaries who had suffered the most under the Primus Pilus. They could not simply avoid him or manfully ignore his harassments, as Belius had done. They had to bow to him, day after day, year after year. Wasn't it inevitable that one day one of them would take up the axe? Or even several of the men?

Yes, several, that was how it must have been! One alone could hardly have taken on Falco. They must have followed him in the evening on his way to the Villa, ambushed him on his way home, overpowered him, and took him to the barbarian side of the river to cover their tracks, where they executed him with a barbarian weapon.

Perhaps even the patrol boat that supposedly found Falco's body in the early morning hours had transported him across the river itself. He might have been stunned or tied up, in any case defenseless against the superior force that had then executed him on my jetty.

That's exactly how it could have happened. And then there was something else that pointed to the legion: whoever it had been whose arrow had pierced me, he had known how to handle his bow. To hit a horseman in almost total darkness, who had already escaped several hundred feet away, and to do so with deadly precision—that took a master marksman. And where in Vindobona did one find men who fit this description? Correct: in the legionary camp.

I was not tired of life enough to share these considerations with the Tribune but had nevertheless convinced myself that I had finally discovered the truth. But how could I prove it? How to get at a troop of conspirators within the legion? That was a hopeless undertaking. First, I couldn't just set out and start interrogating soldiers, and second, they would stick together, as had been proven a thousand times over on battlefields around the world. They were used to fighting shoulder to shoulder, even to the death. No one would ever betray the other.

"I have sent a messenger to your house so that they will not be worried about you," the Tribune said abruptly. "There should be some of your slaves arriving soon to pick you up." Jerkily, he turned to Thessalos. "He is fit for transport, is he not, medicus?"

The doctor, who had been standing silently with us the whole time, took a step forward.

"Yes, Tribune," he said quickly. Then he turned to me. "But take it easy for the next few days, Thanar, do you hear! You may have the constitution of an ox, but you are not immortal." A friendly smile flitted across his face.

I could not believe my eyes and ears. Did Marcellus really give me another chance? When I had already been prepared to hear my death sentence from his mouth? Could it be that he secretly shared the same suspicion as me? That Falco had died at the hands of his own men?

Well, if the Tribune really believed that, it was a testament to his greatness that he was inclined to get to the bottom of it. That he didn't just cover everything up and make me the guilty party. It would have been easy for him.

But there was more. Something in the way Marcellus let me go—already for the second time—aroused my suspicion. Was I only a bait for him, with which he wanted to catch the murderer of the Primus Pilus? The one he had long been on the trail of, while playing the clueless to me?

All at once I was almost certain that the Tribune was hiding something from me. That he knew far more than he let on. I would have liked to ask him about it, but I did nothing of the sort. I was glad to leave the legion camp alive and a free man. As quickly as possible.

VII

At the east gate, Darius, my assistant, and two of the lads who usually accompanied my trade shipments as guards were already waiting for me. They had come with the wagon, which I usually made use of only for long journeys, and wanted to take me back to my house by a direct route.

"You need to rest, master," Darius said, "and Layla is almost worried sick about you!"

That warmed my heart, but before I could return home and nurse my wounds, I had something to do. Something that could not wait.

I ordered Darius to ride home on my horse and bring Layla news that I was well. I myself took the wagon and headed toward the Greek's Villa. If I was lucky, there would still be traces of my nocturnal assailant on the forest path. Only a few hours had passed; perhaps something could still be discovered that would lead me to the murderer.

The rumbling of the wagon, especially when we reached the forest path, made my wound hurt quite a bit, but otherwise I felt sufficiently strong again. And it did me good to resume the hunt for the murderer—at least it was much better than staying at home in bed and brooding over the hopelessness of my situation. One could not behave like a weakling on the battlefield! I was not at war, but my life was in danger. In more ways than one.

When we reached the place where I had heard the crackling in the undergrowth during the night, I had the wagon stopped and made my two men search for tracks. I did still lack the strength to crawl through the underwood myself.

The two slaves struggled through the shrubbery for a good two hundred feet along the trail, but all they could find was a spot with broken branches and trampled foliage.

I climbed carefully out of the wagon, was most pleased that my legs carried me without protest, if a bit wobbly, and looked at the tracks personally. Yes, this was clearly where a man had hidden in the undergrowth—this was where the archer had waylaid me, completely covered by foliage and darkness. The spot, however, was surrounded by dense brush, which was intact. Which meant that he must have come on the path and then just ducked into the undergrowth. In other words, he must have already been lurking here when I came riding along the path. And he had been alone. Two men would have had to create much more space for themselves in the bushes.

Street robbers usually gathered in groups, which promised a much higher chance of success. But the man who had waylaid me here had not been out for a raid. He had not chosen me purely by chance as a victim, of that I was almost sure.

No, someone had waited here in the undergrowth until I left the villa, had stepped onto the path behind me, and—with masterful bowing skill—had shot an arrow into my back. Even though I still had not the faintest idea why.

I had to let the wagon drive all the way to the Villa because the path was too narrow to turn around—but when the columns of the Porticus came into view, I decided not to return home right away after all. While I was here, perhaps I could find out something more about the Primus Pilus, whom my friend Belius had seen here the night before last.

And Philippos, the new landlord, should at least be informed that his guests were in danger on their way home. Maybe I was wrong with all my murder theories and it was really just a particularly bold robber who had chosen the forest path as his hunting ground? Not the worst choice, because the richest men in Vindobona came and went in the villa.

Anyway, I climbed out of the wagon, left my men in front of the house, and made it to the atrium on my own. There, however, I had to brace myself against one of the columns and fight off another dizzy spell.

During the day, guests rarely came to the villa, so I was not surprised to find the atrium empty.

I could hear the sound of voices drifting out from an adjoining room used in winter by the porter and the guards. No, not voices, but laughter.

That was as good a place as any to make myself noticed and send for the master of the house. Wobbly-footed, I headed towards the room. The door stood slightly ajar—but then I came to an abrupt halt.

Through the crack of the door, I recognized Chloe, the Greek girl who had long been my favorite here at the villa. She was leaning against the far wall of the room, her head thrown back, her slender legs wrapped around the torso of a black man. Or rather, she was pushed against the wall—the man was taking her in the rhythm of a bull gone wild. I could only see him from behind, but I still knew who he was: Juba, the body servant of the old Greek—the only slave from Africa who worked here at the villa.

Old Lycortas had been in Juba's company on that unspeakable day when the bear had attacked him. Juba had heroically defended his master against the beast, almost falling victim to the bear himself.

At least that was the story I'd heard, and it was also said that Philippos, the son of the old man, had given Juba his freedom for this bravery, even though Lycortas had succumbed to his injuries in the end.

It was nothing unusual that Juba continued to work in the villa. Many freedmen remained part of the *familia*, continuing to serve their former masters in exchange for food, lodging, and a small wage. However, a servant, freed or not, was certainly not entitled to take advantage of his master's most precious possession, a luxury slave girl of the highest quality. As indifferent as Philippos might be to the management of the villa, he certainly would not have approved of such behavior. Apparently, the young Greek had no idea what liberties his servants took, and the rule over his household must have completely slipped away from him.

Well, I wouldn't be the one to put him in the picture. Part of me—probably the one which was only too happy to break all kinds of rules or traditions—couldn't help but admire Juba for his impudence. And of course, I certainly didn't want to betray Chloe, because I had grown very fond of the girl.

So I left them to their forbidden pleasure, crossed the atrium, and went inside the house in search of Philippos.

I did not get far. In the corridor leading to the summer triclinium, I ran into Orodes, the guard slave who had received me last night in place of the master of the house.

Orodes was a Parthian prisoner of war, a member of that

fearsome people who lived beyond the eastern border of the Empire and who so stubbornly resisted conquest by the Romans. A boldness for which one had to truly admire these barbarians of the Orient.

Orodes knew how to instill respect by his appearance alone. He always wore a dark shadow of beard on his face, and the sleeveless slave tunica that clothed him exposed the shoulders of a warrior, such that probably haunted the Romans in their worst nightmares. Yet he spoke cultured Latin as if he had been born in the Empire.

Orodes had been the chief guard slave in the villa for several years, and I had always considered him a capable fellow who would go far. If I had been in possession of the necessary financial means, I probably would have even tried to buy him off the old Greek. With a man like this Parthian, I would have known my goods transports to be in safe hands.

However, Orodes also seemed to neglect his duties since the death of the old man. It was not only his job to protect the villa against burglars and other dangers from outside, as the chief guard he also had to ensure order in the household itself. I wondered if he knew that Juba was getting it on with one of the luxury slaves at that very moment.

I asked Orodes to take me to Philippos, but no sooner had I voiced my request than a pain coursed through my back, causing me to stagger.

Immediately the Parthian was at my side, offering me his arm for support. "Are you not well, sir?" he asked anxiously.

"Just an injury that's still causing me some pain. A chair would be good—and a cup of wine."

"Of course, sir." Orodes led me into the peristyle garden of the house, which I knew well. Around it most of the guest rooms were situated. It was a beautifully manicured green space, with rose bushes and daisy beds, flanked by a shady portico. Next to a gently splashing fountain stood a group of comfortable chairs and a side table made of fine citrus wood.

Leaning on Orodes' arm, I staggered toward the seating area. I settled down with a groan, and the Parthian set off in search of his master.

Orodes' arm, it went through my mind. It was as strong as a thigh. The kind of arm that could take down a Roman veteran with a single blow of the axe? At this thought, two words abruptly entered my head: *Parthian maneuver.*

The Parthians were not only generally feared warriors, but in particular downright legendary archers. The Parthian maneuver consisted of turning backward on a galloping horse and striking down your pursuers with well-aimed shots. A tour de force in the art of war. A Parthian archer would certainly have no difficulty whatsoever in hitting a rider from a safe standing position, even in near total darkness.

What if the assassin had not waylaid me along the way but had followed me from the villa?

Orodes. Could he have been the archer?

As the leader of the guard, this man could move freely around the villa without anyone questioning his steps. Especially since order in the house seemed to have all but broken down anyway.

But was Orodes, for all his apparent strength, such an accomplished fighter that he could have taken on Falco? The Primus Pilus?

It probably couldn't hurt to make more detailed inquiries about Orodes. Did he have such a hatred for the Romans that he became a murderer? After all, that was conceivable in the case of a prisoner of war. Had he chosen the Primus Pilus as a particularly repugnant representative of Roman omnipotence because he knew him as a guest of the villa?

But what about me? Why was I supposed to die?

At that moment Orodes returned, with Philippos, the master of the house at his side. I could not help but examine the bare arms and legs of the Parthian. But they were intact. Not a single scratch.

That did not fit. If he really was the murderer of the Primus Pilus, he should at least have suffered some injuries from this fight. Anything else was unimaginable.

And why should he have attacked *me*? Just to present the Romans with a culprit?

I could not think of any other reason. On the numerous occasions when I had exchanged a few words with Orodes here in the villa, I had not gained the impression that he harbored any resentment against me. On the contrary, I had made it clear to him that I considered him a capable and trustworthy man, and he had appreciated that. At least that had been my impression.

No, it just didn't fit. Orodes might have the necessary martial skills, but he was not the murderer I was looking for. The idea which I had come up with this morning in the legionary camp—that some of the legionaries might have conspired against their sadistic Primus Pilus—was much more credible.

VIII

Philippos stepped in front of me, extended a limp hand in greeting, then dropped into a chair as if the weight of the whole world rested on his shoulders.

A slave poured him and me a cup of honey wine, while Orodes took his leave with a bow and disappeared between the columns of the peristyle.

Philippos was only a few years my senior, hardly more than forty, and yet he looked like an aged man. His hair was thin and almost completely gray, and he eyed me with the short-sighted look of a scribe. Yet he was not unfriendly. "You wanted to see me, Thanar? What can I do for you?"

I told him about the archer who had waylaid me on the forest path in front of the villa and about the dead Primus Pilus in my port, whose murderer had possibly also followed him from the villa.

Despite my terse and sober report, all life, all color drained from Philippo's features. It was almost as if another corpse was suddenly sitting opposite me.

"How terrible," he breathed in a brittle voice when I had finished. "A murderer in Vindobona? Have we angered the gods? I will order Orodes to have every guest who visits us without his own guards escorted to the Limes Road from now on!"

"A good suggestion," I said, even though I didn't think any of the villa's guests were in danger.

I asked Philippos about the last visit of the Primus Pilus. "Do you remember when he arrived at the villa the night before last? And whether he came alone or was accompanied by friends?"

The young Greek, still pale as a sheet, shrugged his narrow shoulders. "I'm afraid I can't help you there, Thanar. Since my father's death, Juba has been taking care of the guests. I myself...well, I'm not like my father. I could never be as accomplished a host as he was."

I nodded in understanding but didn't reply. To agree with him would have been very impolite. As he sat there in front of me, an old man with sunken shoulders and waxy skin, I almost felt sorry for him.

"If you want, I can have Juba called, and you can question him. He—"

"No, that's not necessary," I said quickly. It was possible that Juba was still involved with Chloe, and I didn't want to be at fault for the two of them being discovered doing something forbidden. "I'll talk to him the next time I come over in the evening."

"Yes. A good idea. You are here often, aren't you, Thanar? Together with Belius. You are valued regulars; have thanks for your loyalty." The words came haltingly over his lips, even if his friendliness seemed genuine. He bowed as reverently as a slave.

He seemed to want to say more but didn't quite know how. Finally, he began tentatively, "I would like to ask your advice, Thanar. On a personal matter." His gaze sought mine, held it for a brief moment. Then his eyelids lowered.

This request surprised me, but of course I immediately agreed.

"You are a respected and very experienced merchant, Thanar," said Philippos. "I would like to start a business in books. Do you think I can be successful with them? The classics of my people, the speeches of emperors and philosophers, the famous Roman poets, the great tragedies. I could hire some copyists and then supply Pannonia and the neighboring provinces with books."

"But the Villa?" I asked, astonished. "And your father's slave trade? You don't want to give that up, do you? Surely that is a most lucrative business. Lycortas must have had the best sources and contacts. And what he has built up here in the villa—there are few equals in the entire empire. You can believe me, I've been around a lot!"

"I guess I'm not living up to my father's legacy," Philippos muttered. A melancholy smile flitted across his bloodless lips. "The slave trade, the villa...I don't know anything about that. That's not what I want to do. Books are my passion, and I just want to earn enough to live on. Maybe it's not too late for me to start a family, either." The melancholy smile gave way to a livelier, more hopeful one. "Do you think that's possible? Can I make a living with books?"

I couldn't understand why Philippos was worried about making a living. Or what had kept him from starting a family until now. If he didn't want to continue his father's business, Lycortas must at least have left him an extremely rich inheritance. Chests full of gold, with which Philippos could make do for the rest of his life. But that was none of my business, of course.

My body felt heavy, the wound in my back hurt, but still the businessman in me sensed a unique opportunity at that moment. I knew what prices old Lycortas could get for his best slaves—after all, I myself had bought one of his luxury girls from him only six months ago: Layla.

Before I met her, I would never have thought of spending the sum Lycortas demanded for a slave. For that price, one could buy a nice little townhouse in Vindobona. The expense was not only unplanned but also far beyond my means. While I truly could not complain about my business, I usually reinvested almost every sesterce of profit back into buying new goods, expanding my small fleet, faster travel wagons, and more powerful guards. Not in a glowing-eyed sorceress who clouded my senses.

Almost a year ago, the old Greek had brought Layla back from one of his trips, on which he always acquired only the best that the slave market had to offer. When I saw Layla for the first time, spent the first night in the Villa with her, I knew that I had to have her all to myself—at any price. Unfortunately, I was stupid enough to let the cunning old man notice that, and he quoted me such an outrageously high sum that it left me speechless.

Nevertheless, I sealed the purchase—but not until six months later. My savings were insufficient, and so I had to engage in some business dealings that I would never have dared to undertake otherwise, to ship even more shady goods than I already did, and travel to areas from which hardly any merchant had ever returned. I, however, did get back, finally having raised the sum Lycortas demanded. *Exitus acta probat*, as the incomparable Ovid put it. The outcome justifies the deeds. Layla was worth every risk I took for her and all the gold I laid down to make her mine.

I shook off the thought of my black sorceress and turned back to Philippos, who looked at me expectantly. "If you really want to devote yourself to the book trade," I said, "I'll be happy to help you sell your girls for the best possible price. I'm sure we'll agree on the terms."

I had no experience in the slave business and no intention to get involved in human trafficking in the long term, but to find a buyer for the beautiful girls of the villa, who were well trained in the art of love—that would be easy for me. I knew enough rich men who could afford such an expense.

"I would actually prefer to release the girls," Philippos replied.

I couldn't believe my ears and stared at the young Greek, probably quite aghast. It was not unusual to give freedom to slaves. Many men made provisions for this in their wills or, for example, gave skilled craftsmen in their service the chance to buy their own freedom after ten years of good work. But to release nearly two dozen sinfully expensive luxury slaves all at once? You might as well set your own villa on fire.

Philippos apparently not only had no idea about household management but was also completely clueless in business matters.

"Did not the learned Alcidamas already speak of God setting all men free and nature making no one a slave?" Philippos said, looking at me with strange intensity.

Obviously, the young Greek really was a well-read man. I had a modest library of my own, of which I was quite proud, and liked to stick my nose into scrolls whenever I found the time. However, I had never heard of this Alcidamas.

Anyway, it was time for me to go. I pushed myself up out of the chair and wanted to shake hands with Philippos, but he insisted on inviting me to a fortifying meal. "It's the least I can do for you after the hardship you suffered on the way home yesterday. Chloe is your favorite, is she not? I will send for her to serve you some refreshments and please you with her company."

I was surprised that Philippos knew my favorite when he didn't want to deal with the guest services. He had probably noticed a few things, but that was unavoidable when you lived under the roof of the villa.

I was about to accept with thanks when I remembered that it was not a good idea to send for Chloe. She might still be with Juba, and I didn't want to be the one to blame if she was found in the servant's arms.

So I asked Philippos that Suavis keep me company. Maybe I could use the opportunity to ask her a few questions about Falco. The dead Primus Pilus had even fought with my friend Belius for her sake.

Philippos seemed surprised but nodded immediately. Was he wondering about the complete turnaround in my taste? From the fiery Greek to the icy beauty of the north?

While I waited for Suavis and the promised meal, my thoughts wandered to Layla. I longed to get home to her as soon as possible, even if such delicacies did not await me there as here in the villa.

I old, sentimental fool thought of her far too often. Sometimes even in the way I used to think of my wife when long journeys separated me from her. *My wife.* How strange that sounded, after all the years I had missed her now. Only two summers together had been given to our marriage, then the plague had snatched her away from me.

A dull pulsation in my back brought me back to the present. What took Suavis so long?

When I was already about to get up to make my way home with an empty stomach, she finally came hurrying over. Next to her walked a food carrier with a lavishly laden silver tray—and then I saw that it wasn't Suavis at all. The woman who came toward me looked a few years older but was otherwise the spitting image of the beautiful Germanic girl.

"I'm very sorry, sir, I couldn't find Suavis," she said in an ingratiating voice. "I hope you will agree to let me keep you company in her place. My name is Alva."

"Are you Suavis' sister?" I asked in surprise. I had never seen this woman in the villa before.

"Her mother, sir."

I was astonished. Suavis was in her teenage years, I knew that—so if Alva really was her mother, she must have given birth to her at a very young age. She could be no more than thirty years old.

When she took her seat opposite me, she held herself upright like a queen and tried to smile. Which she failed to do. Her face could have been as beautiful as her daughter's, but it seemed frozen into a mask. And her eyes were those of a dead person.

The eyes of a dead person? Never before had I had such strange thoughts about the appearance of a woman. It was probably because I had almost taken the barque across the river of the dead myself not long ago.

Alva poured me wine from an amphora and placed small bowls and plates full of delicacies before my hungry eyes.

While I was eating, I asked her where Suavis was. There were no guests in the villa, so she couldn't be busy.

At this question, life came into Alva's face. No, not actually life, but rather fear. At least that was how it looked to me.

"I...I don't know, sir," she said hesitatingly. "Maybe she went to the market with the house servants."

I gazed at Alva in amazement, and she immediately lowered her eyes.

I had already noticed several times that things had changed in the villa since the old man's death, but was Philippos really unworldly enough to send one of the province's most valuable pleasure girls to go shopping at the market? I just couldn't believe it.

But what reason could Alva have to lie to me?

"Do you want me to play the lyre for you?" she asked me, while I feasted on a generous portion of caviarium, the fish eggs of Danubius sturgeon.

"I'm happy if you just keep me company," I said. I wasn't in the mood for music; actually, I just wanted to quickly fortify myself a little and then finally return home.

"How come I've never seen you at the villa before?" I asked Alva. "I'm a guest here quite often."

Once more she tried to smile, but again the corners of her mouth barely moved. "I was the body slave of Lycortas, sir. I had to stay exclusively in his private chambers."

"Then I guess he wanted you all to himself, the old geezer," I said with a laugh—but immediately tried to row back. "I'm sorry, Alva. I'm sure his death must have caused you great grief."

"Yes, sir. I miss him very much."

It was not easy to see behind the facade of this woman, but this claim was an outright lie. I could have sworn to that.

IX

When I entered the peristyle garden of my house, where Layla liked to stay in summer, I could not believe my eyes. Layla was there, sitting on one of the marble couches in the shade of the portico—but next to her, no, half on her lap, rested Marcellus. The Tribune.

"*Rosa mea,*" I heard him say to Layla just as I arrived. He was smiling at her like a shy boy. Then, however, he must have noticed my footsteps, straightened up, and in one fell swoop transformed back into the awe-inspiring commander I had come to know over the past few days.

Suddenly, I wondered whether I had merely imagined his words of endearment. *My rose?* Was I already fantasizing in broad daylight? Because of my injury?

Marcellus looked up at me from the marble couch and nodded a casual greeting. As if he was the master of the house here and I was just an annoying visitor who disturbed him during a tryst with *his* slave.

The Tribune was an attractive, handsome man. About Layla's age. And she didn't seem to mind his overtures. Rather the opposite. There it was again, that stab of jealousy I felt not for the first time.

Layla jumped up and embraced me. "You are well, master," she cried, "thank the gods!" She pressed her slender body against me and looked up at me with her night-black eyes.

I gently stroked her head.

"Very impressive," said the Tribune. "The medicus was right, you have the constitution of an ox, Thanar." He rose as well, stepped in front of me, and patted me on the shoulder as if we were old friends.

"To what do I owe the *renewed* honor of your visit, Tribune?" I asked.

His features hardened. He straightened up to his full height in front of me, which still made me look down on him.

"Another man was murdered, last night," he said flatly. "From the looks of it, only a few hours after the attack on you. My men found him this morning, among the graves on the south road, with half a dozen arrows in his back."

"By the gods! Who? Who was murdered?"

"Bricius Iodocus Rufus. One of the most respected citizens of the city."

"The Cattle Prince?" It was just a joking name, but every child in Vindobona knew Rufus by that moniker. He was a Roman citizen, but of Celtic descent. His family had lived in Vindobona long before the Romans invaded, and he owned one of the largest estates in the province. It was located east of the camp suburb and produced the best fillets far and wide. As far as I knew, Rufus was even the legion's main supplier of beef. And now he was supposed to be dead?

"Do you see any connection?" I asked the Tribune, "to the attack on me and the Primus Pilus?"

Obviously, that was a superfluous question. Why else had Marcellus come to my house again? Solving the death of a private citizen and bringing the murderer to justice was the business of the dead man's family—not something a Tribune of the legion had to worry about.

"Don't you see it?" retorted Marcellus. "It was the same arrows, the same night—"

"Roman arrows?"

Marcellus nodded. "Which you can—"

"All right," I sneered, "which you can buy at any arrow maker's."

A smile flitted across the Tribune's features, which was a great relief to me, given the boldness that had suddenly come over me.

"It looks like you actually told me the truth," Marcellus continued. His eyes again wandered over Layla, who was still standing with us.

I didn't understand what he was getting at, just looked at him questioningly.

"Well, Rufus was still seen alive at the time when the medicus cut the arrow from your back in our Valetudinarium. If you do not know the art of magic to the highest degree, you could not have murdered the man."

Of course. Why hadn't I noticed that myself? Perhaps because in the back of my mind I was still pondering the Tribune's strange advances to Layla? What did he want from my slave? And what game was he playing with me?

I was still sure that Marcellus knew more than he admitted. At least as far as the death of the Primus Pilus was concerned. Even if the murder of Rufus destroyed my beautiful conspiracy theory concerning Falco's legionaries. Had Rufus been just another random victim to create a false trail? To lead the search for the killer away from the legion? Would soldiers really go to such lengths just to get rid of their hated Primus Pilus and get away with it? I could not rule it out. After all, they had already tried to involve me in the whole thing. Yes, one had even sought my life. Almost with success.

"You said they found Rufus on the south road?" I addressed Marcellus again. "Among the graves?"

The Tribune nodded. "Just a quarter mile south of the camp suburb."

The Romans did not bury their dead within their settlements; but the roads leading out of Vindobona were lined with tombs. The more magnificently they were decorated and the closer they lay to the city, the more prestigious was the family whose ancestors were buried there.

"Was Rufus murdered among the graves, or was his body merely dumped there?" I asked.

"From the looks of it, he died on the spot. The first arrows probably didn't strike him down right away; he dragged himself along the road for quite a distance. The steps of the grave in front of which he finally collapsed are stained with blood, as if one of his cattle had been slaughtered there."

"Was he shot in the back like I was?"

"Yes, he was."

"And he was traveling alone? No slaves to accompany him?"

Marcellus shook his head. "Apparently, Rufus often went out in the evening without an entourage, that much I could already find out. He visited taverns in the camp suburb, barely a mile from his estate, and indulged in dice addiction in the back rooms. His wife probably wasn't supposed to find out about it. That's why he went alone, taking no slaves with him. I don't have to tell you how prone they are to gossip."

"But you seem to have learned the truth nevertheless, Tribune."

"Well, legionaries like to hang out in these taverns. They knew Rufus well and were aware of his vice. We had no difficulty in locating the innkeeper where our Cattle Prince indulged in wine and gambling last night. Rufus stayed in that tavern until closing time."

"So that's how you know he was still alive while I was already in the camp hospital."

"Right." The Tribune smiled triumphantly, apparently very taken with his own cleverness.

"But Rufus' estate is east of the camp suburb, isn't it?" I said. "So what was he doing on the south road after he'd left the tavern? That's quite the wrong direction for his way home, isn't it?"

"Figure it out, Thanar," the Tribune replied, "I can't tell you. But I will put this murderer on the cross, that much I know. By Jupiter! And you will help me do it."

It was a statement, not a question. But I did not contradict it. Of course, I would not rest until I had hunted down the man who had placed a corpse in my harbor and driven an arrow into my back. And who apparently liked to ambush his victims in particularly secluded places. Rufus had as little business late at night on the grave road as the Primus Pilus had in my harbor. Was this fact significant? Did it conceal a clue to the murderer? If so, I was struck with blindness.

"You can count on me, Marcellus," I said. "I'll take a closer look around Rufus's estate, if you don't mind. I'll ask a few questions and find out if he had any enemies. I think I can do that better than having the Roman legion march on Rufus's heirs."

"Your tongue is quite sharp, *barbarian*," said Marcellus, looking at me sternly. "Your walk along the banks of the river of the dead must have made you foolhardy. But I agree with you. I shall not fail to interrogate Rufus's household myself, but four eyes, as we know, see more than two. We'll find out if anyone tried to kill Rufus. Whether there is a connection to you or the Primus Pilus. And I'll have the road patrols doubled in the meantime. The corpse of this assassin will soon adorn a pole on the Limes Road, I swear to you!"

X

Layla remained leaning against a pillar, lost in thought, as the Tribune took his leave.

I put my arm around her shoulders and stroked her cheek. "I hope we didn't scare you with all this talk of murder, my dear," I said.

Layla shook her head. "I was just worried for your life, master. Last night, when you didn't come home. That's all. For Rufus I will not mourn, any more than for the Primus Pilus. It was the Furies who guided the hand of their murderer, of that I am sure."

"The Furies?"

"The goddesses of vengeance, master."

"I know who the Furies are, dear. But why would they go after Falco and Rufus' lives? Falco was a bad fellow, no question about it. If he had incurred the wrath of the Immortals, for all his misdeeds, I wouldn't have been surprised. But Rufus? He was a rather good-natured guy, as far as I knew him. Addicted to gambling and drunkenness, perhaps, but otherwise quite harmless. And besides, you never met him, did you?"

Layla nodded. "I never crossed paths with Falco either. But I didn't have to. Slaves talk among themselves, you know, master. They like to gossip a lot, because for most of them it's the only pleasure in their existence. We get our meat from Rufus' farm; twice a week his slaves deliver to us. And with the meat they bring the latest news and rumors. That's how I know what kind of man Rufus was."

"Your inquisitiveness is almost as great as your beauty, my dear," I joked.

She smiled. "I am no more curious than any other slave, master. There are open ears and eyes in every household. Everywhere and always. And then there is gossip. In the market, the forum, or the amphitheater when slaves are allowed to attend the games. The guards and lantern bearers talk among themselves while waiting for their masters, in front of the thermae, the theater or the villa of the Greek that you visit so often. And what they hear there they carry on to the house slaves, to the laborers in the fields or in the quarries, to the she-wolves in the brothels, or to the even more pitiable girls who sell themselves along the grave roads. It's like a big net that spans all of Vindobona and even reaches Carnuntum. So, you see, even though I don't leave your house and have never met Rufus or Falco, I know quite a bit about their deeds. Their cruel, deeply evil deeds. And the Furies have finally come to judge them both."

I didn't know what to say. Of course, I was aware that slaves talked among themselves, but the extent of their knowledge and how freely they shared it with their peers was something I had probably never considered. I was extremely uncomfortable with the thought that every slave in Vindobona knew what I was saying or doing in my own house.

But there had been something else in Layla's speech that had made me take notice: *the she-wolves at the grave roads!*

Layla was right—these women were the most pitiable of all. Even though many of them were free or freed women, their lot was harder than that of most slaves. For the equivalent of

71

a loaf of bread, they offered their spent bodies to those men who couldn't even afford—or didn't want—to visit the city's dingy brothels. I had not thought of them at all when the Tribune had spoken of the grave road, where the Cattle Prince had died.

Maybe one of these women had seen something last night? Maybe one of them had even witnessed the archer murdering Rufus?

But was this slave network Layla had just told me about really as tightly woven as she had claimed? Could my sheltered body slave have already heard what had happened at night on the grave road—barely half a day after the crime? It seemed inconceivable.

I immediately asked her about it, eager as a hunting dog that has picked up the scent of game. "Did you learn anything from the she-wolves? What did they report about last night?"

I looked at her expectantly, but Layla shook her head. "You misunderstood me, master. I said the slaves gossip about their masters, about the rich and powerful of the city, not that they're risking their necks with careless talk. Do you think a she-wolf would spread the word if she witnessed a crime? So that the killer would then cut *her* throat the next night? Those women are completely defenseless out there, master."

She fell silent for a moment, seemingly lost in thought. Then, however, she raised her head, looked at me, and said, "But at least now you know what Rufus wanted late at night on the grave road. Please don't say anything to the Tribune— the girls would be scared to death if the legionaries took them in for questioning." A distinct wrinkle creased Layla's dark brow. The fate of the she-wolves seemed to be very close to her heart.

"You mean to say Rufus was a *customer* of the grave-whores?" I asked. "I'm sure you're mistaken, dear. A man like him has enough luxury girls in the house, he would never—"

The crease in Layla's forehead became even more prominent. "Believe me, master, he did," she interrupted me. "He went to the graves regularly. Always late at night and alone, probably worried about his reputation. They say he had very particular tastes. But please don't ask me what they were," she added quickly. "I don't know. And don't want to know."

Layla fell silent. The corners of her mouth were twitching in disgust.

I could not believe it. As was so common with gossip, many a half-truth or plain slander probably spread in this slave network. A man like Rufus, one of the richest and most respected citizens of the city, should seek out the seediest whores in town? To indulge in some dark inclinations there? That was crazy. Nevertheless, I could think of no better explanation for what might have led Rufus to the grave road late at night.

However, the she-wolves would not help me to find the murderer. I could understand that they would keep silent, even if one of them had observed something. It would bring them nothing but trouble if they talked.

Many of the she-wolves were in the service of a pimp. Had Rufus possibly messed with one of them? Did his death have nothing to do with the Primus Pilus or me; had he simply died in a quarrel with a shady scoundrel? Had he been murdered for the few coins he was carrying?

I had to ask the Tribune if Rufus had been robbed. Although, what would that prove? His body had been lying by the road all night—surely his wallet had been emptied there. Not necessarily by his murderer.

No matter how I twisted and turned it, I got nowhere. If anything, this hideous series of murders only gave me new puzzles with every hour that passed.

And then another thought came to me—also not exactly one that was likely to cheer me up.

"Layla," I asked, "what is being said about *me* in your slave network? Do they wish the vengeful goddesses on my neck also? Do they associate me with Falco and with Rufus; do they believe I'm a bad person, too? Tell me the truth!"

Layla looked up at me in amazement. "You are the best master I have ever had, Thanar," she claimed with fervor.

I wanted only too much to believe her.

XI

The very next morning I set out for Rufus' estate.

I felt better; my legs carried me reliably again, and the wound in my back hardly hurt anymore. Nevertheless, for Layla's sake, I agreed to use the wagon instead of swinging into the saddle of my horse.

Rest, Thessalos, the camp doctor, had ordered me, and he certainly wasn't thinking of riding through half the city. And Layla kept talking to me until I complied and agreed to be driven.

For her sake, I even took a guard with me, only to spend the whole trip feeling like a decadent old bag who wasn't even man enough to defend himself in Vindobona on roads that were among the safest in the province.

Rufus' property was located between the civilian town and the camp suburb. The estate consisted of a manor house, to which generation after generation had made additions and alterations, a servants' quarters, and a storage wing. All the buildings crowded around a narrow courtyard and were surrounded by a fieldstone wall. Behind them stretched lush pastures with fat cows as far as the eye could see, as well as a few fields where slaves hobbled around in shackles.

It was common practice to keep those workers who performed the hardest jobs in agriculture or in mines and quarries from trying to escape in this way. These men even spent their nights chained in work prisons—usually dark, underground dungeons.

Looking at the farm slaves, I always had to think of the words of the learned Pliny: agriculture succeeds worst where it is done by inmates of labor prisons, like everything done by people without hope.

Today, however, Philippos' words also forced themselves back into my memory. Or rather Alcidamas' words, which he had quoted. *The gods have set all men free, and nature has made no one a slave.*

What a strange statement. I could not say that I fully understood it. Wasn't it just due to the divine order that some people were born as kings and princes, others as simple farmers, shepherds or craftsmen, as free citizens, and some as slaves? Who was I to question the course of the world? And why was I even pondering such a matter? I was a man of action, who was otherwise really not inclined to profound meditations.

The barking of two guard dogs jerked me back to the present. They were chained next to the entrance gate and greeted me with bared teeth.

The reception in the atrium was fortunately friendlier. An army of slaves, well-fed and apparently in deep mourning for the loss of their master, were bustling about. Rufus' body was laid out under the masks of his ancestors, as was the custom.

The dead man was wrapped in expensive clothes and was lying on his back, which made it impossible for me to take a closer look at his wounds.

Rufus' eldest son, a short, bald man, rushed over to greet me. We exchanged due words in view of the dead pater familias, then the son asked me if I had been a friend of his father.

I thought about it for a moment, but then decided to tell the truth. "I didn't know him well. We got our beef from him, of course—" I faltered.

"I was probably shot by the same assassin as your father," I then said. Crude, brutal words, but I couldn't think of gentler phrasing at that moment.

The little man looked at me, baffled. "Well, then, I'm sure you're as determined as I am to bring that conniving scoundrel to the cross." He jutted his chin forward, looking more comical than dangerous.

"We will," I said quickly. "He will pay for his bloody deeds!"

Then, without further ado, I moved on to the questions I had prepared. "Do you have any suspicions about who might have wanted to kill your father?" I began. "Did he have any enemies?"

The son smiled thinly. "I'm sure he didn't. He was a kind-hearted man. Always friendly to—" His voice failed him. He turned away for a moment to collect himself.

I was uncomfortable stirring up this man's grief with my questions. But what choice did I have? I finally needed answers. I had to find at least a lead that I could then follow up.

"So last night," I continued, "where was your father? What was he doing on the grave road so late at night?"

"The gods only know," said the son. "I can't explain it." He looked at me without really seeing me. He seemed to have really loved Rufus.

"My father liked to pay homage to Bacchus," he finally continued, after looking around to make sure no one was listening to our conversation. "When he left home alone, his destination was usually some tavern or other in the camp suburb. Not a place for a man of his standing, and my mother—

well, she's a woman who speaks her mind. She reproached my father every time she heard about one of his tavern visits. So he undertook them secretly. Surely, in one of these taverns some scoundrel noticed him and followed him on his way home. And then slaughtered him—just for the sake of his purse." Again, the son turned away, pressed his eyelids shut, and swallowed hard.

"So your father was robbed?" I had assumed that much. But it didn't explain how he had come to the grave road.

I couldn't possibly ask this grieving man if his father had been involved with the grave whores. Layla's claim in this regard seemed all the more ridiculous to me in this sprawling, luxurious estate. There was more than one pretty young girl among the house slaves, so why would Rufus take an emaciated, toothless wench on the grave road? It just didn't make sense. And if the Cattle Prince had indeed been the brute Layla's slave gossip made him out to be, I couldn't find any hint of that in his household either. Rufus' son, at least, seemed to think his father had almost been a saint.

"Has your father had any problems with the legion lately?" I tried a different approach. After all, there was the matter of the dead Primus Pilus in my port, which still puzzled me.

The son looked at me uncomprehendingly. "With the legion? We supply the camp with beef. We have for years. Only the very best quality. And they pay well and on time. There have never been any problems."

"Did he perhaps know Falco, the Primus Pilus, more closely?"

"Not that I know of. He was murdered too, wasn't he? But with an axe, as far as I was told?"

I nodded wordlessly. Not only the slaves in Vindobona

were well informed, but their masters no less, it seemed. However, Rufus' son didn't seem to know that I was the man in whose harbor Falco's body had been found. Or he was too polite to emphasize it.

First the axe, then a bow. Did this change of weapons mean something? Just as I was asking myself this question, the son said, "Whoever he was, this murderer, he must have been a real bungler. Five shots to put down a man who was on foot? And all that for the sake of a purse that my father would have handed over to him without hesitation! Father was a peace-loving man. Almost a little fearful, if I'm honest."

His hands clenched into fists. "That fiend didn't have to kill him just to get his money!" he cried with bitterness.

Now it was my turn to stare at him, baffled. "On foot? Your father wasn't on horseback?"

"No. He hasn't ridden for many years. He usually took the wagon or the carrying chair. But as I said, some evenings he didn't want any companions."

I must have been mistaken. That was, not I, but the Tribune. As a matter of course, Marcellus had assumed that Rufus' murderer was the same man who had attacked me. And I had followed him in this assumption without questioning it.

But an archer who was able to hit a fleeing rider in the deepest darkness and at a considerable distance with just a single, deadly accurate shot—surely such a marksman didn't have to waste five arrows to take down an elderly man who was on foot?

Again, this was something that made no sense at all. I almost uttered a curse in the presence of the mourning man and his laid out dead father.

No matter how hard I tried, these strange attacks only became more inexplicable the more questions I asked. How was I ever going to find the murderer? Or rather the murderers, because as it seemed, it could not possibly be one and the same man.

XII

Like a beaten dog, I made my way home and also caught myself constantly watching for suspicious characters on the side of the road. When the wagon bumped into a pothole, I winced.

It could not possibly go on like this.

I instructed my coachman to make a short detour through the civilian town and had him stop in front of Belius' house. It was an elegant town house in the immediate vicinity of those brickworks to which my friend owed his enormous wealth.

Belius himself, however, was not at home. I briefly considered waiting for him, but his body servant could not tell me when he expected him back. Some administrative matter had led him to the forum of the camp suburb.

I could not have said what I hoped to get out of Belius either. Maybe I just wanted to lament my suffering to a friend. To wail in his ears how much these ghastly murders were affecting me. Pathetic, I know.

I feasted on a few grapes offered by a slave, then left word for Belius to meet me tomorrow evening at the Greek's Villa. Perhaps my always well-informed friend could at least give me some more information about Rufus. Was the Cattle Prince now a fiend, as Layla wanted me to believe, or the man beloved by all, whom his son saw in him?

I took my leave and set off on my way home.

As I approached the bridge over the Danubius that would take me to the north bank and my house, a familiar figure came riding toward me. A Roman on a tall white horse, proud and confident in the saddle like a commander.

Tribune Marcellus.

He turned onto the Limes Road before I had quite reached the bridge and didn't seem to have noticed me. Where did he come from? What was he doing on the north bank of the river, in barbarian territory?

I received the answer from Layla shortly thereafter—although it was not even a remotely satisfactory explanation. Marcellus had paid another visit to my house. He had waited for a while to see whether I would return home but then had left again without having achieved anything.

"And what did he want?" I asked Layla. "There hasn't been another death, I hope?"

Layla did not answer, she seemed to have to ponder first.

"Didn't he leave me a message?" I probed.

"No, master." Layla seemed uncertain, confused—which was not usually her style. Normally she knew an answer to everything and anything, even without being asked.

"Are you sure? I mean, he didn't come here just for fun, did he? How long did he stay?"

Layla lowered her head as if I had reprimanded her. "Quite a while, sir. He chatted about this and that, about last week's gladiator games, about the emperor's new gold coins... He wanted to know how long I'd been part of your household and where I'd been before that. Things like that. I asked him, of course, if there was anything new. About the murders, I mean."

"So?"

Layla shook her head. "If there was, he didn't tell me about it. Maybe he just wanted to talk about it with you in person?"

"But he didn't leave me a message to come see him? Or to let me know that he will return at a later hour?"

"I'm really sorry, master."

"No, no it's okay, dear. It's not like it's your fault. It's just...I can't figure this man out. What is his role in all this, what does he know about the murders, what is he hiding? And why this continued interest in me when he supposedly no longer thinks I'm the guilty party?"

Marcellus had claimed the latter, at least after the murder of Rufus—which, according to his own words, I could not have committed. But who was able to know what the Tribune really thought? Was he spying in my house in my absence? Had he chosen Layla to question her about me? It was highly suspicious, after all, that he was so interested in her. What other Roman nobleman liked to have such long conversations with a slave girl?

Layla was loyal and devoted to me, I was sure of that. Even if I could not hope, of course, that she could show me the same affection that I felt for her. After all, she had no choice in the matter. She had not come into my house voluntarily; she was not my wife. Even if I seemed to forget that more and more often. And the Tribune was a powerful man who could become very dangerous very quickly. For Layla as well as for myself. I'm sure she was aware of that.

I left her at home and made my way down to my port. I had a shipload of Roman goods to get on its way, destined for the northwestern provinces. And after that I had to load another boat—with precious amber, which I was delivering to an intermediary in Carnuntum.

I made every effort to concentrate fully on my business. I supervised the packing, assigned men to guard and transport duties, then wrote some letters and sent out messengers— but it was all to no avail. I was only half focused; my thoughts kept drifting. To the dead Primus Pilus, to the inscrutable Tribune, and to the archer who had hit me so masterfully, only to shoot at Rufus like a beginner.

Finally, I gave up work and instead made a libation to the gods on my home altar. "Please give me enlightenment," I pleaded. "Just one tiny lead! Help me find this murderer! I'll soon lose my mind if you don't." I promised the immortals a fat bull if they came to my aid and hoped desperately that they would hear my plea.

That same evening a messenger arrived with a letter from Belius. My friend was looking forward to meeting me tomorrow evening at the Greek's villa.

I have a theory that might interest you, he had scribbled in his barely legible handwriting on the wax tablet.

Leaving my own house the next evening proved difficult.

Layla tried to talk me into an escort that I wouldn't have assigned even to a trade wagon full of gold and pearls. Besides, I had had enough of wagon rides. I wanted to get back in the saddle and move freely and carefree on Vindobona's streets again.

It happened that due to my two shipments yesterday, most of my guards were on the way. And I really did not want to leave my house—including Layla—unprotected. Thus, there was no man to spare for an escort. With this argument I finally managed to convince my worried slave. But maybe she just knew me well enough to understand when I was determined to get my own way. I did that far too seldom with her anyway.

So I sent for my horse, armed myself with a well-sharpened long knife, and swung myself into the saddle under Layla's saddened gaze. Because of my back injury, I didn't manage nearly as smoothly as I had intended, but at least without help.

I still had to promise her to make my way home through the darkness together with Belius and his entourage; then I finally managed to ride off.

I think part of me was crazy—or desperate—enough to hope for another attack by the killer. Now I was prepared and would not be such easy prey. I would hunt down the villain and then thrust him, dead or alive, at the Tribune's feet. I had sworn to bring the man to the cross and, by the gods, I was determined to do it!

Dusk was just falling over the land when I reached the junction to the villa. No sooner had I turned into the narrow forest path than my stallion suddenly spooked.

Directly on the path stood a hulking man whose hand went to the pommel of his sword when he saw me. I pulled my own knife from my belt, but at that moment he stepped aside and nodded at me with a friendly smile. Then I recognized him too: he was one of the guard slaves of the villa. So Philippos had taken the matter seriously and placed the forest path under guard. The lives of his guests were obviously close to his heart.

Halfway to the estate, I met another guard, just as armed with sword and shortbow as the first, and this time it was I who nodded to him, identifying myself as a guest of the

Greek.

That evening, the villa itself also seemed almost as it did in the days of the old Lycortas. Orodes, the Parthian, guarded the entrance, and no sooner had I entered the atrium than I was greeted. Juba hurried toward me, the old man's former servant, to whom Philippos had entrusted the reception of guests.

On a whim, I asked him how the beautiful Chloe was doing—but he was not flustered by my innuendo. Neither with words nor with the slightest gesture did he betray his secret tryst with the young Greek woman, which I had unintentionally witnessed.

I let him lead me to the summer triclinium, the great hall where Belius liked to be entertained. But there was no trace of my friend. I also hadn't noticed his chair bearers in front of the villa this time. Probably Belius was still on his way here.

"I'm going to stretch my legs a bit in the garden and wait for my friend," I said to Juba, who then bowed and hurried back toward the atrium.

Halfway across the room, however, Suavis came toward me. In a sleeveless tunic, barefoot, and with flushed cheeks, she pranced toward me like a young deer. In her left hand she balanced a silver tray from which she took a cup and handed it to me. "Welcome sir, would you like some refreshment? Some well chilled mulsum?"

I was delighted to help myself. There was nothing better on an oppressively hot summer evening than cold honey wine. And the villa's ice cellars were always just as excellently stocked as the wine warehouse, I could rely on that.

"Belius sends his regards," Suavis said as I drank in thirsty sips. "If you agree, he would like to dine in the garden today. May I show you to your arbor? He himself is still in the bathing grotto but will join you presently, I am to tell you."

She gave me such an innocent smile that I had to laugh. I had noticed that her hair, which she wore pinned up, was wet at the nape of her neck. So it wasn't hard to put one and one together and know what had lured Belius into the bathing grotto before supper and what he was just recovering from.

The old philanderer! It was actually not like him to retreat to a cozy tête-à-tête with his favorite girl right after his arrival at the villa.

"The old boy is falling for you more and more every day, sweet Suavis," I joked, earning a girlish eye-roll in return. The young woman was really adorable. She certainly knew exactly what effect her innocent act had on men. And Belius was probably particularly susceptible to it.

You yourself are not one bit better off, it went through my mind. Layla had me at least as much in her grip as this beautiful Germanic woman had my old friend. With this thought, I settled down in the arbor where Suavis led me and lost myself in reflections about the power of women.

Suavis scurried away among the tall trees that overshadowed the garden to inform Belius of my arrival. In the meantime, I feasted on the appetizers that were already waiting in the arbor. There was cheese, olives, flatbread, and fresh plums. And another well-chilled amphora of mulsum.

I poured myself a drink and made myself comfortable on the softly upholstered marble couch. I wondered what Belius' theory, which he had hinted at in his letter, might be all about. Would I finally get to the bottom of the murders with his help?

Time passed, but my friend did not appear. What took him so long, I asked myself impatiently. Had he pulled Suavis into the pool with him once again, the old lecher, instead of finally dressing and coming to me?

I leaned back and looked up at the evening sky. *What a wonderful place the villa is*, I thought. Then a sudden tiredness overcame me, and I decided to close my eyes for a bit until Belius would finally join me.

XIII

It was a sharp woman's scream that woke me from my stupor. Startled, I pulled myself up. It took me a moment to remember where I was. In the Greek's Villa, in the arbor where I was waiting for Belius—

That was as far as my thoughts got, because at that moment I saw him: Belius. He lay stretched out on the marble couch facing mine, his eyes wide open, his tunic full of blood. So much blood! I still had to be dreaming; this was a nightmare, for sure!

"He's dead!" the woman's voice now screamed. I turned my head, and there stood Suavis. Her eyes seemed about to pop out of their sockets at any moment; she stared first at me, then back at Belius, then turned on her heels and ran wailing toward the house.

It was not a nightmare. In Belius' neck stuck the hilt of a knife—*my* knife, I now realized. My friend was dead, murdered, right under my eyes. Under my closed eyes.

That was impossible! I couldn't have been asleep the whole time while Belius was being slaughtered like a sacrificial animal not five feet away from me. I rubbed my temples, struggling to clear my head. I felt as if I had drunk an entire amphora of honey wine, but I had not. Or had I?

Everything was such a blur. Suavis had led me here to the arbor, that much I remembered. Then she had gone to inform Belius of my arrival.

And after that?

Nothing more. I lacked any memory.

Rapidly approaching footsteps jerked me back to the present. Then suddenly Orodes stood before me, the muscular Parthian, with two men at his side, hardly less impressively built. He just nodded wordlessly to them, and they positioned themselves where the arbor opened onto the garden, thus blocking the way out.

They did that because of me. They wanted to prevent me from escaping. It took me far too long to comprehend this. My head was still not working properly.

Only now did I realize what this must look like. My friend dead on the bench, with my knife in his throat.

I followed Orodes' gaze as it traveled down my body, and there sheer horror gripped me: my clothes were stained with blood, just like my hands.

I stammered wildly, trying to make it clear to Orodes that I didn't understand any of this any more than he did, that I was innocent...

I don't know what words came out of my mouth and whether they made any sense. I simply could not comprehend what I saw with my own eyes.

Belius was dead. It was not a nightmare. It was much worse. My dearest friend. Dead.

At that moment, two more men entered the arbor. Orodes' guards willingly cleared the way for them. They were Philippos, the master of the house, and Juba, the African servant.

Philippos flinched at the sight of Belius' dead body, while Juba's eyes immediately darted over every detail of the arbor—only to linger on me.

"I didn't murder him!" I shouted before any of the men

could say anything.

Juba's dark eyes reflected suspicion. Philippos, on the other hand, who had now stepped between Juba and Orodes, simply stood there and stared into nothingness. Between the tall African and the muscular Parthian, he looked and acted like a boy. Which did not surprise me. What else could one expect from a man who was already overtaxed by the management of a household?

Fortunately, the chaos in my head now cleared a little, even if I hardly felt anything other than the pain over the loss of my friend. This was another murder they were trying to pin on me! Just like the death of the Primus Pilus in my port.

"What happened here?" asked Juba, while his master was still staring into space, transfixed. "Did you two have a fight?" The servant's voice sounded remarkably matter-of-fact.

I shook my head vigorously. Then I reported everything I could remember. Up to the moment when I had fallen asleep.

"You were overcome by fatigue an hour after sunset?" Orodes asked suspiciously.

I shrugged helplessly. After all, I couldn't explain it to myself. I generally didn't tend to go to bed early.

Juba bent over the table, lifted the amphora, and looked inside. "Empty," he commented.

I could not remember having poured more than one cup from this vessel, and it certainly held enough to fill five or six cups.

"The murderer must have given me a sleeping draught!" I cried. "In the wine or in the food! All this was already prepared when I came here. Everyone had free access to it."

Orodes rubbed his chin. "A man falls asleep at the table—

91

and wakes up hours later, over a dead body?" he said. "That's what you want us to believe?"

"I did not make up this atrocity! Probably the murderer also drugged Belius, just like me. He was alone in the bathing grotto. He must have been dragged here from there and then stabbed with my knife."

The bathing facilities were located in the back of the villa. Not a hundred steps separated them from the arbor. A strong man could have carried Belius here unseen. A *very* strong man. My friend had accumulated a considerable corpulence over the years. He had certainly not been a light burden.

"And how did the blood get on your clothes?" Orodes probed further. "And on your hands?"

"I don't know! Maybe Belius was—" I fell silent. I could not and would not imagine it. It was just too cruel. Had my friend been killed right above me and only then dumped on the couch across from me?

"The murderer must have dipped my hands in Belius' blood," I said. "After the murder. However he managed to do that."

Orodes looked at me doubtfully, then turned to Philippos.

The Greek, however, did not utter a word. Even when Orodes addressed him with a reverent "Master?" he showed no reaction.

The Parthian straightened his powerful shoulders. "I'll go get Suavis," he said, this time addressing Juba. "Maybe she saw something. Though I'm not sure we'll get a sensible word out of her."

"The poor thing," grumbled Juba. "The sight here is truly not for a woman." He made a sweeping gesture over Belius' bloodied corpse.

Orodes hurried away with quick steps, but his men did not take their eyes off me for a moment.

When the Parthian returned with Suavis, she clung to his arm and half ducked behind his massive body. She looked more childlike and fragile than ever.

It was I who addressed the first question to her, "You led me here and then went to the bathing grotto to Belius, didn't you, Suavis? Did you meet him there?"

The girl stared at me fearfully for a moment, as if I were a bloodthirsty predator, then she nodded, barely perceptible.

"Good, and then you came back here with him? You must have found me sleeping then, right?"

"No...sir," she replied in a shaky voice, clinging even tighter to Orodes' arm. "When I went to the bath to inform Belius of your arrival, he told me that he was about to set out for you. He did not want me to accompany him. And he specifically said he didn't want any disturbance in the arbor. Therefore..."

Her voice failed. A tortured whimper, reminiscent of an injured bird, escaped from her throat.

She swallowed. Then she continued, "That's why I didn't check on you, that is, not all evening. But then, in the end, I did want to ask if you required more wine or food." She sniffled, looking at me from her sky-blue eyes, which were now swimming with tears.

Orodes put his massive arm around her and pressed her against him. Whereupon Suavis sobbed even harder.

I felt sorry for her, but I had to know if she might not have seen something that could help me. "Did you notice anyone else here near the arbor during the evening?" I asked. "Anyone going into the garden or coming back into the house from the garden?"

"I really wasn't paying attention to that, sir. I have taken care of other guests in the meantime. As is my duty," she added, with a fearful sideways glance at Philippos.

He just nodded absently. Still, he had not spoken a word. He stood there as if he were the slave who respectfully stayed in the background while his masters would somehow settle this nasty affair.

I continued to try my luck with Suavis. "When you discovered Belius' body, you must have seen that I was asleep, right? It was your scream that woke me."

Suavis did not reply.

"Is that true?" inquired Orodes, lifting the girl's chin with his index finger. When she looked up at him, he gave her an encouraging nod. There was something strange in his gaze as he did so. Something soft and tender that I would never have thought this Parthian warrior capable of.

"I...don't know," Suavis stammered. "I just saw the...the dead man. All the blood."

"You didn't notice Thanar?" Orodes probed. "Was he even here when you found the body?"

"Yes, yes, he was present. He was lying here." She pointed to the couch, from which I had long since risen.

Then she hesitated. "I don't know if he was asleep," she said barely audibly. At the same time, her gaze darted fearfully over the faces of the men present but avoided me.

"There you have it," I tried to make use of the little Suavis had supplied me. "If I had murdered my friend—which I absolutely had no reason to, for I loved that man like a brother!—then I should hardly have lain here after the deed was done. I tell you, someone is trying to frame me, and it is not the first time!"

Juba and Orodes exchanged a meaningful look. They too must have heard about the dead Primus Pilus in my harbor. If the slave gossip provided Layla with information as excellently as she claimed, it surely reached here to the villa as well.

"Perhaps Thanar was not asleep, but the gods struck him with a fainting spell," Juba said to Orodes, as if I were not even present. "So that he would not escape his just punishment." At this, the African clasped the amulet he wore around his neck.

XIV

Anger flared up in me. This was really going too far. I had enough of being interrogated by slaves and servants as if before a high court. Enough of slander, which now went so far as to invoke a judgment of the gods upon me.

"Send for Tribune Marcellus!" I cried, before Orodes could make a reply to Juba. "He is in charge of solving this series of murders. He can vouch for me and investigate this crime here."

That was a bold statement, born of nothing but desperation. Whether Marcellus would believe me, when I was accused of murder for the second time within a few days, only the gods knew. But he was a man of reason—at least that was the impression I had of him. He could be convinced by facts and sound arguments. And he could help me search for the real murderer. We would question the rest of the slaves in the house to see if anyone had seen anything. At least that was a start.

The murderer must have followed me here to the villa. The wall surrounding the mansion was not a real obstacle for a halfway dexterous man. Or the villain had walked in unhindered through the atrium. Was he possibly to be found among the guests of the villa?

Philippos took the floor for the first time. "I think that's a good idea," he said. "Let the Tribune decide what to do. Send a messenger to the legion camp."

This time it was Orodes who sought Juba's gaze. Whatever he wanted to say, the African seemed to understand him. He shook his head almost imperceptibly.

Orodes then turned to Philippos. "I think it is better that we take our guest to the Tribune, master. I'll ride out with him myself first thing in the morning. We can have him spend the night with us. In safety."

The Parthian knew how to choose his words well. What he meant by letting me *spend the night in safety* was all too clear. He wanted to lock me up.

I did see the point why neither he nor Juba thought it a good idea to let the Roman legion invade the villa. The guests who were enjoying themselves in the house would surely not be pleased. And it would certainly not be good for business if word got out that a guest had been murdered in one of the arbors.

I, however, could not take this into consideration. I had to talk to Marcellus, to prove my innocence with his help. On the other hand—to get away from here, to ride to the legion camp, that was just fine with me. But I did not intend to wait until the next morning.

I was about to protest loudly, to insist that I be taken to the Tribune immediately. But then I paused. When I thought about it, I could really use a few hours. I had to figure out what I was going to say in the first place. How was I going to prove my innocence to Marcellus again?

Moreover, I was desperately longing for some sleep. I had to have a clear head when I faced the Tribune, otherwise I would follow Belius all too quickly across the river of death. Through the stomach of some bloodthirsty beast that would feast on me in the arena should I be found guilty.

Why had my friend had to die? Belius was the most kind-hearted and peace-loving man I knew. What hatred could the murderer have for him?

Without resistance, I let Orodes' men lead me to the basement of the villa. They took me to an empty storage room, the door of which was secured with an iron lock.

I couldn't have told how long I lay in that dungeon staring into the darkness, unable to make any sense of the evening's events. Or how often I dozed off in between. Surely someone had given me a sleeping draught after my arrival at the villa, of that I was now quite certain. I hadn't drunk five cups of wine, I wasn't intoxicated—at least not in the way one gets intoxicated from Bacchus' gifts. I had been tricked and made a murderer again, that much was clear to me. But why kill Belius, my beloved friend?

He had announced in his letter that he wanted to present me with an interesting theory. And he had ordered Suavis not to disturb us at our meeting in the arbor. That had to mean that he had found out something. About the murders. Or the murderer. Something that could expose the villain— or at least a solid lead that would eventually lead us to him. That had to be it. The killer must have found out about it.

Had Belius possibly confronted him with his knowledge?

No, my friend would not have been that reckless. He had never taken big risks, had never set foot outside the door without his guards. But that had not been able to save him in the end.

I had my best friend's death on my conscience. It was I who had involved Belius in the murder investigation. I would have to live with this guilt for the rest of my days. A short period of time only, if I didn't think of something soon.

A sound startled me out of my gloomy thoughts. A metallic scratching somewhere in the darkness. I jumped to my feet and pressed myself against the basement wall. Then I realized where the noise was coming from and what it was. Someone was turning a key in the iron lock that separated me from freedom.

Had the night already passed? Had Orodes come to present me to the Tribune?

My guts clenched in cold panic. I was not ready yet. I had nothing to show, nothing to say, no finely honed arguments to prove my innocence.

The door opened slowly and almost silently. The faint glow of a tiny oil lamp fell through the crack.

The figure carrying the lamp was not Orodes. I could only make out a human outline, but it was much too small and narrow for the massive body of the Parthian.

"Thanar?" the figure whispered.

A woman's voice!

I detached myself from the wall and crossed the room with quick steps. Then I knew who was standing there in front of me. "Suavis? What are you doing here?"

"Shh," the girl said, pressing the index finger of her free hand against her lips. "They mustn't hear us," she said, so softly that I barely understood her.

She quickly glanced over her shoulder, then gestured for me to follow her. I didn't let her tell me twice.

Her lamp barely illuminated the darkness of the basement hallway, but Suavis guided me with a sure step to the stairs and then through another narrow hallway. She walked on bare feet, as silently as a deer in the woods, while I plodded along behind her like a drowsy bear, confused and ponderous.

"Why are you helping me?" I whispered as she came to a halt in front of a door. A massive wooden door that was latched from the inside. "And how did you get the key to my dungeon?"

Suavis pressed her lamp into my hand and stemmed the whole weight of her delicate body against the massive latch. With a squeak that seemed to penetrate my every limb, the door burst open. Cool night air rushed in.

"I know you're innocent, sir," Suavis whispered, looking around hurriedly, then shoving me through the door with her child hands. "Here on the left is the garden. At the far end, the wall is easiest to get over, I think. Be quick!"

"Wait! What do you know, Suavis? Have you seen the killer? You have to tell me!"

Again, she squinted fearfully over her shoulder. "I did indeed find you asleep, as you said, sir. At the time I returned to the arbor, and Belius—" She faltered.

"And Belius was dead," I completed her sentence.

She didn't react; wanted to scurry back into the house. I just caught her by the arm and held her back. "Why didn't you confirm that I was asleep?" I asked.

She tried to escape my grasp but had to realize that it was useless. "I was afraid, sir," she whispered, "I did not dare to speak for your innocence. Forgive me."

"Afraid? Of whom?"

"You should really escape now, sir."

"I'm not leaving until you tell me everything. Tell me what you know. I won't betray you."

A low moan escaped her throat. "I don't know anything, sir. I just figured you certainly wouldn't go to sleep after murdering your friend. But if it wasn't you who killed him—"

"—someone else must have done it," I said. Possibly one of those men who had so self-righteously held court over me? Orodes? Or Juba? Whoever, if this man got the impression that Suavis knew too much, her life was no longer worth a sesterce. Anyone who could cut down a Primus Pilus with an axe would break this girl's neck with his bare hands. Probably without a thought about her death. No wonder she had not dared to speak freely.

With a jerk, Suavis freed her arm from me, whirled around, and scurried back into the house. She had already pulled the door shut behind her before I could say anything else. I only heard the latch, which squeaked again like a tortured animal.

I stood alone in the darkness of the night, unable to move.

What should I do now? Flee as far as my feet would take me? Over the garden wall, to the river, and from there north to my house? I could pack my most precious possessions into the travel wagon, take Layla with me, and flee to the far north.

Where I would be on the run for the rest of my life. Branded as a murderer who was blamed for two deaths, one of them a Roman Primus Pilus. The Tribune would have me hunted down, and no one who cared for his own life would give me shelter. The barbarian lands might not be a province of the Empire, but the power of the Roman army reached everywhere.

No, that was not a solution. I had to face the Tribune, voluntarily, as a free, innocent man. Right now. I had to calmly recite to Marcellus what had happened, convince him that

Belius had to die because he had gotten too close to the murderer. I didn't have anything better.

I hurried off in the direction Suavis had pointed out to me. I would return to the Villa as soon as possible, accompanied by the Tribune. Perhaps some trace of the murderer could still be found, if one searched thoroughly.

The sky was cloudy, the night black as the depths of Hades. I wandered over garden paths, on which I had already walked carelessly a hundred times during the day, expecting at any moment that my escape would be noticed and that henchmen would pursue me.

But I listened in vain for footsteps in the darkness, peered in vain for the glow of torches rapidly approaching me.

Finally, I found the wall. Or rather, I stumbled blindly into it. Groping, I searched for a foothold between the rough stones—then something struck me down from behind that felt like a bolt of lightning from Jupiter. Fiery pain flashed through the back of my head, then my eyes went black.

XV

So now the time had come. My execution in the amphitheater. I could already hear the roar of the beast, which would instantly pounce on me under the cheering shouts of the audience. I knelt in the sand of the arena, tasting blood in my mouth. The pain in my head was hammering so brutally that I could perceive nothing but blackness around me.

I wrenched my eyes open, forcing myself to look, wanting to face the beast that would maul me in the next instant. A bear, unmistakable. Its roar was already very close, threatening to shatter my thudding skull.

Why couldn't I see anything? Why couldn't I remember my accusation before the judge, my death sentence, or how I had been dragged here to the arena? Had I not just been in the garden of the Villa? Yes, I had been—until I was struck down by Jupiter's lightning at the wall.

At that moment it came back to me.

Dazed, I touched the back of my head, where pain was pounding. My fingers felt wetness, probably my blood, and a large bump.

Not a stroke of lightning had hit me; much rather something like a club blow. And not the divine Jupiter had struck me down, but a human henchman. The murderer?

The dungeon in the Villa at night pushed itself back into my memory. Suavis, who had helped me to escape and was now possibly in danger herself. And how I had wandered around in the night-black silence of the garden until that blow on the back of my head.

The night-black silence. Apart from the eerie roar of the beast that pulsated in my ears, it was still completely silent around me. And almost pitch black. Where was the audience in the tiers of the amphitheater, where was their bloodthirsty cheer? And why was it night? Surely executions in the amphitheater were not held in the dark?

I scrambled to my feet, rubbing my eyes to finally regain my sight.

That helped a little. I noticed that it was not completely dark around me. A little above me, at a distance of perhaps thirty feet, I could make out a torch. It was stuck in a holder and gave off flickering light. Next to it was a door, and in front of it were the rows of seats of the amphitheater.

No, there was only one row. But it *was* an amphitheater that I was in, although much smaller than that of the camp suburb or the civilian town.

Above me, no night sky was stretching, that much I realized now. I was in a building, in a windowless room.

I stood on the floor of the arena, in the sand, and all around me loomed the audience seats. But they were empty. Not a single spectator was staring down on me. Only the bear was still roaring. Where was he?

Swaying, I turned around. I felt dizzy, and the pain in the back of my head almost robbed me of my senses.

To my right, I saw the outline of a grate that closed off a tunnel. The roar of the bear came from over there, but I could not see the beast. Behind the bars of the grate, I could make out nothing but a black hole.

Something moved on the gallery directly above the grille.

The light of the single torch left large parts of the room in semi-darkness, the far end even in complete blackness. But could that silhouette up there on the gallery belong to a human being? It wasn't much more than a dark shadow. No, there were two of them! Three or four feet to the right crouched another shadow. He had to be sitting on the spectator's bench, for he loomed far less high than the other figure, and he did not move.

"Who are you?" I called to the phantoms. "What is this place?"

I received no answer. Instead, the upright shadowy figure bent down, and a loud crunch sounded. At the same time, the grating in front of the tunnel started to move. It shifted upward handbreadth by handbreadth.

The man up there was operating a rope winch! He let the beast, which now roared even more bloodthirsty, into the round of the arena. Where I stood.

This might not be one of the amphitheaters of Vindobona, but still an execution was to take place here and now. *My* execution! The two figures up there on the spectator stand were about to unleash a beast on me.

The grate in front of the tunnel had already lifted halfway. In a few moments, the beast would pounce on me. With staggering steps, I headed for the side of the arena where most of the light from the torch fell. I pressed my back against the wood of the enclosure, knowing for certain that it was far too high to climb.

There was no escape from this arena. And I had nothing to defend myself but my naked fists. Already the bear stormed out of the tunnel, stopped, and straightened up, roaring on his hind legs. He must have smelled the two people on the stand above him, because he turned to face them. He dropped back onto all fours and charged the few steps toward the rail. There he got to his hind legs again, striking upward with one paw, but the spectator seats were out of reach even for him.

Suddenly, there was a new sound. A rumbling above my head.

Steps.

The vague inkling of murmuring voices.

There was someone up there!

I hesitated for just a single breath, then screamed at the top of my lungs, "Down here! Help me!"

I knew that my yelling would draw the beast's attention to me, and it did. And maybe those people up there were just the cronies of the two villains who had just unleashed the bear on me. After all, I didn't even know where I was or what was above my head. Still, it was my only chance.

I screamed once again.

The bear charged toward me.

I yelled even louder. I stared directly into the ugly face of the beast and jerked both arms above my head to make myself as tall as possible. This was how one behaved when suddenly facing one of these brown-furred beasts in the forest and not carrying a weapon. Which would never have happened to me. I never crossed a forest unarmed.

The bear paused. Not five feet in front of me he came to a halt, reared up again on his hind legs, jerked his massive skull up, and growled at me from his fetid mouth.

I was a dead man. A bear was two times as fast and five times as heavy as the strongest warrior. He was armed with teeth and claws as sharp as the best Celtic steel. In the small round of the arena there was no escape from this monster.

I was already preparing to commend my soul to the gods when the door on top of the gallery shook on its hinges. In the dim light of the torch, it groaned agonizingly, then the wood splintered, the door burst open, and several men rushed in close behind each other. Men with lanterns and flashing swords.

The bear jerked its head around, confused as to who was trying to steal its prey. Drool was dripping from its bared fangs.

The first of the men reached the railing of the grandstand, jumped over it with a spirited leap, and landed not an arm's length from me in the sand of the arena.

It was Marcellus, the Tribune.

At that moment, the beast attacked.

The monster lunged at me. I escaped its bared teeth with a diving leap that sent a ghastly pain through my back. I landed on my belly and quickly rolled to the side to escape the beast's paws as well. But a blow struck me, the claws digging into the flesh of my upper arm. I cried out.

Marcellus drove his sword into the bear's flank just as it was about to strike at me again. Now it was the beast's turn to howl in pain. It let go of me and wanted to rip out the Tribune's throat, but his blow had been well aimed. The bear was already staggering when two legionaries rushed at it from behind and finished it off with their swords.

With a final bloodcurdling roar, the beast sank to the ground.

For a time that seemed to last forever, I just lay there in the sand of the arena. I spat out what had come into my mouth and rubbed my eyes to be able to see clearly again, but then the pain overwhelmed me. My back stung as if the archer had struck me down again, and my upper arm felt as if it had been torn out.

The Tribune and one of his legionaries helped me to my feet.

"I was never so glad to see you, Marcellus," I said, and the words came from my heart. "You saved my life."

The Tribune made a hand gesture as if it were not worth mentioning. "What, by all the gods, is this?" he cried. "An underground arena? In a brothel?"

A *brothel*? So, we were still in the Greek's Villa? That couldn't possibly be.

"How...did you find me?" I stammered. "How did you know—"

"Your slave made sure that I was woken up and thrown out of bed," Marcellus said as naturally as if this statement made any sense. But it didn't. Tribunes did not have their sleep disturbed by slaves.

"Layla," he added, a most peculiar smile flitting across his face. "She must have convinced your servant that you were in danger because you hadn't come home from your visit to the Villa. In so much danger that only the Roman legion could save you. With this message, the two of them presented themselves at the East Gate, desiring to speak to me."

There it was again, that smile. A mixture of triumph and— I didn't know how to name the other. Amusement at Layla's audacity to show up at the legion camp in the middle of the night and ask for the Tribune?

So it was my beloved Nubian to whom I owed my life. I had

smiled at her concern for me and bragged that I could take good care of myself. This vanity almost became my undoing.

"What happened to you?" asked Marcellus. "How did you get here?" He looked around the arena in disbelief, gazing down at the motionless body of the beast he had so fearlessly taken on.

"I was knocked down—" During my escape, I almost said. Because I had been imprisoned as the murderer of Belius.

But this was neither the time nor the place to explain that to Marcellus.

"I came to myself here in the arena," I said instead and left it at that for the time being. That I had feared in my first confusion to have been condemned *ad bestias,* I also preferred to keep to myself. The Tribune did not need to know how close I'd considered myself to be to execution.

"Who?" asked the Tribune, "who did this to you?"

"I don't know. I couldn't make them out in the dark."

Marcellus uttered a curse.

I looked up at the gallery, where two legionaries had positioned themselves with lanterns and drawn swords. Next to them crouched one of the Villa's guard slaves, who must have been on night duty at the gate today and had let the legionaries into the house. The man looked around the amphitheater as if seeing it for the very first time. However, there was no trace of the two figures who had set the bear on me.

"There's probably another exit back there," I said, pointing to that side of the arena where the beast tunnel opened.

Marcellus instructed two of his legionaries to investigate. "Would be good if we found the exit unlocked," he turned back to me afterwards. "Hoisting you up into the stands in your condition might be difficult."

I let go of his arm, on which I was still leaning. I wanted to show him that I wasn't in such bad shape as he assumed.

My legs did carry me, but the pain that raged through my body just wouldn't subside.

"Take off your tunic," Marcellus said. "Let me see the wound."

I did as I was told. Carefully I pulled the garment over my head. Then I squinted down at my naked shoulder myself. The bear's claws had dug deep into my flesh, but I could still move my arm. I breathed a sigh of relief.

Marcellus tore off the part of my tunic that wasn't stained with blood and folded a bandage from it with deft hand movements. He knotted it tightly around my arm. "This will do until we get you to the Valetudinarium. Then Thessalos can patch you up expertly—again." He grinned at me.

"I'll be fine," I said with more bravado than I felt.

XVI

One of the two Marcellus had sent out returned from the beast tunnel. "This passage leads only into a large cage, which is locked from the outside, Tribune," he reported.

The second legionary stepped up beside him and rattled the ironclad door in the wooden enclosure of the arena just a few feet to the left of the beast tunnel. This must have been the way I was dragged in, but now, of course, this door was also locked.

The legionary threw himself bravely against it but could do nothing. The door and its lock were designed to withstand a bear.

"Slave," Marcellus called to the guard crouched at the top of the gallery. "Who has the key to this door?"

"I-I have no idea, Tribune," the man stammered, bowing deeply. "I'm t-the first time down here. Shall I wake the master?"

"Do that. And hurry up. He owes my friend here a lot of answers. Aculeo, you go with him," he ordered one of the legionaries.

My friend here. Oh, how the words made me feel good. So, Marcellus didn't think I was a murderer anymore? I breathed a sigh of relief, which, however, came out as a tortured groan, because the pain just drove through my arm again as if with red-hot iron.

The Tribune looked at me with concern, stepped toward

me, and once again checked the makeshift bandage he had put on me. "It's holding well," he said, and I squeezed out a smile and a few words of thanks.

Some minutes later, the legionary that Marcellus had sent off with the guard slave came running through the broken door at the top of the gallery.

"Do you have the key?" asked Marcellus.

The soldier came to a halt at the rail and bent down to us. "No, Tribune," he said hesitantly.

"What is the matter?" Marcellus hissed at him.

"We found the master of the house dead, Tribune."

"Philippos?" I cried. It couldn't be. Another murder?

Marcellus uttered a curse. His gaze slid restlessly over the enclosure of the arena that held us captive. "We'll have to climb, then," he ordered. "Come on, men, form a ladder for Thanar!"

The soldiers promptly obeyed. Like a troupe of acrobats, the three legionaries who were in the arena with us piled up against the enclosure. Two formed the base, the third climbed onto their shoulders and held out his hand to me.

I could only reach for it with my right hand; the left arm, which the bear had mauled, wouldn't be able to carry my weight. Marcellus pushed me upwards; from above two more soldiers bent down to me, and with combined forces they finally hoisted me up to the gallery. Then they pulled up the Tribune and the other legionaries, which was much quicker.

"Take us to the dead man, Aculeo," Marcellus ordered, then he offered me his arm for support, and we set off at a rapid pace.

We climbed through the door that the legionaries had broken open, or rather through what was left of it, followed a long, winding corridor, and finally climbed a staircase. It ended in a hallway that lay directly behind the atrium.

The Villa was bustling with activity. Slaves came running from all parts of the house, looking startled or sleepy. They froze or ducked away as soon as they saw the legionaries.

Marcellus ignored them, and I struggled to keep up with him. The spiraling events made me forget my pain for the moment.

A bear in the Greek's villa? Philippos, dead? None of this made any sense. Not in the slightest. The questions raged in my mind: why did they keep such a beast in this house? What was the underground arena all about? Who were the two villains who had thrown me to the beast? Surely, they were to blame for the death of Philippos as well. And for all the other killings. For the murder of Belius, my beloved friend.

The legionary we followed led us into a part of the Villa I had never entered. Apparently, here were the private rooms, which were not accessible to guests.

We arrived at a door that stood half open. In front of it, the guard slave, whom Marcellus had sent out for the key earlier, had positioned himself. At his feet crouched a sobbing, golden blond girl. Suavis? She was crying so desperately that it literally shook her delicate body.

"What's going on here?" Marcellus shouted at the slave.

The girl jerked her head up, and that's when I saw that it wasn't Suavis at all. It was Alva, her mother. The resemblance between the two women was truly astonishing.

"We found her next to the dead man, Tribune," said the legionary who had led us here. "In this condition."

The guard slave stepped sheepishly from one foot to the other, clearly overwhelmed by the crying woman.

"Then she killed the master of the house?" the Tribune asked incredulously.

Alva emitted a sound reminiscent of a deer wounded in a hunt, then suddenly jumped up and wanted to scurry past us. But Marcellus had excellent reflexes. His arm shot forward and got hold of her shoulder. "Take care of her," he ordered the legionary, shoving her toward man.

Impetuously, he pushed open the door that the slave had been guarding. The room behind it was a study, furnished with a carved chair, a desk made of precious wood, and a huge iron-bound chest.

On the chair sat Philippos—no, he hung more than he sat. His right hand was slack around the hilt of a dagger stuck deep in his chest. The floor beneath him was swimming in blood. The master of the Villa was indeed dead.

"What's this?" said Marcellus, reaching for a double-winged wax tablet that lay unfolded on the table. The accompanying stylus had rolled into the pool of blood at Philippos' feet.

"I have no regrets," Marcellus read aloud. "Death to the oppressors! Signed: Philippos."

The Tribune shoved the tablet into my hand. A deep wrinkle appeared on his youthful forehead.

Confused, I read the words again. My gaze wandered over the corpse once more, and then I realized the meaning of what I had noticed before but had not grasped: Philippos' right hand had wielded the dagger. His fingers were still clinging lifelessly to the hilt of the weapon and were stained all over with blood.

The young Greek had not been murdered but had taken his

own life. And what I held in my hand was his suicide note—in which he confessed to the murders! He was not another victim, but the perpetrator who had murdered three men. Falco, Rufus, Belius. And it was only thanks to Marcellus that I had not become the fourth. Or rather my faithful Layla, who had alerted the Tribune. I couldn't wait to take her in my arms.

I have no regrets. Death to the oppressors! I could not say that these sentences made much sense to me.

But then Layla's words came back to me, her fixed idea that the Furies had slain the bad men, as she had put it. Falco, the Primus Pilus, and Rufus, the Cattle Prince. Had Philippos seen in them both the same as my slave had done? Oppressors from whom the world had to be freed?

But what about Belius—or me? Belius had been a kind-hearted man, and as for myself, I could be accused of many things, but I was certainly not an oppressor!

"So Philippos is our murderer?" I heard Marcellus say. It sounded like an echo of my own thoughts. "The man must have been completely out of his mind." The Tribune shook his head, then turned to Alva, who was still being held by one of the legionaries. The soldier's eyes wandered up and down her body incessantly, as if it were Venus herself he was holding captive. Which was not surprising. The average legionary didn't set eyes on a slave girl of Alva's beauty and grace in his entire lifetime.

"Woman," Marcellus addressed her, "tell me what you saw!"

Alva turned to me with a pleading look, probably because she already knew me. Or because Marcellus instilled fear in her. The Tribune was really good at that.

I went to her and freed her from the legionary who was

holding her. She pressed herself against me, trembling.

"Don't be afraid," I said, "no one is accusing you. We just want to know what happened here. What were you doing in Philippos' chambers so late at night?"

"My chamber...is next door," Alva whispered with bloodless lips. "I was asleep, but then noise in the house woke me. Footsteps. And voices. I just went to see what was going on...and that's when I discovered the master." She started sobbing again.

I gently stroked her hair. A terrible thought came to me: surely the young Greek had not killed himself before the eyes of this poor woman?

"Philippos was already dead when you found him?" I asked cautiously.

To my great relief, Alva nodded vigorously a few times. "Yes, sir. I found him like this." Her voice failed. Her eyes filled with tears. "Why did he do that?" she wailed, "Why? How could he do that to me?" She buried her face against my chest.

I wondered at her words, and from the way Marcellus looked at me, he seemed to feel the same way. But now was not the time to get anything more out of Alva. Her tears were flowing like the waters of the Danubius and did not seem to want to dry up.

"Let's go, Thanar," said the Tribune. "You belong in the hospital and should catch a few hours' sleep. I'll have my men guard the Villa, and in the morning we'll investigate at our leisure. I still have plenty of unanswered questions. Agreed?"

I nodded wordlessly. As far as the open questions were concerned, I could only agree with him. But the thought of a soft bed was more tempting than anything else right now.

Marcellus turned to the guard slave, "How big is the *familia* of this villa? How many people live here?"

"About forty, all together, lord," the slave mumbled, his eyes widening in fear.

"Good, we will have some questions for all of you in the morning. For today, you can retire."

The slave scurried away as if the Furies themselves were after him. I let go of Alva, who had completely wet my skin with her tears. She headed for the door on our right like a sleepwalker. Her room was indeed right next to her master's chambers.

"You three guard the house," the Tribune continued, nodding to the legionaries standing to our left. "One the gate, one the entrance here to the master's chambers, one the slave quarters. No one enters or leaves the mansion. I'll hold you accountable for that."

"Yes, Tribune," the soldiers replied, as if from one mouth.

XVII

"Who do you think Philippos had in mind when he wrote *Death to the Oppressors*?" the Tribune mused to himself while the medicus doctored me in the camp hospital. "Us Romans? Was he an agitator, is that why he killed the Primus Pilus? Because he hated us?"

"I don't know." I moaned through clenched teeth. Thessalos, the doctor, was cleaning my wound, which felt as if the bear was once again tearing the flesh from my bones. This time slowly and with relish.

"With Falco, that would still make sense," the Tribune continued his consideration. "He was a Roman soldier and also a...well, let's say a rather brash fellow who liked to get his way. But the other men Philippos murdered—Rufus and your friend Belius—though Roman citizens, were both of Celtic descent, were they not? And you are—" He faltered.

"A barbarian, I know," I completed his sentence.

Marcellus was right. That Philippos should have committed all the murders simply did not make sense. Had the young Greek really fallen prey to madness? He had always kept himself in the background during his father's lifetime, and after the old Greek's death he'd left the management of the business largely to Juba, the former body servant.

The old Greek! it flashed through my mind—no, I must have shouted it out loud, because the medicus flinched.

"Can you hold still until I'm done here, please?" he complained. He had finally stopped pouring fiery pain into my wound and was just getting ready to apply a bandage.

"What about the old man?" asked Marcellus.

"He passed away recently. Fell victim to a bear attack."

"What, you mean in the underground arena? He was murdered too?"

I nodded slowly. "They said he was attacked in the woods. But don't you think that's a strange coincidence if there was a wild bear living in his own house?"

"So he was the first one Philippos murdered? His own father? Was *he* then an oppressor?"

"I knew him only as the host of the Villa, but he certainly ran the household much more strictly than his son does now. And Philippos was quite in his shadow during his lifetime."

"Until he couldn't stand it anymore and turned into a patricide?" Marcellus mused, sounding like a philosopher. "There are people like that, Thanar. They let themselves be subjugated; they lead completely invisible lives. They seem completely harmless to the outside world, even fearful. And then suddenly they can no longer bear it. Maybe it only takes a small thing—and they lose their mind. Biting blindly like a beaten dog."

"But then why murder all the other men?" I interjected.

The Tribune rubbed his chin while his forehead was in deep wrinkles. He seemed very comfortable in the role of philosopher and thinker. "Well, maybe Philippos found pleasure in killing," he said. "It felt good to get rid of the tyrant. Maybe afterwards he fell for the idea of ridding Vindobona of more oppressors? That is, of men he perceived as such?"

"Belius was all kinds of things, but certainly not a tyrant. And as for me—"

The Tribune waved it off. "I didn't mean to offend you, Thanar. Perhaps Philippos simply saw you two as particularly demanding guests? Did you often stay under his roof?"

"Well, yes," I admitted.

"Wait!" Marcellus exclaimed abruptly. Something lit up in his eyes, as if he were following a sudden inspiration. "Did you perhaps speak with Belius in the Villa about the murders?"

"Yes, I did," I said, unsure of what he was getting at. "I asked Belius for advice when you accused me of...when your men found the body of the Primus Pilus in my harbor."

"When I accused you of murdering Falco," the Tribune stated what I had actually wanted to say.

I nodded wordlessly.

"Now, that may have driven Philippos to seek the lives of both of you as well. He overheard your conversation in the Villa and felt threatened. He feared you might expose him as the killer."

"Oh well," I said, finally realizing, "and there was something else. Belius sent me a message that he had a theory about the murders. And he had a secluded arbor reserved for us in the Villa last night, where we were not to be disturbed."

"There you have it," said Marcellus. "Philippos became aware of this, drew his conclusions from it, and unleashed his sinister plan."

Again, I nodded. That was exactly how it could have happened. Which meant that I was indeed responsible for my friend Belius' death. He had been killed because I had involved him in the murder. Would I ever be able to forgive myself for that? I did not know. I had only the faint consolation that his death had already been avenged. Even if not by my hand.

But the underground amphitheater? Surely Philippos had not had that built. He could not possibly have done it in the few weeks since his father's death.

So, was this arena the work of the old man? If so, he couldn't have been sane either. Who in his right mind kept a bear in the cellar and built an arena for private games?

And what poor souls had had to compete against this beast? This last question sent an ice-cold shiver down my spine. Had the old Lycortas already been a murderer? Had he let innocent people be mauled by the brown-furred beast?

"In any case, this Philippos was a very clever fellow," Marcellus snapped me out of my gloomy meditation. "He was a master at framing you for his shameful deeds. Already from the beginning. And if his sinister plans had been crowned with success again tonight, you would probably have been found tomorrow morning somewhere in the forest near the Villa, mauled by a bear. It would have looked as if you had murdered your friend Belius, escaped from the mansion during the night, and fallen victim to the beast during your escape. A truly ingenious plan, I must say!"

I nodded mutely and silently thanked the gods that they had foiled this plan, which I found simply abominable, at the last minute. That they had sent Marcellus to my rescue.

"When Philippos saw us storming the amphitheater, he must have stolen away through the back exit," Marcellus continued his reflections. "He knew he was lost, that there was no escape for him—and so he slipped back into his chambers, grabbed a dagger, and disemboweled himself. An ignominious death, but less agonizing than the one we would have given him. I think he knew that."

"There, done," announced Thessalos, the medicus. He took one last, scrutinizing look at the bandage he had put on me, then helped me put on a clean tunic. "Maybe tomorrow you'll manage not to get mutilated again," he joked with the gallows humor of the military doctor.

I assured him that I firmly intended not to become his patient again anytime soon and thanked him profusely for his service.

My next thought was for Layla. Another short ride across the river, then I would be with her. I asked Marcellus to have my horse brought to me.

But he shook his head. "You're not riding anywhere, my friend. You'll be a guest in my house tonight and will catch some hours of sleep. Your servant and your slave girl are already waiting for you."

"They're here? In the camp?"

Marcellus nodded. "I told you they alerted me for your sake. Do you think I just sent them on their way after that? I had to vow to your slave to bring you back to her in one piece. I think she would have preferred to ride to the Villa herself." A smile stole across his face. "She's a true lioness, your little Nubian."

He hesitated for a moment, seeming to ponder something. Then he patted me brotherly on my unharmed shoulder and said, "I hope you forgive me for being so hard on you. That I took you for a scoundrel and a murderer. You are a good man, Thanar."

"For a barbarian, you mean?" I added with a grin, and then we both laughed.

Perhaps I too had wronged the Tribune. The courage and the vigor with which he had saved my life from the bear showed a noble character. Yes, Marcellus was really all right. *For a Roman,* I added in my mind and smiled quietly to myself.

XVIII

The spacious and elegant houses of the Tribunes were located on the main street of the legionary camp, directly opposite the Principia—the staff building and flag shrine of the legion. Each of the six villas was built two stories high around a spacious atrium and equipped with every comfort. Worlds separated them from the accommodations of the common legionaries. The men crowded into cramped dormitories ten at a time.

I had never seen the inside of a Tribune's house myself. Slender marble columns welcomed me as Marcellus led me across its threshold.

Crowds of slaves came running to give their master a worthy welcome. Artful paintings decorated the walls, and a magnificent mosaic covered the floor. It showed the god Mars in one of his glorious battles.

Between Marcellus' slaves, Layla pushed her way through and rushed towards us with a cry of joy. She threw herself at my neck, so that I almost lost my balance, but her eyes also flitted over the figure of the Tribune. "Thank the gods, you two are unharmed!" she cried.

Then she kissed me and bowed to Marcellus. When she stood up again, she brushed his arm with her cheek as if by chance.

A strange smile flitted across the Tribune's youthful features. The next moment it was gone again.

Marcellus turned and started moving briskly. "This way," he said, again in the commanding voice I already knew so well from him.

He led me to a spacious room on the upper floor, where a slave was preparing a bed for me for the night. The bed was wide and thickly padded; a pitcher of water and an amphora of wine stood ready on a small bronze table, and next to it a plate with fruits, nuts, and cheese.

Only now did I notice that I was ravenously hungry. I dropped down on the soft bed and started munching on the delicacies.

Layla joined me and wanted to know everything that had happened to me. So, while I feasted, I described to her once again the events of the whole night. Even to my own ears, what I had to tell sounded completely unreal. Like a never-ending dark dream.

Layla listened to me, her eyes widening in horror. When I described the fight against the bear, her gaze wandered several times over the figure of the Tribune, who was leaning casually against one of the walls and looking down on us with an almost fatherly look.

With a nonchalant hand gesture, he dismissed his heroism in the arena as a matter of course. "Your master would have done the same for me," he said to Layla.

Would I now?

For a moment, all three of us fell silent. I drank a cup of heavily watered wine and enjoyed the pleasant tiredness that started to spread through my limbs.

"Are you sure you saw two men on the gallery?" the Tribune abruptly broke the silence that had fallen. "That doesn't fit the picture...or did Philippos have an aide to assist him in his outrages?"

I looked up. Marcellus was right. Why hadn't I noticed that myself?

I pondered what I had actually seen in my panic—and what I had not. The arena had been largely in darkness. I had just awakened from a faint and had tortured my mind with how I could escape the death that was imminent. Had I only imagined the second figure on the gallery? It had sat there motionless—perhaps Philippos had merely deposited something on a seat and I had mistakenly seen an accomplice in this bundle?

"I can't say for sure," I told Marcellus. "Maybe it was just one man I saw."

The Tribune said nothing in reply. He ran his hand over his clean-shaven chin and then began pacing up and down the room.

I struggled to remember more details from the arena, but I did not succeed. Fatigue was already weighing heavily on my eyelids. I only wanted to sleep.

Marcellus came to a halt. "Layla," he turned to my slave, "you were once part of the Greek's familia yourself, weren't you? You lived under his roof for a few months, barely half a year ago?"

Layla gave a hardly noticeable nod.

"And you didn't know about that bear? Or about the amphitheater in the basement? Surely that must have existed in your time."

Layla's face darkened. Quite a while passed before she answered. "One of the girls once told me a rumor about it. I think it was Suavis. Or Chloe? I don't remember. Anyway, the rumor was that the old master was playing some kind of cruel games. Secretly at night in the cellar. And that there was a monster down there. It was a horrible story, but I thought it was just an old wives' tale. And even if I had believed the rumors, what could I have done about them? What could any slave have done? Should we accuse our master? Where and to whom?"

"I don't blame you at all," Marcellus said quickly, then fell silent for a few minutes, but without taking his eyes off Layla.

"Had you never heard anything?" he finally asked. "The roar of the bear? Screams, perhaps?"

"Screams are nothing out of the ordinary in a house full of slaves," Layla replied with a bitterness I had never noticed with her before.

Marcellus, at a rare loss for words, looked down at the floor in dismay. I myself reached for Layla's hand and squeezed it gently.

"If a crime happens in a familia," she continued unasked, "it can bring the entire slaves of that house to the cross. That's why we don't hear, see or know about anything that happens under our roof. Especially not about what the master might be up to. All we can do is hope and pray that his deeds won't be discovered and charged to us in the end."

"You don't have to tell me about that," Marcellus replied. His voice sounded warm, full of compassion, but I just couldn't get used to the way he was looking at Layla.

What was there in his eyes? Desire? And how did he even know that Layla had lived in the Villa? He seemed to be very well informed.

"We'll sort out what this amphitheater is all about tomorrow," Marcellus said, still addressing Layla, "but for now we really should let your master get some sleep."

He got up, wished me a good night, then left my room together with Layla.

"Tell me again how you defeated the bear," I heard her say to Marcellus outside the door. She spoke with that flattering, dark voice that always warmed my heart. And while the footsteps of the two were quickly moving away, the Tribune began a new description of his heroic deed.

XIX

The next morning, I became certain of something I had suspected for quite a while: my Layla was a sorceress.

And I the purest wax in her hands.

Even before I had fully awakened, she had already cajoled me so artfully that I promised to take her along to the Villa. She had good arguments why I had to take her with me: the slave girls were her friends, and she would like to stand by them in this difficult hour. And the girls would certainly be more talkative if she were present. Marcellus and I were so awe-inspiring that they wouldn't say anything out of fear. And so on and so forth.

I still made the pitiful attempt to claim that it would certainly not be okay with Marcellus if she came along. You could probably guess what I got in reply: she had already asked the Tribune for permission, and he had no objections.

I really would have preferred Layla to be safe in my house, but what could I do? I couldn't deny her that wish. If she hadn't proven her assertiveness last night and persuaded Marcellus to rescue me in the Villa, I would already be wandering through the depths of Hades.

So Marcellus gathered a crowd of legionaries around him while I climbed into my wagon with Darius and Layla.

In front of the Villa, we met again.

In the house, everything seemed to be in order. Under the columns of the portico, a somewhat sleepy legionary greeted us. He was leaning on his spear but had apparently fulfilled his duty obediently all night. "No special incidents," he reported to the Tribune.

Aculeo, the soldier who had been guarding the private quarters, even stood at attention at his post and greeted us with the same message.

Marcellus turned to me. "Who might know best about what was going on here in the house? Who is the chief slave?"

"Juba," I said after some consideration. "He is no longer a slave, for Philippos set him free after his father's death, but in a sense he runs the household."

"Well," said Marcellus, "let's start with him, and then we'll take another look at this concubine of Philippos. Hopefully she'll have composed herself a bit by now and be able to tell us more."

"Alva, you mean? She was the concubine of Lycortas, the old Greek, not the son."

The Tribune raised his eyebrows. "Was she? The way she cried for Philippos yesterday, I would have assumed—well, never mind. Where do we find this Juba?"

"The African?" Aculeo, the legionary, asked officiously. "His chamber is just around the corner here. I had a few words with him last night."

We followed the legionary to a closed door, which Marcellus pushed open without knocking.

Then we all froze on the threshold.

Juba lay on the floor in front of the bed, limbs frozen like in a spasm, mouth wide open as if still gasping for breath in death.

Because there was no doubt that he was dead. His eyes stared at us with pupils dilated in fear, in which there was no more life.

Marcellus was the first to react; he crouched down in front of the dead African and touched his arm. "Rigid and cold," he said, "the man has been dead for some hours."

Aculeo, the legionary, pressed himself against the door-frame and was stammering a hurried prayer. "The gods must have struck him down," he cried. "I stood guard here all night! No one was in his chamber, certainly not!"

I stepped out into the hallway and looked around. Juba's chamber was the last room in this part of the house. Who-ever wanted to get to his door had to pass by the place where Aculeo had stood guard.

Marcellus eyed the soldier sharply. "You didn't leave your post? All night?"

Aculeo turned pale. "I visited the latrine once briefly, Trib-une," he stammered. "But it was after that that I spoke to the African. He was in good health then, I swear it!"

Marcellus snorted. He turned to me. "Then I suppose this Juba has also judged himself. With poison?"

"Looks like it," I said, stepping back into the room and bending over the body. Juba had no visible injury, and there was no blood anywhere.

"The second man on the gallery," I heard Layla mutter.

I startled when I heard her voice. Over the discovery of the body, I had completely forgotten that she was with us. The sight of the dead African was really nothing for a woman.

But Layla seemed unmoved. She stood right next to me and examined the corpse with that expression of utmost concen-tration on her face that I had observed many times—when-ever I found her in my library. My book collection was Layla's greatest passion. She could stare into any scroll for hours—

just as she was now staring into the face of the dead African. Yes, that was it. She studied the corpse with the utmost attention and without any disgust, as if it were nothing more than the writings of a famous philosopher.

Layla repeated her words, "Maybe he was the second man you saw in the arena, master. I thought to myself last night that you must be right about that. That you did indeed observe two perpetrators, I mean. Philippos was not—" She faltered.

"Yes?" Marcellus encouraged her.

"I didn't get to know him as a man of action, that's all," Layla said, looking modestly to the ground. "That's why I don't believe him capable to murder so many people."

"She's right," I intervened, "Juba must have been Philippos' accomplice." Why hadn't I thought of that before?

I turned to Marcellus. "When the old Greek fell victim to the bear, Juba was supposedly at his side. Philippos set him free afterwards because he is said to have defended his master so heroically."

"Which is a lie, if we assume that the old man died in the arena and not on a road in the woods," Marcellus said.

"That's right. No one would have believed that the old man went out alone. So Philippos needed the servant's help if the father's death was to be believed. And *for that* he rewarded him with the gift of freedom, not for his heroism."

But there was more that could be explained if one assumed two perpetrators. I truly did not consider Philippos to be a great warrior. Perhaps it had been he who had so bunglingly riddled Rufus, the Cattle Prince, with arrows—while Juba knew how to place a well-aimed shot, in my back, and how to wield the axe that had struck down the Primus Pilus.

Yes, that was how it must have been. Philippos had bought the servant's assistance in his murderous plan by promising him freedom. There was hardly a better motivation for a slave.

But then, when the legionaries invaded the villa and Philippos took his own life, the African must have known that he too was facing execution. Even if he had not been arrested immediately, it was only a matter of time. Perhaps Juba had even assumed that I had recognized him on the gallery of the bear arena. And so, he had followed his master to his death during the night.

A strange satisfaction came over me. The feeling of finally having found a halfway coherent explanation for all the murders and attacks. Even if I could not claim to understand Philippos' motives. *Death to the oppressors.*

Well, it might be in the nature of things that the deeds of a madman remained incomprehensible to a sane person. I had to be content with that.

An agonized groan snapped me out of my thoughts. I looked up and saw Alva, who had appeared at the doorstep. Aculeo reacted immediately. He grabbed her by the arm, preventing her from entering the room.

"Is he dead?" she stammered in a brittle voice.

I nodded wordlessly. Layla went to her and put her arm around her shoulders.

"We have some questions for you," Marcellus said. "Where can we talk in peace?"

Like a sleepwalker, Alva led us to the other end of the corridor, where a quiet peristyle courtyard opened up. A small ornamental garden surrounded by a portico, which had probably served exclusively as a retreat for the master of the house. Besides a marble water basin, there were some laurel bushes and flower beds with roses, daisies, and other decorative plants.

In the portico there was a luxurious sofa and some chairs. The Tribune took a seat on the sofa, and I sank into a marble chair. Despite the excellent medical care that the camp doctor had given me, I was still very weak on my feet. The few steps through the house had already exhausted me. I felt twice as old as I actually was.

Alva preferred to stand, and Layla stayed by her side. She hugged the trembling blonde and spoke soothingly to her.

"The death of the young master yesterday seemed to have affected you very much," Marcellus began.

Alva did not react. Only when the Tribune repeated his words did she nod her head, barely noticeably.

"But you were the old man's body slave, weren't you?" Marcellus asked.

Alva's sky-blue eyes widened. "Yes, Tribune," she replied tonelessly. Then she looked at Layla, seeking help.

"You can speak freely, dear," my intrepid Nubian assured her. "No one means you any harm." She gently stroked the woman's light-blond hair.

Alva swallowed. Then she began tentatively, "Lycortas claimed me all for himself, but I—"

Tears welled up in the corners of her eyes, but she quickly wiped them away. "I loved Philippos," she whispered, "and he loved me. When Lycortas found that out, he wanted—" A new flood of tears filled her eyes. Quickly, she turned her head away and buried her face against Layla's shoulder.

It took quite a while before she was able to continue speaking. She pressed a cloth that Layla had handed her into her eye sockets. Alternately in the left and the right eye, as hard as if she wanted to crush them.

I already feared for her eyesight, but Layla grabbed the cloth from her hand and took it upon herself to dry her tears, much more gently than Alva had done.

Alva mumbled something I couldn't understand, then she pulled herself together. "When Lycortas found out his son loved me, he wanted to make me a gift to the Legion. As a camp whore."

XX

Layla audibly sucked in her breath. She gave me a pained look.

I could only share her horror. Alva, a camp whore? The old Greek must have truly been a monster to devise such a punishment.

The fate of those girls who served the legionaries as pleasure slaves was perhaps even worse than that of the grave whores. There were only a handful of she-wolves in the camp—feasted upon by a few thousand soldiers. The life expectancy of these girls was correspondingly short. A woman of Alva's exquisite beauty would probably have died within a very short time—no, I didn't even want to think about that.

Was Alva telling the truth? I could hardly believe it. What had angered the old man so much? It was not unusual for a father and son to share a concubine. In fact, it was the norm in less wealthy households. Lycortas must have been consumed by jealousy.

"When was that?" I heard Marcellus say. "When did Lycortas find out about you and Philippos?"

Alva didn't have to think. "Two days before he died."

I could read in her eyes that she knew all too well what that meant.

Marcellus put it into words. "Well, there we have the perfect motive why the old man was murdered. Philippos threw him to the bear so as not to lose you."

Alva let out a muffled sob. "I didn't know anything about it! You'll have to take my word for that. I would have talked the young master out of it! To kill the *Pater familias*—such an act draws the vengeance of the Furies!"

Marcellus nodded mutely. The murder of Lycortas had been avenged, there was no denying that. Philippos had paid for this outrage with his own life. Just like Juba, his accomplice.

"What do you know about the bear arena?" the Tribune turned to Alva again. "Was it Lycortas who had it built?"

It hardly seemed possible, but at these words Alva became even paler. Her tears were no longer flowing, but the last bit of vitality disappeared from her beautiful face.

She nodded stiffly. "Yes, Tribune. Many months ago, already. The bear was not the first beast he kept."

Marcellus looked at her in dismay.

"In the beginning, the master owned a lion," Alva said. "He was very proud of the fact that his games resembled those in the great city of Rome. Bears and wolves, that was something for the backwoodsmen in the provinces, he claimed. But the lion died under his hands, in the underground dungeon. And a new one was very difficult to obtain. So, the master finally bought a bear—and somehow he took the beast into his heart. It was the only creature he loved at all."

"And what did he want with the beasts? With the bear?" Marcellus continued. "Was the old man holding private games down there in the basement?"

Alva snuggled so close to Layla, as if she wanted to disappear under her armpit. "You tell them," she whispered to my Nubian in a brittle voice.

Layla raised her hands in a dismissive gesture. "I've only

heard rumors," she protested, "how can I—"

"The rumors are true," Alva interrupted her. "They're all true."

Layla's eyes widened. As if struck by lightning, she stared at Alva, who returned her gaze and nodded, barely noticeable. Then Alva turned away from us, headed swayingly for the pillar that towered close behind her, and let herself slide to the ground against it. She no longer cried, she just sat there dead silent and huddled up.

"Layla?" the Tribune turned to my slave, who was now fighting tears herself. His voice sounded changed, soft, and warm—and yet it was clear that he would not rest until he learned the truth.

Layla swallowed. Her mouth opened, but it was quite a while before the first stumbling words crossed her lips. "I was only told about the bear once by one of the girls," she began, "and she didn't know exactly for what purpose Lycortas kept the beast. But I also heard about Lycortas holding his own games with gladiators, at night in the underground arena." She squinted over at Alva, but there was no sign of life from the slumped, motionless bundle.

Layla wet her lips with her tongue. "With *gladiatrices*, I should say," she continued tonelessly. "Women. It was said that from the girls Lycortas acquired all over the world, he always chose some for himself. They were not resold or rented to guests of the Villa. I never got to see any of them at all, so I thought—" She fell silent.

"—that they didn't even exist," I finished her sentence.

Layla nodded, barely noticeable. "I don't know what exactly Lycortas did to them. I heard about him making them fight each other—without weapons and completely naked. A fight to the death in which there was no mercy. Supposedly, only one of the duelists could leave the arena alive. I assume he then gave the winner her freedom, but perhaps he did sell her on after her wounds had healed? I have no idea."

Alva's blond mop of hair stirred. She raised her head, as slowly as if time had frozen around her. "No girl has ever left the arena alive," she whispered. "Though the master promised it, to spur them on to battle. I know it. I was there. The one who survived the duel was thrown to the bear. The master used to watch it all, feasting on wine and fine food, and when the beast had mauled the girl, then...then he took me on the gallery in the face of her bloody corpse. At first he did this only every few months, but lately more and more often. He just lived from one execution to the next, talking of nothing but his games and becoming more and more ill-tempered the more time passed between them. He seemed to find it increasingly difficult to procure new girls; I don't know the reason. He would walk up and down in front of the bear cage for hours, talking down to the beast and then taking his bad mood out on the house slaves. Or on me," she added in a toneless voice.

Alva's words were flowing now as unstoppably as her tears had been before. Her lips were moving as if by magic. She herself seemed to be in a place far beyond our small courtyard.

"Then one night," she continued, "when Lycortas found me in Philippos' arms—I was sure that I would now end up in the bear pit myself. But, no—oh, how he laughed, like a hideous demon! 'The bear is so greedy' he sneered, it would finish me off much too fast. The legionaries, on the other hand, those good, disciplined Romans—it would certainly take them a week or two to ravish me to death. That's why he wanted to make me a gift to the camp. He thought that was an appropriate punishment for my betrayal."

A sound of horror escaped me. That sadistic, old bastard! How rotten of heart and character did a man have to be to find pleasure in such atrocities?

For quite a while, no one spoke a word. We were just standing there, as if paralyzed. I fought against the images that forced themselves into my head. The huge, furry monster to which I myself had almost fallen victim. Its roar, which made your blood freeze in the veins. His foul breath, the razor-sharp teeth and claws that could tear the flesh from your bones within the blink of an eye.

Marcellus was the first to regain his speech. "What, by all the gods, drove the old man to this?"

I didn't think the Tribune expected an answer to this question, but someone whispered, "I think I know." It was Layla who had spoken.

Marcellus looked at her questioningly.

"Lycortas hated us girls," she said. "He was convinced one of us had bewitched him, put a curse on him. The divine Priapus had withdrawn his favor, you must know, and struck Lycortas' manhood with impotence. He was no longer able to perform the act of love."

Marcellus' mouth dropped open, but then he composed himself. "Hasn't Alva just told us that she had to be at the old man's will after the bloody spectacles in the arena? So surely his virility must have been intact?"

"It was," Alva whispered, keeping her gaze fixed rigidly on the ground in front of her. "However, only if he had sacrificed a girl in the arena. That was his counterspell, he always used to say. His revenge on us whores who had cursed him. The carnage the beast caused excited him so much that he could take me, right there in the stands, until—"

Her voice failed. A spasm seized her slender body and shook her so violently as if she would throw up at any moment. She buried her face in her hands, and no further sound escaped her throat.

Layla knelt on the floor beside Alva and wrapped her arms around the trembling woman. "It's over," she said, in a voice that seemed to come from the darkest depths of Hades. Unconcealed, seething anger resonated in her words. "He can never hurt you again, that rotten old monster. Never again, do you hear? Cursed be his soul for all eternity!"

I could understand Layla's feelings all too well; indeed, I shared them completely. For the moment, I forgot all the other people Philippos had killed and felt nothing but deep satisfaction over his murder of the old man. That he had fed this monster of a father to his own beast. Such a deed could not bring the revenge of the Furies, patricide or not!

A man could deal with his slaves as he pleased, for they were his property. No court in the world forbade him to punish them if they lied, lazed around or even stole. But to throw completely innocent girls to a bear for the mere pleasure of killing them—I had never heard of such an abominable act. Old Lycortas deserved the cruelest death a mortal could devise—even the gods had to come to that conclusion.

For a while we all sat dazed and silent, each absorbed in his own thoughts. Then the Tribune asked, "Did Juba, the old man's body servant, know about these outrages?"

"He did," came the muffled answer from Alva. She had hidden her face in Layla's arms. "He was in charge of feeding the bear. And he and Orodes always had to take away the bodies of the girls."

"Then Philippos will not have found it difficult to make Juba his accomplice," I said. "In addition to promising him the gift of freedom."

Marcellus nodded somberly. He was silent for quite a while, then he seemed to remember something that had probably been bothering him for some time. "Did Philippos have children?" he asked. "Who are his heirs?"

Alva did not respond, so I took it upon myself to answer. "I think he was childless," I said. "And unmarried, as far as I know."

Layla confirmed my suspicions. Gently, she nudged Alva. "Do you know if Philippos left a will, dear?"

Alva composed herself. For the first time, her heavily reddened but all the more intensely shining eyes turned again to the Tribune and me. "Philippos told me that he had made a will. In favor of the entire familia, he said. I never asked what exactly he meant by that. He was still so young, after all, I...I thought we could finally be happy together." She pressed her lips together, her eyelids closed for a moment, but no more tears came.

"Where can we find the will?" asked Marcellus. "Did Philippos deposit it in the temple?"

Alva shook her head. "No, Tribune. He kept it in his money chest, as far as I know."

"Let's go and see, then." Marcellus looked relieved to be able to devote himself to such routine tasks as executing wills. Part of him already seemed to have returned to the intrepid commander's demeanor he was so fond of displaying. With a determined look on his youthful face, he rose from the sofa. Only his eyes were still reflecting the pain of a man who had just looked into the abyss of evil.

XXI

We found the key to the money chest on a chain that the dead Philippos wore around his neck. Marcellus took it and used it to unlock the chest.

It was made of heavy wood, studded with iron and of impressive size. To everyone's astonishment, however, it did not contain the rich gold treasure we had expected. On the contrary, the chest was almost empty, just the bottom was covered with coins.

How was that possible? I had always thought the old Greek to be a very rich man, and his villa, the epitome of *luxuria*, bore eloquent witness to this. His son could not possibly have squandered so much gold in the short time since he had taken over the estate.

The Tribune seemed as dismayed by the sight of the nearly empty chest as I was. "Philippos was robbed," he said. "Before or after his death." His gaze wandered to Alva, who stood behind us with Layla.

"No, Tribune," she replied, startled. "Certainly not! None of us would—"

"Nor have I accused any of the servants," Marcellus interrupted her. "Not yet. But a rich man's chest does look much different."

Fear flared up in the blue of Alva's eyes. "Neither Lycortas nor Philippos talked to me about their business dealings," she said hastily. "But Philippos was worried about money when he took over the house, that much I know."

"She's telling the truth," I interjected. "Philippos also expressed concern to me about how he was going to make a living. Which made me wonder a lot at the time."

"When was that?" asked Marcellus.

"Just a few days ago."

"I think I know where all the gold has gone," Layla said. Marcellus frowned.

"The games Lycortas held in his secret arena," she explained. "They must have cost him a fortune. I don't know anything about business, but I know the amount of money you have to raise to pay for a—" She hesitated. "For one of us. For all the girls he killed."

"Of course," I exclaimed, "Layla's right!"

I silently scolded myself a fool for not having thought of it myself. "It was the old man's vile pleasures that emptied his money chest. He wasn't robbed," I said.

Marcellus nodded slowly but did not seem fully convinced. He turned to the legionary Aculeo, whose presence I had long forgotten. The young soldier had stayed in the background all this time but now jumped forward, eager to serve.

"Gather the men," Marcellus ordered him, "and then search the entire estate. Cellars, utility rooms, slave quarters, everything! Understand? If Philippos was robbed, the gold must still be in the house. No one had a chance to take it away during the night."

At this last statement, he gave Aculeo a searching look, which the latter probably interpreted correctly. "No, Tribune, no one had left the estate during the night. I swear to you! The entire house was under guard."

"And yet Juba has succeeded in judging himself," Marcellus

remarked. "Practically under your eyes."

Aculeo looked as if he longed to sink into the ground. He stammered something, but the Tribune silenced him with a commanding wave of his hand. "We'll talk about that later. And now let's get going. Turn the house upside down."

"Right away, Tribune." The legionary hurried away.

The respect Marcellus instilled in his men was truly amazing. I wondered if he was considered a similar tyrant in the legionary camp as the murdered Primus Pilus. It could not be ruled out, but it was none of my business, I decided. The Tribune had saved my life, and for that I was deeply indebted to him.

He seemed to be pondering something. He remained motionless next to the open chest for quite a while, but then he bent down, reached in, and pulled out a bundle of wax tablets. The will.

The tablets had been properly tied up and sealed by seven witnesses. Everything seemed to be in order. Marcellus broke the seals, opened the tablets, and studied the text.

Finally, he lowered his hands and fixed Alva with his gaze. "Philippos releases all his slaves, and you are his sole heir," he announced.

Alva let out a small cry. With widened eyes, she turned to Layla. "Free," she whispered, "free!"

Layla smiled at her, then pulled her into a hug. "You truly deserve this, dear! After all you've been through."

"Free," Alva repeated, as if she were casting a magic spell.

"Did you know about it?" Marcellus interrupted her joyful frenzy. "Did you know the contents of Philippos' will? "

Alva winced as if the Tribune had startled her out of a dream, woken her from a sweet, far too short slumber. She tilted her head, seeming to have to search for the right words first. "Philippos spoke a few times of wanting to set us all free," she finally said. "But he never put it into practice. And he confided nothing to me about his will."

Marcellus nodded absently, then delved into the wax tablets once more.

"I think everything is in order with this will," he said after quite a while had passed.

I must have lost myself in some musing in the meantime, because when I looked up, Layla and Alva were no longer with us.

Marcellus did not seem to be bothered by this. Perhaps the two women had set out to deliver the joyful news to the other slaves of the house. That the death of their master had set them all free.

The Tribune turned to me, eyed me piercingly with his dark eyes, then said, "Let's go, Thanar. We're done here."

When we had exited Philippos' private chambers, Marcellus left me and went to check on his men. In the meantime, they had probably turned half the house upside down, but I doubted that they would come across any stolen gold anywhere. Philippos had obviously had money troubles—after the old man had fed the profits of his whole life to a monster.

I walked aimlessly through the house for a while, traversing all the splendid rooms in which I had spent so many carefree evenings with Belius, and lost myself in thoughts of my murdered friend. Never again would he preach to me within these walls about frugality and modesty, only to immediately order another amphora of the most expensive wine or pull a creature of luxury like Suavis onto his lap. Never again would he entertain me with gossip about the citizens of Vindobona, never again would he offer me advice or lend me his sympathetic ear whenever I had a problem. It felt like I had lost my father—for the second time.

In the garden behind the summer triclinium, I finally came across Layla. She was standing with a group of slaves who were talking excitedly. When they saw me, however, they immediately fell silent. Suavis, who had just nestled in the arms of Orodes, the guardian slave, tore herself away from him, startled.

"Don't worry," I reassured them, "you have nothing to fear from me."

Suavis looked at me uncertainly, then the burly Parthian pulled her back into his arms, and she let it happen. Next to the massive man, she seemed even more childlike than usual.

She was Alva's daughter, born in the house, it went through my head. Which had to mean that the old Greek had fathered her. As jealous as he was in claiming Alva for his own, even toward his own son, he certainly wouldn't have shared her with any other man. So Suavis had to be Lycortas' child and thus Philippos' half-sister.

Well, it didn't matter. The daughter of a slave was born a slave, no matter who her father was. No master of the house acknowledged the offspring he produced with his servants. It was simply an inexpensive way to ensure the supply of slaves in the house. Especially in peacetime, when there were no prisoners of war to fall back on, and the price of slaves used to climb inexorably.

Next to Suavis and Orodes stood Chloe, the young Greek woman who had always been my favorite at the Villa. She seemed strangely absent and didn't seem to have noticed my arrival.

I also saw her now with completely different eyes. She was no longer the seductive, mysterious beauty who had always enchanted me so much, but simply a young girl who seemed completely lost. A child that one wanted to protect from all harm.

The Villa and the sensual pleasures that this mansion had offered my friend and me were a thing of the past. Behind the beautiful glow on the surface, a place of horror had come to light.

"What will happen to us now?" Orodes asked me. "Are we all going to—" He hesitated and looked down at Suavis, who was still nestled against him.

He didn't have to state it; I knew what he meant. *Are we all going to be executed now?*

Layla had certainly already told Philippos' slaves about the will that made them freemen—but Orodes probably knew that it was only valid on one condition: Philippos had to have actually died by his own hand.

If the Tribune had even the slightest suspicion that someone had helped in the demise of the master of the house, this could mean death for the slaves instead of the freedom that was within reach. If a murder in a household remained unsolved, it was common practice to execute all the unfree who had served under that roof.

I did not know what judgment Marcellus would come to. I could not and would not speak for him.

That Philippos had had all too good a reason to kill his father could not be denied. And also for the murder of Falco, Rufus and Belius a motive could be constructed from his point of view. His hatred of tyrants might have moved him to kill Falco and Rufus. Presumably, these men had reminded Philippos of his father. And the fear of being exposed as a murderer could have driven him to murder my friend Belius.

Juba had been the young Greek's accomplice in all these deeds. In the end, they had both taken their own lives to avoid execution. It all made sense.

And yet...

I truly did not wish death upon Philippos' slaves. They had more than earned their freedom. But if I was completely honest with myself: deep inside me, a persistent doubt was nagging. By far not all the questions that preoccupied me had been answered. I couldn't shake the feeling that something was wrong with this series of murders.

Just what?

I decided to remain silent to the Tribune. I would find the time to investigate my doubts—without bringing a few dozen innocent people to the cross.

A few moments later, a legionary came rushing to us in the garden. He was not one of the men who had ridden here to the Villa in the Tribune's entourage. Probably a messenger from the camp.

"I'm looking for Tribune Marcellus," he called out, bending over, gasping for breath. "It is urgent."

I was about to reply that I had no idea where Marcellus was, when the Tribune stepped out from behind one of the fountains that dotted the topmost part of the garden.

Had he just been on his way to us? Had one of his men

alerted him to the messenger who was looking for him? Or had Marcellus been lingering near us for some time without revealing his presence to us? I don't know how I came up with the latter thought. And yet I could not help thinking that Marcellus had overheard us.

Probably after all the events of the last few days and because of the pain that still plagued my body, I was no longer completely sane.

The messenger hurried toward Marcellus, greeted him hastily, and pressed a closed wax tablet into his hand.

Marcellus skimmed the letter, then took the messenger aside and gave him some instructions. He spoke so quietly that I could not understand anything.

The legionary hurried away.

"I must return to camp immediately," the Tribune announced to us. "I will assign Aculeo to finish the search of the house and then take care of the bodies. Besides, my men can escort you home, Thanar."

"That won't be necessary," I assured him. On the streets of Vindobona, I was no longer in danger from the murderer.

Marcellus was already about to leave, but I held him back. "These slaves are awaiting your judgment, Tribune," I whispered to him.

XXII

"My judgment?" asked Marcellus.

"Do you absolve them of all blame for the death of their master? Did Philippos actually commit suicide?"

Marcellus looked at me in surprise. "Of course, he did. Do you doubt it?"

"No, Tribune," I said, anxious to sound fully convinced.

Marcellus nodded silently. Then he turned, straightened to his full height, and addressed the slaves. However urgent his affairs in Vindobona might be, there was probably still time for a grand gesture. "Your master—and his servant—are guilty of several heinous crimes," he began. "To escape their just punishment, they cowardly, by their own hand, departed this life. Their bodies will be disposed of in the Danubius without funeral rites. Philippos' last will be executed tomorrow, you will all be given your freedom, and Alva will inherit the remaining fortune."

I was not an advocate and could not claim to know Roman law. Nevertheless, if Lycortas had had other interested heirs besides his son, they probably could have contested Philippos' inheritance and, as a consequence, the latter's own will. A patricide was certainly not entitled to inherit.

Or was he?

It was probably true, as so often: *ubi non accusator, ibi non iudex*! Where there is no accuser, there is no judge. And anyway, neither Lycortas nor his son had been Roman citizens.

Why was I racking my brains here? In the end, all decision-making power in this case lay with the one who took it. Specifically, the Tribune of the Roman legion. That was the way of the world. As far as I was concerned, Marcellus had made a wise and just decision.

"Should my men come across stolen gold during the search of the house, the thief will, of course, be severely punished," the Tribune added, but it was obvious that he no longer thought that likely himself.

Suavis and Orodes burst into cheers; Chloe raised her head, looked around as if she had to make sure where she was first, but then joined in the shouts of joy

Layla suddenly sprang forward and embraced the Tribune with a passionate "Thank you!"

I could not believe my eyes, but Marcellus did not seem to be angered by this unseemly gesture. He did not push Layla away from him, as befitted a Roman commander who was pulled into a hug by a slave girl in public. On the contrary, his arms closed around Layla as a matter of course, and for a moment he held her tightly against him.

Then my slave came to her senses. She detached herself from him, took a few steps backwards, and lowered her head. "Excuse me, Tribune," she said in a strained voice.

I couldn't explain what had gotten into her. Layla had otherwise always kept herself perfectly under control and had the best manners.

"We've all been through a lot," I muttered, more to myself than to the Tribune.

Marcellus turned without another word and walked away.

For him, this seemed to be the end of the matter. Apparently, he was no longer even interested in the search of the house by his men. And that, although he had seemed quite skeptical earlier, when Layla had presented him with her explanation for the empty chest.

Well, presumably Marcellus only cared about finally having closed the case. And successfully. The murderer was caught and also already judged; the public order in Vindobona was restored.

A foreigner—a Greek—had been convicted as the culprit, which certainly suited the legion well. The Greeks still thought of themselves as something special, something better. They had never really come to terms with Roman rule, even though their once proud homeland had been part of the empire for centuries. Marcellus could not have found a more suitable murderer.

It was certainly not lost on the Tribune that many a question had remained unanswered. Nevertheless, his hasty return to the legion camp was probably for the best of all concerned. The slaves of the Villa had gained their freedom, and I could discreetly pursue the questions that still occupied me—without immediately bringing the entire household to the cross.

"I want to take another look at Juba's body," I said to Layla, "before the legionaries take it away."

My slave girl looked at me, startled.

"You're welcome to stay here with your friends in the meantime," I told her, "and I'll pick you up when we're ready to return home."

I could not blame Layla for not wanting to take another look at the corpse that looked as if frozen in agony. However,

I was concerned about how exactly the African had died.

But it was apparently not the gruesome sight that Layla shied away from. "Is something wrong, master?" she inquired. "I can tell something is bothering you."

"Just a couple of loose ends I'd like to tie up for myself."

"Then I will come with you, master."

I felt compelled to give Layla an explanation. "You don't have to worry for the sake of your friends, dear. The Tribune has acquitted them, and I mean them no harm. It's just—"

"Yes, master?"

"I want to get clarity so I can bury Belius with a clear conscience. That's all. I need to make sure that my friend has truly been avenged. I don't want to carry that debt of honor around with me for the rest of my days."

Layla nodded slowly. "I understand you, master," she said softly.

I directed my steps back to the house, and Layla followed me silently.

Juba was still lying in his chamber as we had found him, with twisted limbs frozen in spasm and eyes wide open. As if he had stared into the face of the god of death himself and lost his mind in the process.

"You don't think the Furies struck him down?" Layla asked after I had been kneeling on the floor next to the corpse for quite a while, pondering.

"I think he died of poison," I replied. "I am not able to say whether the goddesses of vengeance drove him to drink it. Perhaps he simply wanted to evade arrest by the Romans, in order to die an easier death than they would have prepared for him. But if he took the poison here in his chamber, where is the cup, the vessel, from which he drank it? He could not have carried it away, for outside in the corridor a legionary was keeping watch."

"He could have taken the poison before he retired to his room," Layla said but immediately contradicted herself. "No, that would be strange. If he was in possession of poison, he certainly hid it here in his chamber. Surely, he didn't want to risk someone else finding it and possibly accidentally drinking it. Although—yes, of course, that must be it!"

She knelt down beside me and stared into the eyes of the dead African. "Those dilated pupils, I thought they spoke of the fear that consumed him when the Furies pounced on him—but perhaps there is another possibility."

"Yes?"

"Do you think he drank the women's beauty poison, master? No need to hide that in his chamber; everyone here in the house had access to it at all times."

"The women's beauty poison?"

"Yes, master. Look at his eyes. How big and shining they are."

"Because the pupils are dilated," I said. "You're right about that."

"Just like with beautiful women. *Atropa*, the sacred juice of the goddess of fate, makes the pupils become so wide. The girls apply it in the evening before showing themselves to guests."

"The girls drink poison?"

Layla shook her head. "They drip the sap of the plant into their eyes. Just a few drops. You have to be very careful with it. Every pleasure slave knows about the deadly power of atropa. It can blind you if you use its gifts too often. But it is also a way out when—"

"When?"

"Well, when there is no other way. When you no longer want to wait for the goddess of fate to cut off the thread of your life with her dreaded scissors. When a girl comes into the possession of an owner who makes her life more terrible than death."

She hesitated, then continued in a whisper, "I myself once just managed to keep Alva from drinking atropa. *One must never lose hope,* I told her then. I had no idea what she was really going through. How terribly Lycortas tortured her." Layla fell silent and her eyelids closed for a moment.

"Where do the girls keep this atropa?" I asked.

"In their quarters, sir."

"Where Juba had access at all times?"

Layla nodded.

"So he may have drunk it there, shortly after the legionaries invaded here and Philippos was found dead," I said. "Then he returned to his chamber—and waited for death."

"That's how it must have been, master."

"Hm. Just look at the way he's lying there. Doesn't it look to you as if, in his death throes, he was still trying to reach the door of his chamber? To get help?"

"Yes, master. I think so."

"Why would he have done that when he had drunk the poison himself and had already laid down to die?"

"Maybe his pain was so severe that he tried to save himself after all?"

"Is there an antidote for this atropa, then?" I asked.

Layla shook her head. "I don't think so, master."

I gazed silently down at the frozen corpse for a while. Juba had tried to leave his bed and his chamber while already in his death throes, I was sure of it. But there was something else that bothered me.

XXIII

I stepped in front of the simple wooden shelf that covered one of the walls. On it stood some vessels, on one of the boards lay a neatly folded tunic, and below that two wax tablets leaned askew. I took them from the shelf and flipped them open, but both had been carefully smoothed and were ready to be reused.

"I wonder why Juba didn't leave a suicide note like Philippos did?" I said to Layla. "He had writing materials here in his chamber." I showed her the blank tablets. "Surely he didn't want his death to look like murder, did he? He had to realize that he was endangering the entire slave household."

Layla's dark brow furrowed. "Juba certainly wasn't murdered—that is, by any of the slaves. He was a popular man. Do you think any of the guests could have—"

"There were no more guests in the house last night, dear," I interrupted her.

"But Juba could have been given the poison in the evening. Or he could have drunk it himself at that time."

"Before the Romans showed up here and his master disemboweled himself? I doubt it. Why would he have done that?"

Layla began to brood. It was obvious that she wanted to protect the slaves of the villa.

"Someone could have snuck into the mansion from the outside," I said—more for Layla's sake than because I really believed in the possibility.

"The walls around the estate aren't really an obstacle, I suppose," she replied. Her eyes lit up hopefully.

But immediately her face darkened again. "How could the murderer have gotten past the legionaries?" she asked. "Surely the chambers here were guarded all night?"

I shrugged. Layla wanted to protect her friends, but she was also a woman with a very sharp mind who wouldn't delude herself.

"I would like to look at the slave quarters," I said into the silence that had arisen. "Will you show me where this atropa is kept?"

In the average household, slaves usually slept in the corridors outside their masters' rooms. Here in the Villa, however, the servants, including the luxury girls, had their own sleeping quarters. It was a single large hall, which had been furnished only with the bare necessities. Narrow bunk beds crowded next to each other, and simple wooden shelves lined the walls. Only Juba, as a body servant, and Alva, as the old man's concubine, had their quarters in the private wing of the villa. Orodes and his guards shared a small chamber behind the porter's lodge in the atrium. All other slaves were housed here.

The hall, which resembled a legionary barracks with its bunk beds, lay almost deserted. No doubt the slaves were busy exchanging and celebrating the news about Philippos' will and the Tribune's fortunate verdict. Only in the back of the hall a single man was kneeling, but he rose when Layla and I entered the room.

It was not a slave, but one of Marcellus' legionaries. The man named Aculeo, who had guarded the master's chambers overnight. The search of the house the Tribune had ordered was apparently not yet complete.

"So far we have found nothing," the soldier reported to me, although I had not asked him to do so.

At that moment the door opened behind us, and a woman came running into the hall. It was Chloe, the young Greek girl.

She stopped in astonishment when she saw me. She probably wanted to say something, but her mouth opened and closed without a word coming out. Then she noticed Layla, who had headed straight for one of the shelves on the left long wall of the room.

"What are you looking for here?" Chloe addressed her old friend.

Layla gave me a questioning look, and I nodded back. I didn't owe anyone an explanation, but I didn't want to make a big secret of why I was still snooping around the Villa either.

"Do you still keep the atropa here?" Layla asked casually as she eyed some of the vials lined up on the shelf. Next to them were pots of ointment and a bowl with those strange utensils that women used to put on makeup.

Chloe didn't seem to find the question strange in any way. "Over here," she said, stepping up to the shelf and handing Layla a small jar.

Layla opened it carefully and peered inside. "Almost empty," she remarked, glancing over at me.

I went to her, took the vessel from her hand, and held it under my nose. An odor that aroused nausea, somewhere between bitter and pungent, emanated from the jar. I quickly closed it again and put it back on the shelf.

"Tell me, Chloe," I began, trying hard to sound as casual as Layla, "was Juba here in your quarters last night?"

She didn't seem to have to think about it but replied promptly, "Juba? No, he has no business here. He has his own chamber in the master's wing."

"Indeed," I said hesitantly, not knowing how to proceed for the moment.

Layla came to my rescue. "What where you up to last night?" she asked, "you and the other girls? After the master had been found dead."

Chloe looked at her a little suspiciously now. "We sat here together. We chatted for ages because we couldn't find any sleep. But Juba wasn't with us, definitely not."

A sudden change occurred in her beautiful face. "Oh—do you think he took his own life with atropa?"

"Could be," I said noncommittally.

Chloe's eyes widened. "How awful. But he must have obtained it earlier. I'm sure of it. He wasn't here last night, I'm sure of it."

I nodded. "That's probably how it happened," I said, earning a meaningful look from Layla. I knew what she was thinking: if Juba had taken the poison to his chamber, we would have encountered the vessel there; and that he should have drunk the juice before the legionaries had shown up made no sense. Nevertheless, I saw no way of ever knowing how it had really happened.

"Who prepares the atropa juice, by the way?" I asked Chloe.

"Alva does that," came the reply. "She cultivates the berries in the kitchen garden. She's extremely knowledgeable about herbs and all that stuff."

Chloe walked up to one of the bunk beds, which must have been hers, pulled out a tiny chest from under it, and removed something I couldn't make out. Then she scurried out of the room.

Layla and I remained alone with the legionary. The man had worked his way to the farthest corner of the room, scrupulously looking under every cot. He had rummaged through all the bedding and opened every box and chest.

"Nothing here either," he said now, rising. "I'll see if any of the other men have found anything, then we'll take care of the bodies and move out." He nodded to me and prepared to leave the room.

"Just a minute," I held him back. "Aculeo, right?"

The soldier nodded.

"You stood guard outside the private chambers overnight, didn't you?"

Something flickered in the man's good-natured eyes. Something that he got under control again in the next moment. Fear?

"That's right," he replied. It sounded more like a question than a simple answer.

Was it just my imagination, or was this soldier suddenly on guard? "I just wonder if Juba might not have left his chamber after all," I said. "To obtain the poison he used to kill himself."

"Certainly not," Aculeo replied hastily.

The man definitely had something to hide.

"And you didn't see anyone stealing into Juba's chamber either?" I probed further.

"No, Thanar. Shall we leave now? The men and I must return to camp. The Tribune must be expecting our report by now." He made a deferential hand gesture to escort me out of the hall.

"I think I'll stay a little longer," I replied. "There are still some small things that are bothering me. I want to question the slaves about them."

"Question the slaves?" echoed Aculeo. All color suddenly seemed to have drained from his tanned cheeks.

I looked around the room. The legionary, Layla and I were still all alone. With a few quick steps, I was at the door that Chloe had left half open behind her and pulled it closed.

Then I returned to the soldier and put my hand on his shoulder. "Won't you tell us what's bothering you, Aculeo? I'm not concerned with how well you're fulfilling your official duties, I just want to know what really happened last night. You saw something, didn't you? What was it? I promise you, it will stay between us."

"You're a friend of the Tribune, aren't you?" the man whispered while eyeing me fearfully. Beads of sweat suddenly shone on his youthful forehead.

"Nevertheless, I have no interest in causing you any trouble. As I said, I'm only interested in the truth. My friend died in this house last night, and I want to make sure that his killer is indeed dead."

Aculeo heaved a deep sigh. "Mithras help me!" he cried. "After all, if you speak to the slaves, you will know." He slapped his hands in front of his face.

"Know what?" I asked.

XXIV

"There was this boy," Aculeo began. "One of the slaves, no, surely it was an evil demon, in boy form, who bewitched me! I really didn't want to...I couldn't...oh, by all the gods, he was so beautiful! I forgot my duties and let him seduce me. Marcellus will throw me to the wolves!"

"Marcellus won't know," I tried to placate him. "So you left your guard post to, um, devote yourself to this demon, yes?"

"Only very briefly!" replied Aculeo. "I don't think that during this time anyone—"

"Where did the boy take you? To one of the guest rooms?"

Aculeo nodded wordlessly and then cast down his eyes.

That complicated everything. So Juba had not been isolated in his chamber. He might have left it, but just as well someone could have crept in on him while Aculeo had been indulging in the pleasures of Eros. Someone could have murdered the African during that time.

"What did he look like, this demon in boy form?" I asked the legionary.

"He had reddish-blond hair that fell to his hips," Aculeo enthused but immediately interrupted himself. In a more sober tone, he added, "He said he was from Britannia and called himself Lons—but he was certainly not human. No mere mortal could possess such radiant beauty, such incredible—" Again, the young soldier faltered.

He bit his lips. The rapturous glow disappeared from his

eyes. Instead, he begged me once again not to tell the Tribune.

I promised him and sent him on his way. He darted out of
the room like a fleeing deer.

I turned to Layla. "Doesn't it seem unusual to you that a
pleasure slave would seduce a legionary—and on the very
night that two people are killed in the house?"

Behind Layla's dark brow, a lot seemed to be going on. "You
think Lons deliberately tried to lure this soldier away from
his post?" she said.

"Do you have a better idea? Aculeo is a nice young fellow,
but that this Lons found him so attractive that he absolutely
had to seduce him, I would rule out. Our good legionary is
truly not blessed with an irresistible appearance, or how do
you see it?"

Layla nodded hesitantly. "But why would Lons have lured
him away?"

"Isn't the answer obvious, dear? So that another slave—
Lons' accomplice—could sneak into Juba's chamber."

"I'll never believe that, master! None of the slaves had any
reason to murder Juba. No one would—"

"It's all right," I placated. I put my arm around her and
pressed a kiss to her forehead. "Let's go find this demon from
Britannia and hear his side of the story."

Just outside the slave quarters we came across Chloe. When
she caught sight of us, she pretended to be on her way somewhere in a hurry. Had she been standing in front of this door
the whole time, listening?

She tried to scurry away, but I held her back. "Wait a moment, Chloe. I have a question or two for you."

"Yes, sir?" Her large dark eyes scrutinized me curiously. But there was something else in them that I couldn't quite put my finger on. Was it suspicion? Or simply fear? It seemed like an echo of the expression with which Aculeo had just looked at me. Had Chloe overheard the legionary's confession? Or did she already know about his nocturnal tryst with Lons without having to eavesdrop first?

"You said earlier that Juba didn't come here to the slave quarters during the night..."

"Yes, sir. He was not with us."

"You sat with the other slaves for a long time, you said. Because you couldn't sleep. And outside your door a legionary kept watch, didn't he? All night long."

"I can't say that, sir. After all, the door was closed. I could not see him."

"Of course. But what about the slaves? Were they all in the quarters? Did you notice if anyone was missing? Did one or two perhaps leave during the night?"

"No, sir. No one." The answer came far too quickly to be even halfway credible.

I was fond of Chloe. Before Layla came into my life, I had spent many unforgettable hours with her here in the Villa. And it was really not my intention to harm her and the other slaves, who were about to gain their freedom, in any way. But if there was one thing I could not stand, it was when people blatantly lied to my face.

Annoyed, I struck a harder tone with Chloe. "You're lying, girl," I told her outright. "With all the slaves housed in this room, you can't tell me you'd even have noticed the absence of one or the other."

Chloe looked at me, startled.

"Lons, for example, was not with you," I continued before she could say anything back. "Or he left the room sometime during the night. Am I not right?"

"No, sir. Certainly not. I saw him. He was—"

With an impatient gesture, I commanded her to be silent. It was pointless to question this girl. She shamelessly told me one lie after another. If I didn't resort to measures that I didn't want to take at all, I couldn't get anything sensible out of Chloe.

I looked at Layla and noticed that her face had darkened. She fixed Chloe with her black eyes, and the young Greek stared back defiantly.

"Were you Juba's lover, Chloe?" I asked abruptly. Satisfied, I registered how much this question upset the young woman. Perhaps she could be dealt with in this way.

She gasped for air, like a fish that has been pulled out to dry land. "No, sir!" she cried when she had regained her composure. "You'll have to take my word for it. I swear it!" she added, but of course I was not satisfied with that.

Instead, I said, "I saw you the other day, you and Juba. With my own eyes. You were making love in broad daylight, right next to the atrium."

I squinted over at Layla but noted to my dismay that this revelation didn't seem to surprise her.

It was she who beat Chloe to the answer. "Juba used to take the girls as he pleased," she explained to me. "Even in the old man's lifetime."

The way she looked at me could only mean one thing: Layla was speaking from her own experience.

"What, he got you too—" The words froze in my throat.

Layla nodded. Her eyes had narrowed to black slits. "There was nothing we could do about it. As the master's body servant, Juba enjoyed his complete trust. If one of us had talked, tried to accuse him—"

"That would have been suicide," Chloe chimed in. "Of course, what Juba did wasn't right, but as far as I was concerned, it wasn't a big deal either."

"No big deal?" I exclaimed. "Juba made a grab at his master's property!"

"Yeah, so?" Chloe retorted defiantly. "Do you think we women cared, the way that old monster treated us?"

I could not believe what I was seeing and hearing. The always friendly and well-mannered girl I thought I knew so well had vanished. Instead, I now had a pugnacious young woman in front of me who was a complete stranger to me. And who didn't mince words. "Juba was just another man we had to serve," she said. "Do you think any of the girls cared, with all the men who abused us day in and day out?" She stared at me angrily.

I did not know what to say. Part of me understood her all too well, but another part of me was appalled by this outrageous accusation.

Reluctantly, I shook my head. I myself had been one of the men about whom she had just spoken so disparagingly. Never had the thought occurred to me during my meetings with Belius in the Villa that I might *abuse* a girl, as Chloe put it.

But from her point of view, it had been so. It was a stance that I'd undoubtedly have shared had I been in her position.

A strange sensation came over me—as if I had been struck with blindness the whole time and now all at once I had become sighted. Only that I could not bear the sight of what was revealed to me.

I sent Chloe on her way, but even that felt wrong. She was a free woman now. Who was I to give her orders?

"Are you all right, master?" I heard Layla say. I didn't know how much time had passed. How long I had stood there like I was stuck, lost in dark thoughts.

"What...yes, dear. Come on, let's find this Lons."

"Chloe spoke the truth, master," Layla said when we had walked a few steps. "About Juba. She certainly didn't give herself to him willingly. It is Orodes to whom her heart belongs."

She caught my astonished look and quickly added, "At least that's how it was when I was still part of the familia. But that doesn't matter." She put on her sphinx smile and quickened her steps.

Layla was obviously uncomfortable that she had let herself get carried away with this bit of gossip about Chloe. Nevertheless, I took up her remark, perhaps only because Chloe had behaved so hot-tempered toward me just now. Or because I simply no longer knew what mattered in this puzzle I was so desperately trying to solve. What was important and what wasn't. "Does Orodes reciprocate Chloe's feelings, then?" I asked. "Are they a couple?"

Layla shook her head. "No, master, I think not. Orodes only ever had eyes for Suavis. And it seems to me that he still does."

"Suavis?"

I remembered how the brawny Parthian had hugged the

170

delicate blonde to him when the two of them had stood together with Layla and Chloe in the garden earlier. I had assumed he was just trying to comfort Suavis, but now that gesture took on a whole new meaning.

My head was spinning. I was reluctant to pry into the personal relationships of these people. I was a merchant, not a spy. Investigating a murder or even digging through the entanglements of this Villa's familia was really not my thing. I had no experience in such matters, and whichever way I turned, I always had the feeling of running into a wall. The more I learned about this house, about its dead as well as about the living, the less I understood. At least that's how it seemed to me.

XXV

It took quite a while before we finally managed to track down Lons. The young Britannic had retreated to the farthest part of the garden. He was alone and did not seem pleased to see me. He eyed me suspiciously, and I couldn't help thinking that he had gone to this secluded part of the estate to avoid the Roman soldiers.

Did he have something to hide?

As for his appearance, Aculeo, the legionary, had not exaggerated. Lons was perhaps sixteen or seventeen years old, a handsome young fellow who possessed the proportions of a Greek statue. His features also radiated an almost classical beauty and grace. Copper blond hair flowed around his shoulders like the finest silk fabric. One could not blame Aculeo for not being able to resist this youth. All the young legionary probably knew of the pleasures of Venus were the camp prostitutes or the she-wolves of Vindobona. Lons must have seemed to him like a son of Eros himself.

It was Layla who finally made the Britannic talk. She vouched for me, so to speak, and assured Lons that he could trust me.

"It's not about trust," the youth countered, eyeing me suspiciously. "You really just want to talk?"

I didn't understand right away. Only when Layla said, "Thanar is not interested in your love services. He only has a few questions for you," I realized why Lons was acting so dismissive. And at the same moment, I began to suspect that the seduction story Aculeo had told us might not be entirely true. I was eager to hear Lons' version of events.

"I was standing with some slaves in the kitchen," he began when I asked him about it. "Only for half an hour or so before the legionaries sent us to our quarters. The Romans shared the meal with us, and when we were done, this one soldier took me aside."

"Aculeo?"

"He didn't tell me his name. He dragged me away with him to one of the guest rooms, where he—oh, the usual." Lons made an unwilling hand gesture. "He wanted fellatio first, then he took me until he couldn't go on any longer. Without paying, of course. He didn't even tip me."

"And after that?"

"He took me to the slave quarters."

"I see. Was there a guard standing outside the entrance to the quarters?"

Lons shook his head. "No, there was no one there. And the legionary left again, too. That much I still saw."

Just as I had thought. This account of events only remotely resembled the demonic seduction story Aculeo had told me. I was sure that the truth lay closer to Lons' version. The Britannic youth had spoken of the Roman's deeds with a resigned indifference that seemed more convincing than any grand affirmation. Now I understood why he had retreated to the farthest corner of the garden while the Romans were still in the house. Probably for no other reason than to avoid new labors of love.

The legionaries had no right to help themselves to the slaves of a foreign house, but what simple man, free or unfree, would dare to deny a Roman soldier what he wanted?

In any case, I concluded that Lons had probably not intentionally lured Aculeo away from his post. And I now also knew that the slave quarters had been unguarded. At least at the time Lons returned there. Probably the legionary in charge would also have affirmed to me that he had been seduced by a glowing-eyed demon.

I sighed loudly. In plain language, that meant that everyone had been able to go his own way last night under the roof of the Villa, as he pleased. Whether one of these paths had led to Juba's chamber—and to his death—I would probably never know under these circumstances.

Suicide or not? Had Juba voluntarily departed from life, or had he been murdered? If the African servant had habitually helped himself to the slave girls, as if he were the master of the house, then perhaps one of his victims might have sought his life?

Or not. Judging from Chloe's reaction, Juba's assaults were a nuisance to the girls, but not one that was worth a murder.

A nuisance. I wonder what the slave girls had seen in me—and in all the other men who regularly visited the Villa? Had they all detested us behind their lovely smiles and seductive cuddliness? Or even hated us? Was I myself one of the easier guests to serve, while a man like the Primus Pilus, who could hardly control his foul temper, was considered a feared fiend?

For the second time that day, this nasty feeling of having wronged the slave girls of the Villa for so many years came over me. Especially Chloe, whom I had claimed on so many evenings.

Hastily, I chased the thought away.

"Is that all?" Lons asked, whose presence I had almost forgotten. He looked me inquiringly in the face.

I nodded wordlessly, and the young Britannic hurried off.

There I stood, in the well-tended garden that I knew almost as my own, surrounded by the lively splashing of ornamental fountains and cheerful birdsong, and didn't know how to go from here.

Layla asked for permission to check on her friends one more time. I gladly let her go.

For a while I wandered aimlessly among the trees, lost in all sorts of dark thoughts. Until I finally found myself in front of the wall that surrounded the estate. I followed it for a few hundred paces, not knowing why I was doing this or what I was looking for. If I was looking for anything at all.

Of course, I also found nothing that seemed to be of any significance. I passed a gate that probably led into the forest, but it was locked, and discovered countless places where a reasonably skilled climber could have easily overcome the wall. So, it was possible after all that a stranger had sneaked into the house last night and later left it the same way. A murderer whose motives I did not know and who was still at large. Possible—but not very likely. How could an outsider have known about the bear arena in which I had almost lost my life?

I returned to the house and questioned a few other slaves who crossed my path. Two of them were love servants, the others belonged to the household staff.

I didn't learn anything I didn't already know. Everyone claimed to have slept soundly that night. Everyone swore to me that they had neither heard nor seen anything. No one admitted to any knowledge about the underground bear arena. Not even by rumor. No one had entered the cellar, no one had passed by the master's chambers or had been able to observe Philippos hurrying into his study to kill himself. Practically everyone asked me if it was really true that they were being set free.

I gave up.

Was this the end of my lofty investigations, on which I had set such high hopes? Could I claim to see more clearly now than before? Did I know more than the Tribune who had already passed his sentence hours ago, seemingly without any doubt?

Oh, how I longed to ask Belius for advice! My old friend had always given me the feeling that there was a solution to every problem, no matter how difficult it was. And it was usually he who had actually presented it to me. I missed him already, even though Belius had not been dead for a whole day yet.

Had his murder been avenged? I hoped so, but I could not be quite sure. And I saw no possibility to change anything about that fact. The only thing left for me to do was to help his sons prepare the funeral procession and make a generous contribution to a worthy celebration at his grave. Games, music, a sumptuous banquet—Vindobona should keep my friend in honorable memory. I would personally see to that.

I looked around for Layla. I only wanted to leave this house of death as quickly as possible now. I found her in the kitchen, a vaulted hall, which, judging by its size and equipment, also served as a dining room for the slaves.

At the top of a long, roughly carpentered wooden table sat Layla. Chloe was leaning against her shoulder, cuddly as a dark cat. An ancient slave, who must have been the cook, was talking in a barely understandable gibberish that only remotely resembled Latin. He was addressing Suavis, who had taken a seat on Layla's right. Every few moments he put a treat of some kind into the girl's mouth, and when she let out a pleasurable purr, the old man clapped his hands enthusiastically. Orodes, who was sitting next to Suavis and had his arm protectively around her, smiled quietly to himself.

When Layla caught sight of me, she sprang up and came running toward me.

"Let's go home," I said, "I admit defeat."

"No more new insights?" she asked, as if we were two scholars working on a difficult philosophical problem. Without waiting for an answer, she added, "May I speak to you for a moment, master? I have a request to make of you."

"Sure. Let's talk about it in the wagon."

"Can we discuss it here? It's about my friends." She pointed her head at the two girls at the table. Suavis was in the process of now feeding Orodes something that looked like cold roast.

Layla pulled me out into the hallway, where she was straightforward with her request. "It's like this, master. The girls are free now, but—"

She seemed to be searching for the right words. "Chloe and Suavis don't know where to go now, and they don't want to stay here in this house. Alva will have to sell the property, because it probably can't be maintained without the income from the guests. And then there are all the bad memories, all the people who found death here. The girls are afraid, master, and they are both like sisters to me. So, I wanted to ask if you would let them live under your roof for a while. Just until they know where to go. Of course, they'd make themselves useful, help around the house, in the kitchen. Chloe is an excellent—"

I raised my hand, and Layla, who had rattled off her request without taking a breath, gasped.

"Your friends are welcome as guests in my house as long as they wish," I answered her. "We really don't lack free rooms."

I had once built my house in the sure hope that the gods would bless me with a large offspring. A hope that I had buried long ago together with my wife.

"Oh, thank you, master!" Layla pressed a big kiss on my cheek, then scurried back to the kitchen, no doubt to immediately deliver the invitation to her friends.

I followed her to see how the girls would take it. There was a great whispering, shouts of joy, hugs, then they both came rushing toward me to thank me.

Orodes was the last to stand up, stepped behind Suavis, and gently put his hands on her shoulders. In a serious voice, he turned to me. "Your invitation is most generous, sir—"

"Call me Thanar," I interrupted him. "You are now a free man like me."

He nodded, and a barely perceptible smile flitted across his angular face. "Suavis and I—we belong together," he said solemnly. "Where she goes, I want to be too. Do you perhaps need a servant in your house, a guard or otherwise? I can do the work of two men, you won't be disappointed. A place to sleep in the stable or the cellar and daily bread will be enough for me, as long as I can be with my beloved." He smiled down at Suavis' shock of blond hair, which was a good hand's breadth below his chin. The girl stood motionless with her back against his broad chest, gazing up at me from under her thick lashes.

The passion with which Orodes had made his request

stirred something in me. This man loved deeply and faith-fully, of that I was sure. "You too are welcome as a guest un-der my roof as long as it pleases you," I said.

The Parthian thanked me with few but all the more forceful words.

We agreed that he would come to my house with the girls the very next day. After all, none of the three had extensive belongings to pack.

XXVI

The will of Philippos was read the next day in the forum, and every single one of his slaves received freedom according to his last wish. The body of the young Greek, together with that of Juba, was thrown into the river without funeral rites, as was customary for criminals.

Chloe, Suavis and Orodes moved into my house as agreed. I gave each of the three a nice spacious room all to themselves and kept them from becoming my servants. They were my guests, and I wanted them to feel comfortable. They should leave the horror of the murders and all the fears that the girls in particular had gone through behind them as quickly as possible.

The two young women brought something with them that I had not known before and that made Layla really blossom. My house was suddenly filled with the laughter, the noise, the high spirits of young people gathered in a pack. And Layla, Chloe and Suavis made a magnificent pack.

Chloe seemed to feel at home under my roof from day one, while Suavis took a little while to shed her shyness. After three or four days, however, the house virtually shook with the whirl of their activity. Whether one was in the library, the peristyle garden, or the dining room, lively chatter or girlish giggles could always be heard somewhere, not too far away, and on many a sunny afternoon the three friends romped through the garden like young dogs. Only when

Orodes joined them, a change occurred in Suavis and Chloe—one that I didn't quite understand.

Suavis sometimes showed a certain shyness towards the Parthian, which I found strange, since they were a couple. Chloe, on the other hand, seemed to love Orodes all the more obviously, although she had to know that he did not return her feelings. All his attention was always focused on Suavis; he seemed to have found in her the woman of his most secret dreams. Once, when he and I sat together over a cup of wine in the shade of the portico behind the house, he confided in me that they wanted to get married as soon as possible.

Although I made it clear to the Parthian several times that he was a guest and not a servant in my house, he didn't mind helping out in my stables for a few hours a day. He had a knack for horses and was fascinated by the animals in my possession. I owned some of my brother's breeds, and his steeds were the best and most sought after for a hundred miles around. Orodes did not talk much about himself, he was not a man of great words, but I got the impression that he must once have been a gifted horseman in the army of the Parthians.

For me, it was long past time to get back to my business. A few new deliveries had arrived, including some highly valuable pieces of jewelry of dubious origin, which I had to get out of the house as soon as possible.

The arrow wound in my back was still bothering me, however, and so after a few days I decided to entrust my trade assistant Darius with the journey north, which I had actually wanted to make myself.

It was not the first time that I had placed a delicate trading trip entirely in his hands, so we loaded the treasures onto fast travel wagons that night, I gave Darius six heavily armed men, and they set off in good spirits.

I was relieved to know the dangerous goods were out of the house, because the new residents of my home were joined almost daily by an unexpected visitor: Tribune Marcellus. That was, at first he came unexpectedly, but after a few days he was already as familiar a sight as the chattering and giggling pack of girls who romped through the house and garden.

Marcellus usually came two or three hours before sunset—without my inviting him and without any apparent reason for his visit—and often stayed until long after supper. Sometimes he would ask Layla to read to him or play the flute for him. On one occasion I couldn't resist offering him a room in my house, since he seemed to like it so much. Of course, he refused. He didn't even seem to notice that I was teasing him.

What did he want in my house? Didn't the man have official business in the legionary camp that needed his attention? Of course, the rules of hospitality forbade turning him away, especially since he was such a high-ranking guest. He seemed to see his new best friend in me. I would not be able to get rid of him anytime soon, and unbelievably I found myself enjoying his company.

Two days after Orodes and the girls had moved in with me, I received a visit from Alva, the new owner of the Villa. She seemed tense, even downright distressed. She obviously had something on her mind, but only after making polite conversation with me for quite a while did she suddenly lower her eyes and haltingly come to the reason for her visit. "Forgive me for bothering you with this, Thanar," she began, "but I don't know anyone else in Vindobona to whom I could turn."

"What is it about?" I asked. "If I can, I'll be glad to help you."

She raised her head and eyed me shyly. "I need to find a buyer for the villa, but I don't know how to go about it," she said. "You, on the other hand, are an experienced business-man, and that's why I was hoping that you—well, that you could help me. In exchange for a share of the proceeds of the sale, of course," she added quickly, "whatever is customary in this regard."

"Do you want to leave Vindobona then?" I asked.

"Not really, but I don't want to stay in the mansion. The house is full of ghosts of the past. I wake up at night and hear the bear roar. Or the screams of all the girls he tore apart with his claws. In almost every room, something reminds me of Philippos, whom I lost."

She faltered. "Do you think a buyer could be found? And that the proceeds of the sale would be enough to support myself? Could I afford a small house in the civilian town? It's supposed to be safe there, I've heard. A couple of the girls would like to stay with me too; they've never lived in freedom and don't know where to go. Of course, we can look for work—" The questions just poured out of her, and she fixed me fearfully with her beautiful blue eyes.

I raised my hand and tried to reassure her. "Don't worry, Alva," I said. "You can count on me. We'll find a buyer for the villa, though probably no one will pay you its true value. There are not many men in Vindobona who can afford such an estate. However, the art objects in the house can be sold off regardless—I can even buy some of them from you myself, if you want. I can resell them in the *Germanicum* without any problems. And with that, I'm already generously compensated."

I was confident that Alva could finance her livelihood from the sale of the villa's inventory alone—without having to accept wage labor. The tribal leaders in the north certainly appreciated exquisite art objects from the Imperium Romanum. With the exception of my brother, that was. And even a modest purchase price for the villa would be enough to acquire a handsome townhouse in Vindobona that could accommodate a larger familia. A home behind the secure walls of the civilian town that would offer the women access to the markets and stores, the public baths, the temples, and the amphitheater.

I promised Alva that I would take care of everything, and she thanked me with a radiant smile. The tension and worry with which she had come to my house fell away from her.

We sealed the deal with a good cup of wine, and I had fruit and some honey treats served. It was probably the first time for Alva to be entertained in a house as a guest. She ate and drank like a child lost in her favorite fable.

After a while, she said, "I also wanted to thank you for taking my daughter in, sir. I'm sure she's very happy to be with Layla. I hope she won't be a burden to you?"

"On the contrary," I assured her, "Suavis is welcome to stay with me as long as she wants. Until we find you a nice townhouse—then I think she'll want to live with you, won't she?" I smiled encouragingly at her.

However, this did not have the intended effect. Alva's face suddenly darkened. All of a sudden, the tension and worry that had previously lain on her like a heavy dark veil were back.

"Suavis and I are not close," she began tentatively. "She certainly won't want to live with me. Perhaps she will find her home with Orodes? He loves her very much, doesn't he? I think a tribal leader, as he once was, will want to return to his homeland. And perhaps Suavis would like to go with him? She herself has never seen the lands of her ancestors and feels no longing for them."

"She was born in the villa, wasn't she?" I asked. "Was Lycortas her father?" The question slipped over my lips. I had not intended to stir up Alva's painful past again.

A low but all the more agonized groan escaped Alva. "He sired her, if that's what you mean. But he was everything to her but a father. He didn't even allow me to be a mother to her; he always claimed me all for himself. Suavis grew up in the slave quarters. In the beginning, a woman who had just given birth to a child herself took care of her, but she died soon after. From then on, my little girl was on her own—and Lycortas made her a love servant far too early."

Alva sucked in an audible breath and pressed her lips together. "I couldn't help her for the life of me, but still, I don't think she ever forgave me for not being there for her. And after Lycortas' death, when I confessed to her that I loved Philippos, she turned away from me all the more. No, she will not want to live with me at any price, as much as I would like her to. I only hope that someday she can be a happy mother herself."

I didn't know how to express the compassion I felt. Or my growing hatred for Lycortas, even though he was long dead. The way Alva now sat up in her chair, inconspicuously wiping a tear from the corner of her eye, told me she didn't want to be pitied. Behind her delicate, girlish exterior, she seemed to be a strong, if not tough, woman. Even though she had hardly chosen that for herself. It was Lycortas who had made her that way with his atrocities.

"Your Layla was the best mother Suavis ever had," Alva continued abruptly. "Or at least an older sister, at least one of the few people I ever saw my girl happy around. Even though Layla only lived with us for a few months, she took such loving care of Suavis! She is quite a wonderful person. Just like you, sir," she added.

"Thanar," I corrected her, swallowing down the thick lump that had suddenly formed in my throat.

"Thanar," Alva repeated with a sheepish smile. "I'll have to get used to that."

XXVII

Contrary to my expectations, I did not have to search long to find a buyer for Alva's villa.

I had made sure that every man in Vindobona who possessed prestige and, above all, wealth knew about the pending sale. However, I would never have thought of the interested party who appeared in the atrium of my house only three days after my conversation with Alva—without having sent a messenger beforehand. It was Servius Asinius Blandus, but in Vindobona everyone called him only the *lupanarius*.

Blandus owned a good three quarters of all those brothels in the city, which were called lupanars by the Romans. The name was derived from lupus, the wolf, from which the girls—the she-wolves who served in these sad houses—also took their name. They were dark and dirty places, more reminiscent of the underworld of Hades than of a flourishing home of Venus.

What did it actually say about the Romans that the divine Romulus, the founder of the city of Rome, was supposedly suckled by a she-wolf? A real four-legged one, but still. I had often asked my friend Belius this question when we got into philosophizing over a nice cup of wine. It didn't seem to me to cast a particularly good light on the Eternal City.

Well, Belius was dead, and Blandus, the lupanarius of Vindobona, my guest tonight.

Winning the favor of a new business partner by way of his

palate was a strategy that had often worked for me. In the Villa itself, however, there was no longer any kitchen or serving staff, so having dinner there was out of the question. But the lupanarius knew the estate anyway from his own intensive inspection, as he had expressed it in his pompous way, and it was only a matter of coming to an agreement regarding the price.

Blandus was himself a libertus, a former slave, and although he had achieved considerable wealth, he still spoke and acted like the mill worker he had once been. This, however, did not diminish his self-confidence. He had announced to me grandly that not only did he intend to live in the Villa himself, but that he would continue to run it in the manner of the ancient Greek—"only more luxurious!"

Where he wanted to get the appropriate girls for it, I did not ask him. I was happy if I could get a good price for Alva for the house. The affairs of the lupanarius were entirely his business.

For the banquet, at which I wanted to seal the sale with Blandus, I also deliberately invited the Tribune this time. He dined with me almost every day anyway, and on this special occasion he would lend the evening the necessary glamor. The lupanarius had certainly never shared a dining couch with a Roman nobleman in his entire life—I was sure of that.

Marcellus arrived before the appointed hour.

He seemed strangely nervous, drained his first cup of wine in one go, and then went into a strange monologue about the weather and other inanities. That was not usually his style, so I asked if anything had happened to him. And to my astonishment, I found that I was actually concerned about his well-being.

Had Marcellus now really become my friend without my own intention? He certainly would not talk to me about problems within the legion, but what else could have put this usually so self-confident young nobleman in such a nervous mood?

"There is something I wanted to discuss with you, Thanar," he said after starting to talk several times but immediately breaking off.

I cannot say why a strange uneasiness came over me at these words—but it did.

What Marcellus had to tell me, however, I was not to learn, because at that moment a slave entered the room and announced the arrival of Alva. Of course, being the seller of the villa, I had also invited her to the banquet.

To my astonishment, she came accompanied by the lupanarius, who escorted her into the room as if she were his queen. "Took the liberty of looking at the villa after all before I put a whole bunch of gold on the table for it," he explained with a wry grin. "And was allowed to escort the mistress of the house here."

He indicated a bow to Alva, looking like an aging bird of prey pecking at a grain of corn. He was a thin, bony man, with a giant nose, tousled head, and beard hair. He was dressed in a garishly colorful tunic that might have been expensive but hung from his shoulders like a sack.

I led my guests into the dining room, where Layla, Suavis, Chloe, and Orodes had already gathered. They greeted each other—partly with a joyful embrace, partly with no more than a polite nod, then we settled down on the sofas and I signaled my servants to let the meal begin.

The lupanarius immediately seemed to feel at home. However, he had probably never heard of how to behave as a guest in a foreign house.

As the guest of honor for the evening, I had him take a seat right next to me on the sofa. To his left lay Layla, who attracted his attention from the very beginning. Blandus tasted the offered dishes without looking, he participated in the conversation at the table only when he was directly addressed, but I could hear him whispering one insinuation after another into Layla's ear. At the same time, he moved closer and closer to my poor girl, and I caught a pleading look from her to rush to her aid. But how could I do it without offending this lecher?

Suddenly, the lupanarius turned to me, tapped me on the shoulder as if I were his old drinking pal, and loudly announced, "So if you add this pretty black jewel here to the deal, I'm sure we'll come to an agreement as far as the villa is concerned!" He pointed his thumb over his shoulder at Layla, licking his parched lips as he did so.

"Layla is not for sale," I countered, trying hard not to let my annoyance at his unseemly offer show.

Across from me, Tribune Marcellus slammed his cup down on the table so hard that I could hear the wood groan.

"Of course, she would serve only me personally," the lupanarius replied, grinning at me lecherously. "She's far too precious to be a she-wolf. We wouldn't want to throw pearls to the chickens, would we?" His hot breath, reeking of fish, hit me in the face.

"She's not for sale," I repeated firmly, and at that I must have stared at Blandus so grimly that his eyes widened in fright. For Alva's sake, I didn't want to jeopardize the deal with this creep—but there were limits to my good will.

Blandus mumbled something unintelligible, then turned to the food on his plate, leaving Layla alone for the rest of the meal. Which didn't stop him from undressing just about every other woman in the room with his glances and winking lustfully at them when he felt unobserved.

XXVIII

After we had dined in a very subdued mood for almost two hours, I invited Blandus to retire with me for business negotiations. I left the other guests, including Alva, in the dining room. Even though she was the owner of the villa, I could better represent her interests if the lupanarius didn't keep staring holes into her breasts during the negotiations.

I led Blandus into the room I jokingly called the *Barbarian Chamber*. It was a room in the traditional style of my people, filled with plain wooden chairs grouped around a heavy oak table. The front wall was decorated with a large mural showing fishermen on the Danubius. The men were in the process of using all their strength to drag a great sturgeon out of the waters—that fearsome monster that could reach a length of a good twenty feet and fight like a pack of wolves.

I liked to use this room when I received Germanic or Celtic trading partners, guests who preferred to eat in a sitting position instead of stretching out on a Roman dining sofa.

I went down to the cellar myself and selected an amphora of the best Gallic wine, had some sweet treats served, then took a seat at the table with Blandus and got down to business without further ado.

Now that the lupanarius was no longer distracted by his own lechery, we made good progress. He was a shrewd fox who negotiated hard, but he quickly had to realize that I hadn't just been in business since yesterday either. I was confident I could close the deal this evening at a mutually satisfactory price. Then, however, the lupanarius told me in graphic terms that he had to go to the latrine, and I was left alone for the moment.

He did not return.

After waiting for him for what seemed like an endless amount of time, I set out to find him. Surely he couldn't have gotten lost in my house? No, he had probably run into one of the women, and—

I didn't finish the thought, quickening my steps instead. When I pushed open the door to the latrine, I met Chloe. She was sitting on one of the wooden benches and seemed lost in thought.

I asked her about the lupanarius, but she had not encountered him. I settled down opposite her and took the opportunity to relieve myself as well, while I was here.

The young Greek woman and I exchanged a few words, she commented disparagingly on the lupanarius' manners, then I left her alone. I could only agree with her about the character of this old codger, but nevertheless, he had hopefully not simply left my house in the middle of our price negotiation?

Where could he be? I returned to the triclinium where we had originally dined—and found Layla whispering something in the Tribune's ear.

The two of them were alone in the room, so why all this secrecy? What's more, Layla promptly fell silent when she saw me, and Marcellus had put on an expression that I had never seen on him before. He seemed even younger than he actually was and had almost nothing in common with the self-confident commander he was usually so fond of portraying.

I asked them about the other guests, but they had probably left quite a while ago. "I think they wanted to go to the garden," Layla said, and the Tribune just nodded wordlessly.

It was a glorious, cloudless summer evening, ideally suited for a walk in the moonlight. Had the lupanarius chased one of the girls and followed her into the garden? One had to suspect it—I only hoped that Orodes had stayed with the women. In the presence of the Parthian, the old lecher would certainly not dare to offend Suavis or Alva.

I sent two servants to search the garden for Blandus and returned to the house myself. I looked in every room, every corridor, every chamber, but nowhere did I discover any trace of the lupanarius. Finally, I found myself back in front of the door to the latrine. I looked in again, but none of the seats were occupied now.

Directly opposite the latrine, steps led down into the cellar. Perhaps Blandus had been curious and descended here? I took the oil lantern from the hook next to the stairs, lit it, and stepped down into the darkness.

My entire house had a basement, because I needed the space for warehouses, among other things. In the numerous corridors, a stranger could get lost all too easily. And yet, I didn't have to search long for the lupanarius.

I found him, just in front of that cellar compartment where I used to store luxury goods of shady origin. Blandus lay stretched out on his back. His eyes were broken; the hem of his tunic was stained with blood. He was dead without any doubt.

Next to him on the floor, a knife blade shone in the light of my lamp. I knelt down and recognized the weapon immediately. It was a short sax, which usually adorned the wall in my atrium along with some other heirlooms of my ancestors.

The body of the lupanarius, however, seemed unharmed—until I turned him over onto his stomach. Three knife wounds gaped in his back, and where he had lain, a smeared pool of bright red blood covered the floor.

What had Blandus been doing down here? He certainly hadn't tried to break in; he didn't carry any tools with him. He had died just in front of the door to my secret store-room—but he could not possibly have known about the hidden side of my business. Or could he? Was it mere coincidence that he had died here of all places? I thanked the gods that I had emptied this storeroom only a few days ago and had sent the precarious transport on its way accompanied by Darius.

But the even more pressing question, only now drilling into my head, had to be: who on earth had murdered the lupanarius?

Hurried footsteps in the hallway behind me snapped me out of my thoughts. I jerked upright and turned around. It was Marcellus, the Tribune, coming toward me accompanied by one of my slaves. They must have taken the front cellar stairs.

"Ah, here you are, Thanar," Marcellus began, "I was just asking this lad here—" he pointed to the servant, "—about the wine cellar, to pick out another amphora. He didn't know where you had gone, so I came myself. I hope you don't mind, I—"

At that moment, he saw the corpse. It was lying on the floor behind me, and I had probably hidden it from his gaze for a brief moment with my own body in the semi-darkness of the cellar.

Marcellus stopped abruptly and stared at me. Suddenly, I realized what it must look like. My sax, which lay blood-stained beside the dead man—clearly once again a barbarian weapon. I, who had just been kneeling all alone over the corpse. My hands bloody because I had turned the body over. I'd be damned if this sight didn't abruptly remind the Tribune of the death of his Primus Pilus in my harbor.

In a hurried prayer I thanked the gods that at least this time it was not a Roman officer who lay butchered at my feet.

XXIX

"Blandus was murdered!" I said quickly. "I found him moments ago." My voice sounded surprisingly firm given the cold horror eating through my guts.

"Round up the other servants," I instructed my slave before the Tribune could say anything back. "See if a stranger has entered the house! Find the guests, gather them in the atrium, and then you report to me who you found where, in whose company! Understood? No one leaves the house!"

The servant stood rigid and stiff in front of me, staring at me out of empty eyes.

"Go!" I commanded.

With that, fortunately, the lad got moving. "Yes, master," he gasped and stumbled away.

I hurried to explain to the Tribune my own presence down here. "The lupanarius wanted to go to the latrine," I said, "but he did not return. That is why I went in search of him."

The Tribune nodded wordlessly, but there was something dark and strange in his eyes. Distrust, no doubt. Who could blame him?

But was that really all? A completely crazy thought forced itself upon me—probably born out of the horror of the moment: what was Marcellus himself doing down here in the cellar? A house guest helping himself in his host's wine cellar was not within the rules of hospitality. Had the Tribune given the true reason for his presence in my basement? Or had he only come down here to catch me next to the corpse? Next to the dead man he knew was lying here? Because Marcellus had murdered the lupanarius himself shortly before?

No, that was ridiculous. But if not the Tribune, then who?

All at once, all the horror that I had left behind only a few days ago returned. Already the death penalty hovered before my eyes again, like the sword of Damocles. The sight of the dead Primus Pilus in my harbor forced its way back into my mind. Pain flashed through the wound in my back as if the arrow of the treacherous archer pierced me again. I saw the corpse of my beloved Belius before me and was staring once again into the bloodthirsty jaws of the bear that would now finally tear me apart.

I had come to terms with all this as best I could. I had thrown myself into my new, old life, which was now enriched by young people under my roof, and tried to forget.

The criminals who had been behind all the atrocities—they were dead after all! Executed by their own hands. Or were they not?

Here in my basement, at my feet, was a new corpse, another murder victim—on an evening when four former residents of the Villa were staying under my roof. This could not possibly be a coincidence. Even though I had instructed my servant to search the house for a burglar, I was very doubtful about this possibility. The wall around my property was not as easy to climb as the one surrounding the Greek's Villa, and the gate of my house was well guarded at all hours of the day and night.

This could only mean that the murderer of the lupanarius was to be sought under my roof. Among my guests.

I simply couldn't wrap my head around this idea. I didn't

consider Marcellus capable of such a deed. Why would he want to kill the lupanarius of all people? Why would *anyone* want to kill the lupanarius? True, he had been an old, pompous lecher—but that was hardly reason enough to send him on the journey across the river of death.

The questions wouldn't stop crowding into my head. Was it just a coincidence that I had found the body? And that the murderer had used my sax? Perhaps he had merely been looking for an available weapon in the house and had helped himself to it in the atrium. Such a short knife could be easily concealed in the folds of one's robe. And to kill with a sax, it didn't take much strength. Three stabs in the back of a feeble, old codger were quite different from splitting the chest of a Primus Pilus with a single axe blow. This murder here could have been committed by anyone.

I shuddered at the thought.

Apart from the Tribune, Alva, Suavis, Chloe, and Orodes were staying under my roof. I couldn't picture one of the women committing such a bloodthirsty deed, whether they possessed the necessary strength or not, so the Parthian had to be my primary suspect. But he could have killed the lupanarius with his bare hands, instead of having to steal a knife for the deed. Marcellus also carried his own weapon. So, had the murderer wanted to pin the crime on me? Had he made use of the sax for this reason?

"What could Blandus have wanted here in the cellar?" the voice of the Tribune snapped me out of my broodings. Marcellus was now squatting right next to the corpse, looking at the fatal wounds. "He would hardly have suspected the latrine to be down here, would he?"

He rose and pointed with a wave of his hand to the doors

lining up along the corridor. "Do you keep anything valuable down here, Thanar?" he asked. "Could it be that Blandus was trying to steal from you?"

"No," I lied. That was, at the moment it was actually true. Again, I thanked the gods that I had sent Darius off with my shady but very precious goods.

"Here behind us are some storerooms," I explained, "and there in front are the ice cellar and the wine cellar. Then there are pantries, some unused compartments, and the house shrine. That's all. I have no idea what the lupanarius might have been looking for down here."

"A very unusual behavior for a guest," said Marcellus. "To visit the cellar secretly and alone. These nouveau riche freedmen simply have no manners!" The corners of his mouth were twisting in disgust.

I did not reply.

"How many ways are there to get into your basement?" he continued. "Just the front and back stairs?"

I nodded, but then I remembered the gate that led from down here directly out onto the embankment of the Danubius. A path meandered down to the harbor behind that door—so we could move deliveries of goods from the ships directly to the warehouses without having to lug them through the whole house. The gate was in the hallway around the next corner. I walked the few steps ahead, turned, and found what I expected. The heavy, iron-barred door was locked from the inside. Everything was in order.

"I don't think anyone escaped this way," said the Tribune, who had followed me. "And I honestly can't imagine a robber to break in here, at such an early hour, when all the inhabitants of the house are still milling about. Apart from the fact that such a scoundrel would probably look around your atrium rather than search for valuables in the cellar."

Unless the burglar knew what treasures I usually hid in my cellar. But I didn't necessarily want to discuss this thought with Marcellus.

We retraced our steps to the corpse, and the Tribune continued his reflections. He visibly enjoyed the role of investigator. "Did any of your servants have a score to settle with the lupanarius?" he asked. "A lad maybe who caught gonorrhea from one of Blandus' she-wolves?" He laughed throatily but immediately fell silent again. He must have realized himself that the situation was serious.

"I don't think one of my servants is to blame," I said. "Surely such a man could have committed the murder much more easily in a dark alley of Vindobona than during a banquet in the house where he himself makes his home."

"So, it was one of us?" said Marcellus.

I nodded mutely. "The lupanarius must have trusted his killer enough to turn his back on him."

"Not necessarily," Marcellus replied. "The killer may have crept up silently from behind.

"You can't descend here silently via either of the staircases," I contradicted him. "The wood is old and creaks with every step. Blandus would have heard the assassin."

"What if the killer was already lying in wait for Blandus?" Marcellus speculated further.

"Why would he have expected the lupanarius down here? He could only have lured him to the basement himself—which in turn would mean that the lupanarius had to trust him at least somewhat. Otherwise, he would hardly have agreed to meet him in the cellar, of all places."

"Looks like it," Marcellus grumbled. "The lupanarius made the mistake of thinking his killer was harmless."

The Tribune's gaze wandered over the ground beside the corpse. "There's no lamp anywhere here, by the way, Thanar. Did Blandus himself sneak down in the dark? Or did the murderer take his light with him after the deed was done? But what for?"

"There's another possibility," I said, "They may have come down here together. With only one lamp."

"You were very angry that Blandus wanted to buy Layla from you," Marcellus remarked as if in passing. As if he unintentionally spoke his own thoughts aloud.

"That's hardly a reason to lure him into the basement and slaughter him here," I replied coldly, while struggling inwardly to control myself. I almost added: *you yourself, Tribune, are also suspiciously often on the spot when there is a dead body*. But, of course, I said nothing of the sort. Now was not the time to make an enemy of such a powerful man again.

I knelt down and turned the body back into the position in which I had found it. There had been blood on the front, on the hem of Blandus' tunic.

I studied the stains more closely. They could not have been caused by the knife wounds in the back. No, they were more reminiscent of the kind of marks left behind when one cleaned dirty hands with a towel. Some of the stains clearly looked like the marks left by a person's fingers.

Marcellus seemed to have come to the same conclusion as me. "This is where the killer wiped his bloody hands," he said. "Which doesn't surprise me. Otherwise, after all, he could hardly have returned upstairs unnoticed."

And then the Tribune spoke the thought that tormented myself the most: "Do you think there is a connection with the other murders, Thanar?"

"I don't know," I grumbled. "By all the gods, I should hope not."

Marcellus' eyes narrowed to dark slits. "It would mean that we threw the wrong men into the river. That the real killer got away from us."

Yes, I guessed that was what it meant. As much as this thought tormented me.

"Let's go upstairs," I said. "We want to see who was where—while it can still be reconstructed at least to some extent."

XXX

I was pleased to see that my servants were well organized and had done a good job. All the guests were gathered in the atrium and were talking excitedly. However, the conversations immediately fell silent when Marcellus and I entered the room.

Layla, who had been standing with Orodes, rushed toward me and embraced me. "Thank the gods, you two are well!"

There it was again, this 'you two'. It did not escape me that Layla threw herself into my arms but that her eyes sought those of the Tribune. Her relief was for him as much as for me.

"Your servants wouldn't tell us anything specific," Orodes intervened. "Only that there has been a murder. Is that true?"

"Blandus was killed," Marcellus said. "He was stabbed in the cellar."

Sounds of horror were emitted. Alva pulled her daughter to her, but Suavis immediately escaped her embrace and ran over to Orodes. He, in turn, wrapped her tightly in his massive warrior arms. Chloe just stood there, stiff as a board, staring at me with her eyes widened in fear.

Layla whispered in my ear, "Do you think one of the guests murdered him, master?" Her voice sounded completely controlled; at most a hint of curiosity could be discerned in it.

I nodded. "I guess we have to assume that. We'll question each of them individually. Find out who's been where and if anyone might have seen something that will help us."

I wanted to break away from Layla and put what I had said into practice. She, however, held me back. "May I be present, master? Then they will surely be less afraid."

I remembered how enthusiastically Layla had already helped me with the interrogations in the Villa. When I raised my head, I caught Marcellus' gaze. Apparently he had over-heard the whispering between my slave and me. I briefly considered asking his consent but refrained. The lupanarius had been murdered under my roof. In the Germanicum. Marcellus had no official authority here. So, without further ado, I decided myself that Layla could help me with the interrogations. Alva, Chloe, and Suavis would surely be more talkative if they knew a friend at their side.

Marcellus didn't miss the chance to give his consent any-way, with a nod of his head and a generous smile. "Layla was in the triclinium the whole time," he then said, though I had-n't asked him about it. "Together with me."

I could not say that this information lightened my heart, although it proved Layla's innocence. I had to think of how I had found the Tribune and her earlier in the triclinium: ur-gently whispering to each other, over a good amphora of wine. But at least this eliminated the Tribune himself as the murderer. He had first been with Layla and then descended into the cellar with a servant at his side. He had not had the opportunity to kill the lupanarius.

We used my Barbarian Chamber to question the other guests. The room where I had conducted the negotiations with Blandus earlier. Marcellus, Layla, and I took our seats at the large oak table and had a servant present my guests to us one by one, as if we were sitting in judgment on them in the basilica.

The Tribune looked in wonder at the grim great sturgeon wrestling with the fishermen in my mural. The Tiber river in Rome certainly didn't have such monsters, I said to myself with a strangely gloomy satisfaction—which I didn't quite understand myself.

We began the questioning with Orodes. The women might have seen or heard something, or they might be able to confirm who had been where, but they were unlikely to be murderers. They were consummate love servants, not wild women who knew how to assassinate.

"Did you know the lupanarius?" I asked the Parthian. "Before he came to my house tonight?"

"I saw him a few times at the Villa," came the reply. "That's all. He was a guest there occasionally."

"And tonight? Where were you after dinner?"

Orodes claimed that he had gone directly to his room with Suavis. They had remained there until a servant had asked them to come into the atrium.

I had given Suavis and Orodes each their own chamber, but they spent most of their time together in the Parthian's room. So, what he said could well be true—if Suavis confirmed it.

Marcellus had disappointment written all over his face. The Parthian had probably also been his main suspect. But if Orodes was eliminated, who was left? One of the women after all? By the gods, what a crazy notion!

Next, we had Alva come in. She claimed to have been with Chloe most of the time, first in the atrium, then in the garden. The two women had looked at some art objects and then stretched their legs a bit. In the process, they had not encountered any of the other guests. Chloe had once visited the latrine, while Alva had sat alone on a bench in the garden. Only for a few minutes.

"Have you met the lupanarius on a previous occasion?" asked Marcellus.

Alva replied in the negative. "I hardly ever met anyone," she said, sounding most melancholic. "My master wouldn't let me."

Our conversations with Chloe and Suavis proved similarly unproductive. Both had turned into frightened little girls who pressed shyly against Layla.

Once again, I marveled at the cool head of my beloved Nubian. She knew how to calm both Chloe and Suavis down enough for us to ask them questions. She spoke very little herself, but I could see how she followed each statement attentively and immediately seemed to process everything behind her dark forehead. That expression of highest concentration was in her face, which I had already noticed during our interrogations in the Villa. As if she were completely absorbed in studying a scroll from my library.

Chloe stammered something about a curse that must have followed us here from the Villa. In tears, she asked if we would all die in the end.

All the laughter and lightheartedness of the last few days seemed to have fallen off Suavis as well. Her big, blue eyes reflected only incomprehension and fear.

Moreover, Chloe only confirmed what we had already learned from Alva, and Suavis told us that she had made love to Orodes, as she put it. Right after dinner, in his chamber. Where they had then been picked up by a servant, who had refused to tell them what had happened.

We also asked both girls about the lupanarius' visits to the Villa.

"He's been with Chloe a couple of times," Suavis told me, "and behaved quite horribly toward her. Like a wild animal."

"Chloe told you that?" asked Marcellus.

"Yes, Tribune. But she didn't complain," Suavis quickly added. "She never did."

"Of course not. It's okay," I assured her, and Layla gently stroked a golden strand of hair from her forehead.

Chloe had mentioned serving the lupanarius a few times during her questioning just before. But she had said nothing about him treating her badly. Even when I inquired if Blandus had made any special requests, she said, "Nothing different than some of the other customers did." And then she had fallen silent.

"But that's impossible," Marcellus said when we were back among ourselves. "From the looks of it, no one could have done it!"

Layla tilted her head. "And yet I had the impression that they were all telling the truth."

"Me too," Marcellus grumbled. He ran a grumpy hand through his perfectly parted hair.

"Shall we question the servants now?" I suggested. "Perhaps one of them noticed something suspicious? Or actually harbored a personal grudge against the lupanarius?"

The Tribune dismissed the suggestion with an unwilling wave of his hand. "There's no point really. They would cover for each other, like any slave household. And if they claim something about the guests, you can't trust them. For the same reason. Yes, they will swear to you that it must have been one of the guests. They don't want to pay for the dead man with their own lives."

He shook his head. "No, we won't get anywhere like this. Already the statements of your guests are worthless." The way he emphasized the word *guests,* it sounded very disparaging. More like a gang of muggers than friends with whom one liked to have a nice evening.

"May I see the dead body?" Layla asked abruptly.

Marcellus raised his eyebrows. And he also took it upon himself to answer her, although the decision was clearly mine to make. "If you really want to, we'll go down there again," he said. "Maybe the corpse of the lupanarius can still tell us something we couldn't get out of the living. At least he can't lie to our faces anymore."

XXXI

I told two servants to accompany us into the cellar with torches. This gave us more light than the oil lamps could provide. Perhaps we had really overlooked something that could help us.

We rolled the dead lupanarius onto his stomach once more, and Layla looked at the three puncture wounds—seemingly without any disgust. She inspected the sharp blade of the sax and studied the bloodstains on Blandus' tunic. Those on the back, where the garment had turned red throughout, and after we had returned Blandus to his original position, also those on the front, at the hem of the garment. The bloody fingerprints seemed to have particularly taken her fancy.

"The murderer used the tunica as a towel to clean his hands after the crime," Marcellus explained to her.

"Ah," Layla said and gave the Tribune a smile in thanks. However, I was sure that she had long since come to this conclusion herself.

"If only these fingerprints could speak to us by some magic," she said, her brow furrowing deeply. "If they could tell us to whose hand they belong! Then the murderer would be convicted."

The Tribune laughed and shook his head. Turning to me, he whispered, "That girl really has a fertile imagination!"

I myself took another look at the cellar floor. Apart from

the pool that had formed under the lupanarius, there was no blood anywhere. No smeared drag marks, not even a single drop that I could see. The lupanarius had been murdered down here, right where he had fallen, that much was certain.

Apart from the three stab wounds in his back, I could not see any signs of struggle. Blandus had not fought back against his attacker, and from the looks of it, he had not been tied up either. At least there was no trace of it on his wrists, no abrasion, not even a telltale reddening of the skin. So, he must really have come down here voluntarily—whether alone or together with his murderer.

"You know what I'm wondering," I turned back to Layla and the Tribune. "So, the assassin stands behind the lupanarius, he thrusts the sax three times into his back—then walks away, just with bloody hands? Shouldn't his robe also be sullied from the spurting blood?"

The Tribune's eyes lit up. "Yes, you are right. But none of the guests have blood on their clothes. We would have noticed that."

"If the murderer lives under my roof, he could have changed quickly after the crime," I said. "He had the time to do so."

"But he would have risked being seen on the way to his room," Marcellus countered. "A blood-spattered garment would have immediately exposed him as a murderer."

"Not necessarily. If you take the front basement stairs, it's no more than twenty steps to the guest quarters. If the murderer is really to be looked for there, he had only a very short way to go."

Marcellus grumbled unwillingly. "Or our perpetrator knew his business. Blood doesn't spurt in equal measure from different parts of the human body when you jab a knife into them. With the necessary experience, our assailant may have positioned himself behind his victim in such a way that the blood might only have sullied his arm. Which he could wipe as well as his hands. Every one of your guests is wearing either a short-sleeved tunic or even a sleeveless garb, I noticed."

Including you, Tribune, it went through my mind. If anyone here knew the art of killing, it was certainly a Roman officer. But certainly also a former warrior of the Parthians. Orodes.

"But would such a man then have to stab three times?" Layla asked abruptly.

I shook my head. The Primus Pilus had been struck down with only one blow of the axe. The archer who had waylaid me in the forest had shot a single well-aimed arrow. But I still refused to believe that the lupanarius had fallen victim to the same assassin.

"Perhaps the assailant felt great anger toward Blandus," said Marcellus, "and therefore stabbed several times."

"Or," Layla said in her warm, dark voice, "he wasn't a skilled fighter after all, but he was standing in front of the lupanarius, not behind him, when he stabbed."

Her eyes again reflected this expression of highest concentration. *Layla, the thinker.*

This time, however, I could not follow her. "In front of the lupanarius?" I asked. "But dear, the punctures are in the man's back."

"I can see that," Layla said, unperturbed. "What I mean is..."

She interrupted herself, took a step towards me, and embraced me abruptly. She pressed herself against my chest and wrapped her arms around my torso. Then she described a movement with her right hand as if she wanted to ram a dagger into my back.

Marcellus laughed. "Your arms barely reach around him!"

"Perhaps not with a man as strong as Thanar," Layla replied, "but look at the lupanarius. How gaunt and lanky he is. Even the arms of a delicate girl could embrace him completely."

I basked for a moment in the vain joy of Layla calling me a strong man. Had there been admiration in her words?

Only then did the meaning of what my slave had just said dawn on me. *The arms of a delicate girl.*

"Any one of us could have persuaded the lupanarius to a romantic tryst," she continued. "Under the cover of the darkness of the cellar, where no one would be looking for us. As hungrily as he devoured each of us with his gaze, I'm sure he would have been only too happy to be seduced."

Marcellus had lost his laughter. Astonished, he now listened to Layla's words.

"If I had wanted to murder Blandus," she continued, "I would have hidden the sax in my robe and waited for his first embrace. When he was blind to any danger. Then I would have stabbed. A few times probably, not knowing exactly where to hit to kill. My hands would be stained with blood, but the rest of me would be well protected against any splashes by the body of the lupanarius. And such an attack would fit the fact that Blandus fell on his back. I would have pushed him off me as soon as the life drained out of him."

Marcellus and I looked at each other wordlessly. Layla had spoken so dispassionately and calmly, as if she were describing nothing more than the preparation of a meal.

"You don't really think one of the women could have murdered the lupanarius, do you?" the Tribune finally said. He looked at Layla as if he was seeing her for the first time. And as if an icy shiver ran down his spine.

Layla shrugged, seemingly unmoved. "I'm just saying it could be possible. That's all. Of course, a man could have done it in a very similar way. Albeit under a different pretext."

The Tribune's brow furrowed. "Let's search the house for a bloody garment," he finally said, in his usual commanding tone. Even if it didn't sound half as convincing now as it usually did.

We left the cellar by the front stairs. Once upstairs, I ordered the two servants who accompanied us to search the three rooms occupied by Suavis, Chloe, and Orodes in our presence.

The lads did as they were told. They opened cupboards and chests, lifted the mattresses, peered under the bedsteads, rummaged through every corner of the rooms and found— nothing.

I finally sent them away with the order to turn the rest of the house upside down as well. Even though I hardly expected anything from it. The murderer could have simply thrown his sullied garb into the fire in the kitchen. Although, of course, he thereby took the risk of running into one of the slaves who went in and out of there. Or he could have disposed of it in the latrine—where he also had to expect company at any time. If this sullied garment had ever existed at all.

In the end, I returned to my Barbarian Chamber with Layla and Marcellus. We walked in silence with our heads bowed, like a defeated army.

Arriving in the small dining room, the Tribune dropped heavily onto one of the wooden chairs. He stared into the fanged mouth of the great sturgeon on the wall and made a sullen hand gesture. "The death of the lupanarius will go unpunished, it seems. Fortuna is favorable to his murderer. She hides him from us."

He reached for the wine amphora that was still on the table from my negotiation with the lupanarius, poured himself a cup, and emptied it in one go.

I could sympathize with his anger. I myself had had more than enough of this murder hunt which was leading nowhere. I was fed up with interrogations, insinuations, and hair-raising theories about how the lupanarius had met his end. I did not want to see a cold-blooded assassin in my favorite slave, nor in my guests, whom I had grown very fond of. And if I was honest, I could not even imagine Marcellus as the kind of nefarious villain who would stab a feeble, old codger in the back in a cellar. Apart from the fact that I could not, by any stretch of the imagination, think up a motive for this deed.

Finally, the Tribune stood and announced that he had to return to the legion camp.

I nodded. "I'll take the dead man back to his family tomorrow and seize the opportunity to look around his house," I said. "Maybe there will be some clue there as to whether Blandus had enemies or why someone was trying to kill him."

"Do that," the Tribune replied curtly, and that seemed to settle the matter for him.

After seeing Marcellus off, I returned to the atrium, where my guests were still sitting together. I offered Alva a bed for the night, since it was quite late by now. The beautiful Germanic woman, however, refused. So, I gave her at least one of my guards to accompany her, and she abruptly set off for home.

Then I joined my houseguests for a nightcap, during which no one spoke a word, and finally everyone retired to their own rooms.

I was sure I wasn't the only one who couldn't sleep that night.

XXXII

The lupanarius' house was situated in the camp suburb, right behind one of his brothels.

At the gate we met a slave who promised to wake the mistress. Then he left us to ourselves in the courtyard that lay between the house and the lupanar. I said *us* because, of course, Layla had once again wheedled me into taking her with me. This time she hadn't been able to argue that any witnesses—or suspects—would be more talkative in her presence. No, my clever Nubian simply harbored a passion for crime. That was what it looked like.

The lupanar we stood in front of was one of the largest in Vindobona. Next to the entrance, a relief solicited customers, showing the god Priapus. He was busy measuring and weighing his huge phallus. A sight that would make any man green with envy.

I stepped into the hallway of the brothel to take a closer look at how Blandus had conducted his business. However, I found nothing unexpected. At this early hour, neither she-wolves nor interested customers were to be found. To the left and right of the hallway were the small chambers common to lupanars, which were entered through a curtain. Each of the cells was furnished with a stone bunk, on which a tattered mattress offered meager comfort. The walls were decorated with paintings showing the type and variety of love services offered. In between, customers—and probably many a she-wolf—had immortalized themselves with graffiti.

Veneria, you give good blow jobs!

Here I did it with Cytheris and Serena.

Are there no boys here?

Caught the clap here!

The latter was certainly not a good advertisement for the business.

Blandus' widow shed no tears when I told her of her husband's death. "Put him over there," she instructed my men, who carried the body into her atrium. She used a tone of voice as if it were a matter of storing a few sacks of flour.

"None of my children reached adulthood," she explained to me, "and I wept bitterly for each of them. But not for him! Not for that stingy, old lecher. He humped his girls more often than any customer. The horny buck!"

I gently asked if Blandus had had any enemies.

She waved it off. "Enemies? Not him. He was a coward, through and through. He wasn't looking for a fight."

"Did he have any connections to the Greek's Villa that you know of? Before he decided to buy it, I mean?"

"Buy it?" the widow shrieked.

"Didn't he tell you about that? That was the reason for his visit to my house yesterday."

"Was wondering what he wanted up there beyond the river, in the barbaricum," the woman said, eyeing me blatantly. "No offense. Thought he was after some broad again. Buy the Villa? He's out of his mind, the old fool!"

She uttered a curse. "If he could afford an estate like this, he must have hoarded a lot more gold than I thought. He was always skimping on me, as if we were starving. Always had to beg him for a few sesterces of housekeeping money. That scoundrel!" She squinted over at the corpse, and I couldn't help thinking that Blandus probably wouldn't receive an overly festive funeral. For a moment, I almost felt sorry for the old codger.

"The Villa," repeated the widow, who was now talking herself into a frenzy. "He always raved about that, went there more often than he admitted. The old Greek's prices were outrageous, if you ask me. I mean, a fuck is a fuck, right? And when it comes to that, our girls are no worse than those oh-so-fine posh whores, I tell you!"

"Certainly," I replied tactfully.

"We even have a slave girl ourselves from the Villa, an older one that the Greek no longer wanted. Blandus was able to acquire her cheaply—at least that's what he told me. She's blinded, you know, but who cares? Not the guys throwing themselves on her in a dark room, right?"

She giggled, but it sounded more like a grunt. "Oh, how he liked to boast, the old fool! *In my lupanar, you can screw a girl from the Villa!* That's what he told everyone who wanted to know—and everyone else, too."

"May we speak to the girl?" I asked on impulse.

The widow eyed me suspiciously. "No offense, Germanic, but our girls aren't there to chat. And what do you care so much about my old man's death anyway? He wasn't your friend, was he?"

"He died under my roof," I said with as much dignity as I could muster in the face of this absurd conversation. "He was murdered, and I want to know who took his life. And why."

"And what would that have to do with the Villa?"

"Hopefully nothing," I said—and meant it. Even if Blandus had died at a dinner with four former residents of the Villa, and he had wanted to buy the property.

The blind she-wolf—her name was Mina—was fetched after I had slipped the widow a silver coin for her trouble. But we were not allowed to talk to the woman alone.

I asked Mina if she could tell us something about her master. Had he seemed different in the last few days? Anxious, perhaps? Had she overheard anything about disputes at the lupanar? "Some dissatisfied customer, perhaps?" I suggested.

"We don't have no dissatisfied customers!" the widow snapped before Mina could say anything.

The she-wolf smiled thinly and hastened to agree with her mistress. "Blandus was a good master," she added, "he was well liked by everyone." But what could she have said with the old witch breathing down her neck?

Mina seemed anxious, and I couldn't blame her. The last thing I wanted was to cause her trouble. She hardly seemed older than myself, in her late thirties or early forties at the most. Her former beauty could still be guessed at. Moreover, she spoke with a sweet voice and in polished Latin—what a pleasant contrast to her mistress! Otherwise, however, she looked completely neglected and was dressed in the most wretched rags. The poor, battered creature.

"You used to serve in the Greek's Villa," I tried another approach. One that at least didn't involve the widow.

Mina nodded. "Yes, but that was a long time ago."

"Did you know Alva, the body slave of the ancient Greek? Or Suavis, her daughter? Chloe, the Greek, perhaps?"

"Alva," Mina repeated dreamily, as if that name had the power to transport her to a more beautiful place. To a long-lost one. "And Suavis...such a beautiful child."

She couldn't remember Chloe, however. "She must have come along later," she said.

I saw Layla wordlessly take the woman's hand and squeeze it gently. A smile stole over Mina's face. "Such soft skin," she murmured.

"What about Orodes, the Parthian?" I asked further. "He was the chief guard slave at the Villa."

"Not in my time," Mina replied. "Why do you ask me about them, sir? Is there something wrong in the Villa?"

"There have been some changes," I said evasively.

The girls in Blandus' lupanars were apparently excluded from the slave network that Layla had so vividly described to me. It seemed that Mina had not yet learned about the deaths that had ultimately led to the dissolution of the Villa. And I didn't want to be the one to tell her. So, I limited myself to asking her about a possible connection between Blandus and the inhabitants of the Villa.

"What kind of connection? The master liked to be a guest there, and he bought me from Lycortas—is that what you mean?"

"Well...no. I don't know exactly what I'm looking for myself," I admitted, feeling like quite the ass.

I thanked her and did not question her any further. There was no point after all. I would not learn anything here that would shed any light on Blandus' murder, that much seemed certain.

"Are there any high-ranking Roman officers among your customers?" I turned to the widow one last time after Mina had left. Even with this question, I didn't really know what I was getting at. The thought of Marcellus haunted my mind, the nagging question of whether he might not have had something to do with the death of the lupanarius. I didn't know and would probably never know. In truth, I was completely in the dark; who was I trying to fool?

The answer was quite what I had expected. "High-ranking Romans? With us?" the widow snorted, as if she had to choke on a fit of laughter. She glared at me as if I had finally lost my mind.

I said goodbye as quickly as decency allowed, put my arm around Layla, and pulled her away from this dreary place.

"We haven't learned anything that will get us anywhere, have we, master?" Layla put her finger on my wounds as we got into my wagon together. We spent the journey home in silence.

In the afternoon of the same day, I unwittingly became witness to a strange conversation. An argument, actually. Layla was talking to Orodes in a tone of voice she had never used in my presence. Her normally warm voice sounded hard and was quivering with anger.

The two of them were standing in a corner of the colonnade that runs around the peristyle garden of my house. I myself was on my way back to my chambers from the kitchen, where I had given instructions for the purchase of supplies. Layla's tone, however, made me pause in the shadow of a column before she or Orodes could spot me.

I had actually gotten the impression that Layla was fond of the Parthian—just like everyone else in my house. Orodes might look wild and dangerous, but at heart he seemed to be a kind, peaceful fellow. So why this quarrel?

I didn't catch what exactly Layla said to the Parthian. Her tone of voice astonished me so much that I paid no attention to the individual words.

Orodes' answer, however, I could clearly understand. He seemed visibly agitated but spoke soothingly to Layla. "By Zarathustra, I give you my word on it!" he said, then he put his massive hand on Layla's shoulder, squeezed it gently, and finally made off with a determined step.

Layla remained motionless at the spot, looking undecided about what to do now.

I stepped out from behind my column, crossed the garden, and confronted her. "What was that all about, dear? Did Orodes threaten you?"

"No, master," she replied, so hastily that I did not believe her.

I gazed at her wordlessly, and she lowered her eyes. "Won't you tell me what you were arguing about?" I tried again. "You seemed very upset."

"Oh, it's nothing, master, nothing of importance. Orodes was just talking about his future plans with Suavis..."

"And that's what got you all riled up?"

Layla blushed. "Forgive me, master."

"There's nothing to forgive. I was just wondering—"

But Layla had already breathed a fleeting kiss on my cheek and scurried away.

Shaking my head, I turned to leave the garden as well—that was when I saw Chloe's dark mop of hair disappearing behind a bronze statue on the opposite side of the peristyle.

From the looks of it, the young Greek woman had overheard this strange argument, too.

XXXIII

At night I tossed and turned on my bed and could not fall asleep. The summer night was oppressively humid, but it was probably more due to my own thoughts that I found no sleep. Even if the widow of the lupanarius hadn't wasted a single tear for him, the man's death did not let me rest. I felt as if his spirit were hovering over my bed and looking down on me accusingly.

I lit a lamp, put on a robe, and left my bed chamber. Layla's room was right next to mine, and that was where I directed my steps. I always found comfort and peace in the arms of my Nubian, no matter what was bothering me. She had the gift of bringing my thoughts to a standstill.

I opened the door to her chamber, stepped to her bedside, and wanted to lie down with her—but the bed was empty. Where was Layla? Had she not been able to find sleep either?

I decided to look for her in the peristyle garden. There she liked to walk, quite often at night, too, when the divine Somnus denied her access to the realm of dreams.

I paced the colonnade, crossed the courtyard, and called Layla's name softly, but received no response.

Where else could she be, this late at night? With one of her friends, Chloe or Suavis? I hurried through my house until I was in front of the guest rooms.

All the doors were closed. I listened but could not hear voices or other noises from any of the rooms. My guests seemed to be asleep. No sign of Layla.

A little worried by now, I returned to her room. Perhaps we had just missed each other, and she had long since returned. But her room was as empty as I had left it. Had something happened to my slave?

Only yesterday a man had died in my house, and for all I knew, the murderer lived under my roof. At least I couldn't rule that out.

I decided to wake my servants and have the whole property turned upside down to find Layla—that was when I heard a scream.

It seemed to come from my own room. I hurried over and lifted the lamp to see better, but my room was just as empty as Layla's.

Had my ears played a trick on me? But right after I heard it again, this time without doubt. It was the sharp cry of a woman, and it came from—outside!

I hurried out to the terrace adjoining my room. From here, one had a magnificent view over the Danubius during the day, but now I could only make out two shadows on the path along the riverbank. Only a few steps away from the landing stage where the murdered Primus Pilus had lain. Two people, both wrapped in dark robes with hoods, which seemed to me quite unusual garbs on such a warm summer night. But what was even more alarming: the two dark shadows were wrestling with each other!

The one of them cried out again. All I could think at that moment was: not another murder in my harbor!

Suddenly, in the melee, the hood of one of the fighters slipped off their head. A shock of blond hair appeared. And then I also recognized the voice and finally grasped who I

225

was looking at. It was Suavis—and she was under attack!

I ran, taking the quickest route to the atrium, where the slave who guarded the gate at night was squatting. I ordered him to unlock it, grabbed one of the axes that adorned the walls, and urged the man to follow me.

We rushed down the path to the river. There was no one on the footpath now, but I could hear splashing in the water near the riverbank.

There was Suavis! She was flailing, fighting against the waters, visibly panicking. Without hesitation, the guard and I waded into the river and got hold of her. The Danubius was not deep here near the shore, and the current wasn't strong either.

We pulled the girl out of the water, and she managed to crawl the last few feet to the shore on her own. On the embankment, she dropped into the grass and wrapped her arms around her tender body, trembling. With her mouth wide open, she struggled for breath. She stared at me as if she didn't know whom she had before her. As if she saw me for the first time. Fear had made her blind.

"You are safe," I spoke to her. "It's me, Thanar."

Her head bobbed up and down in what was probably meant to be a nod, but nonetheless she continued to stare at me unblinkingly.

I looked around, but there was no sign of the attacker. As far as I could see along the path in the darkness, we were all alone on the shore.

My guard, however, had walked a few steps further and was now bending down for an object lying in the grass at the edge of the path. He lifted it up and came over to me so that I could see what it was. A short sax—that is, not just any sax, but the very one from my atrium that had been used to murder the Lupanarius last night. I had returned it to its place this morning, but someone seemed to have developed a personal affinity for that weapon. Someone who seemed to be able to help himself freely in my atrium. Which left only one possible conclusion: the murderer of the lupanarius was indeed to be found in my house. And Suavis had almost become his next victim.

I hesitated briefly, then wrapped my arms around the girl's quivering body, lifted her up, and carried her back into the house. She stiffened at first, but after a few steps, her limbs went limp, and her head fell against my chest.

I carried her into her room, helped her out of her tunic, which was clinging wetly to her skin, and wrapped her cold, snow-white body in the blanket that lay at the foot of her bed. I had warm honey wine brought and instilled the drink into her sip by sip.

When she was breathing more evenly and calmly again, I asked her what had happened. "Who attacked you, Suavis? Were you able to recognize him?"

She did not respond.

"Suavis? Do you understand what I'm saying?"

She nodded slowly. Then she started to speak, even if her voice sounded thin and timid: "I...don't know, sir. I couldn't see anything. It was so dark. And it all happened so fast. He...had a knife. I somehow got hold of his arm, the blade slipped away, I think, and then he suddenly pushed me into the water."

"And then? Was he going to drown you?"

"I don't know, sir. Then suddenly you were there...and pulled me to shore."

"You didn't see where the attacker fled?"

She shook her head.

"Was it a man? A woman? Couldn't you see anything?"

"I couldn't," Suavis sniffed.

Was it just my imagination, or had she hesitated a moment too long before answering?

"What happened?" a voice suddenly called from behind me, making me jump. It sounded so ghostly, as if it were pushing at my ears from a grave. Suavis was startled, too.

A slender figure with a tiny oil lamp stood in the open doorway and now entered. It was Chloe, not a ghost. Since she was sleeping in the next room, we had probably woken her up.

She took only two steps, then stopped and stared at Suavis. There was an extremely strange expression on her face.

"Suavis was attacked, on the riverbank," I explained tersely.

"On the riverbank?" echoed Chloe. "What on earth were you doing there in the middle of the night?"

A really good question. I couldn't even explain why I hadn't thought of it myself.

Suavis gave Chloe a look that I couldn't interpret any more than the strange expression in the Greek's eyes. What was going on with the girls; they were friends, after all?

"I couldn't sleep," Suavis said after her and Chloe had stared at each other in that strange way for quite a while. "It was such a beautiful night outside, and I wanted to stretch my legs a little."

She turned to me. "I so enjoy being able to leave the house whenever I want. To go wherever I please. Sometimes I get constrained between all those walls. And at night by the river, it's so quiet and peaceful."

It sounded like today's nocturnal excursion had not been her first.

"Quiet and peaceful?" Chloe exclaimed. "Are you tired of life?"

Suavis winced, but I had to agree with Chloe. I could see that Suavis wanted to take full advantage of her newfound freedom, but to go out alone at night was foolish in the extreme. Even under normal circumstances, a young woman wouldn't risk life and limb in such an endeavor. Not to mention the fact that a murderer was on the loose.

Suavis apparently lacked any sense of the outside world—but could you blame her? She had been locked up all her life. The world she knew had ended at the walls of the Villa.

"How did you actually get out of the house?" I asked her, "The gate was guarded after all."

She narrowed her eyes. "I sneaked through the cellar, sir. Through the door that leads onto the embankment. And then I ran down to the harbor."

I wondered how Suavis could know about this exit. She had no business in the basement at all.

"I suppose you unlocked the door from the inside—and slipped out?" I asked. "Which means you opened the way into the house for any prowler. While you were taking your nightly stroll, thieves could have snuck in. Or even worse scum. Don't you realize that?"

"Now that you mention it, sir," Suavis whispered. Still, she kept her head lowered, nervously kneading her delicate hands.

I instructed the guard to lock the cellar door again. When he returned, Layla was with him. I breathed a sigh of relief when I saw her. Where had she been all this time? She owed me an explanation, but that would have to wait.

She entered the room and looked at me in a rather disconcerting manner, but asked no questions. The guard had probably already informed her about what had happened.

Chloe ran up to her, grabbed her arm, and snuggled against her shoulder. Suavis, on the other hand, was still sitting on the bed with her head down.

At the sight of the three girls, a question came to my mind: where was Orodes? He was also sleeping in this part of the house; how come the commotion hadn't woken him up?

XXXIV

I ran out into the hallway and pounded on the door of Orodes' chamber.

No response.

I stepped in without further ado.

The Parthian lay stretched out on the bed, which looked small and fragile under his massive body. He was breathing heavily and seemed to be in a deep sleep.

I lifted my lamp so that its glow fell on his face, but he did not move. Even when I touched him on the shoulder, he showed no reaction. The man really had a blessed sleep. Or was he just faking it?

When I turned around, Layla was standing in the doorway, with Chloe behind her. I pushed past them both without a word, wanting to return to Suavis to ask her some more questions. But as I passed, the glow from my oil lamp fell on Chloe's face, and there I saw something that made me pause: a bloody scratch.

"Who hurt you?" I asked her, perhaps a little too harshly.

Both she and Layla backed away, startled.

I, however, put my hand on the back of Chloe's neck, pulled her face back into the light, and took a closer look at the wound. The area just below her left cheekbone was slightly swollen, red, and marked by two fresh scratches. Blood was seeping from one of them.

It was exactly the kind of wound that a woman's fingernails

could inflict on you. A woman who had resisted an attack on her life? Suavis? Had Chloe attacked her own friend?

The young Greek woman felt her cheek, startled, and Layla now took a closer look as well.

"I must have...scratched myself," Chloe stammered, "while I was asleep! I didn't leave my room, I swear!"

Layla pointed to the reddened swelling under the scratches. "That looks like a mosquito bite, master. They're always so terribly itchy. Happens to me sometimes, too, that I scratch them open."

Chloe nodded vigorously, then snuggled back against Layla.

A groan escaped me. I left them both standing there and returned to Suavis' bedside. I didn't know what to say anymore. Not even what to think anymore. What, by the gates of the underworld, was going on here—under my roof, behind my back? What was up with my guests, all of whom were acting strangely, including Layla, even though she belonged to my own familia? Or was it ultimately myself who was slowly losing my mind and suspecting lies and secrets everywhere?

Were the girls just scared?

No, there had to be more to it, I just felt it. They knew something they didn't want to share with me.

Suavis had curled up on her bed like a tired puppy dog and already seemed to be drifting off to sleep.

I couldn't let it happen. I wanted answers at last. "Suavis, you must tell me the truth," I addressed her. "Our safety depends on it. The one who attacked you was carrying the weapon used to murder the lupanarius yesterday. Do you know what that means?"

I received no answer, only a fearful look from big blue eyes.

"Was Orodes really with you yesterday after dinner? All the time?"

"Yes, sir," she replied promptly. Much too promptly.

"Does it make sense to cover for someone who tried to kill you?" I asked her straightforwardly.

She sat up and shook her head violently. "Orodes would never hurt me! He didn't attack me!"

"Who then?"

"I really don't know! It was so dark, and they were wearing a cape!"

"You're scaring her, master!" whispered a voice at my back. It was Layla.

I whirled around to face her. "Don't all of you understand that there is a murderer among us?" I snapped at her, which I felt sorry for right after. Layla was not a skittish girl, but even she was backing away from me now, as if I had hit her.

"I don't think he wanted to kill me," Suavis said timidly. "What could have stopped him? He had the knife, but he didn't use it. He just pushed me into the river and ran away."

"You could have drowned!" I shouted, upset but knowing at the same moment that it wasn't true. Suavis had been panicked, and she obviously couldn't swim. But the water close to the Danubius' bank was shallow and the current weak. The attacker had to assume that she would survive.

Perhaps he had been on his way into town for another victim and Suavis had just gotten in his way on her foolish night stroll?

"May I sleep now, Thanar?" Suavis snapped me out of my

thoughts. "I am very tired."

I nodded unwillingly and hated myself for being so helpless in the face of all the crimes that were happening around me. The murderer, whoever he was, was playing with me like a cat with a mouse.

"I will sacrifice to the gods," Layla said, "for sparing Suavis' life. I will beseech them that no more misfortune come upon this house. And you should be careful, Suavis, even during the day. Obviously, someone is out to get you. Someone who watches your every move."

There was something strange in those words and in the way Layla spoke them. Something was going on between the girls that I didn't understand.

Or I was really getting paranoid already.

I pushed Layla and Chloe out into the hallway and closed the door behind us. Chloe hugged Layla once more, then scurried back to her own room.

I turned to the guard who had stayed nearby. "I want the guest rooms here watched, every night from now on. And another man will guard my chamber—and Layla's. You'll divide up the shifts and make sure there are no gaps."

"Yes, master," said the guard, then hurried off to set everything in motion.

I wordlessly led Layla to my room and stepped out onto the terrace with her. The Danubius shone silvery in the moonlight. The night lay so still and peaceful at our feet, as if nothing bad could ever happen here in our corner of the world.

"Where were you?" I turned to Layla. "I checked on you earlier but couldn't find you anywhere." I didn't want to ask her that question, loathing the accusation that resonated in my words. I had always trusted her unconditionally. But now I could no longer. Without wanting to, my eyes wandered over her arms, her face, to see if there might also be an injury. But I discovered nothing, not even an insect bite—or something that could be made out for it. Only her hair was flowing unrestrainedly around her shoulders, but it always did that at night.

Layla looked at me silently, for so long that I thought she didn't want to answer me. Thoughts seemed to crowd behind her forehead, but she did not share them with me.

"I couldn't sleep, so I stretched my legs a little in the garden," she finally said, sounding as vulnerable as a small child.

She also looked at me as if I had just threatened her with a beating. She had to sense what was going on inside me, that my trust in her had been shaken—or, even worse, she no longer trusted me herself. For all she knew, I might as well be the murderer! As the Tribune had suspected from the beginning.

I wanted to reach out my arms to her, hold her against me, and reassure her that all was well. That things would be all right. But I couldn't.

I sent her to her room, waited until a servant moved into his guard post outside our chambers, then closed my own door and threw myself on the bed.

My heart ached strangely. I did not find sleep for a long time, and when I finally did, I met my wife in a dream—who had not been by my side in life for so long.

XXXV

At breakfast the next morning, Orodes told me that he had decided to return to his homeland as soon as possible. Together with Suavis.

Four of us were sitting in the Barbarian Chamber: the Parthian, Chloe, Layla, and me. Suavis had breakfast in her room; she was feverish and didn't want to leave the bed.

"A long and arduous journey," I said, surprised by the sudden determination Orodes displayed.

"And dangerous," the Parthian added. "But I will protect Suavis, and if the gods favor us, a good life awaits us in the circle of my family. We own fertile land, are respected—I will be able to offer my bride everything that will make her happy."

I nodded. "This is rather sudden," I said. Was there a murderer sitting here in front of me who was now making his escape? Was Suavis safe at his side? Or was the real danger that threatened her on the planned journey coming from the man who supposedly loved her?

"Layla has awakened a longing for home in me," Orodes replied.

Surprised, I looked at my slave. "You? I didn't know you missed your home."

"I don't, sir," Layla said tersely. "I'm happy here. With you," she added. "It was the land of the Parthians that I spoke of with Orodes."

My heart gave a little flip. It wanted to believe her so much.

Orodes rose to his feet. "I want to check on my beloved to see if she needs anything. Thank you for the meal." He nodded to me reverently.

It wasn't until he had left the room that I noticed Chloe had tears in her eyes. When our gazes met, she also sprang up and ran away.

"What was that about?" I turned to Layla. There it was again, that terrible feeling that I no longer understood anything at all about what was going on under my roof. Orodes' sudden decision to leave. How did he plan to proceed? Where was he going to get the money for horses, for a wagon, for traveling supplies? And now Chloe's passionate reaction.

"She loves him, master," Layla said, "you know that."

"Who loves whom?" I asked, confused.

"Chloe. Orodes. I told you that."

"I thought that was over long ago. Just a crush. Isn't it obvious he only has eyes for Suavis?"

Layla nodded. "It is. But sometimes the heart doesn't want to accept what the head surely knows."

I sighed. Maybe it was for the best of all of us when Orodes and Suavis left my house. Maybe everything could go back to the way it had been before.

I longed for it very much.

Orodes spent the whole day in Suavis' room. Only now and then did he come out to fetch her water, wine or some delicacies from the kitchen. He didn't even let a servant near her. Was he so concerned about her safety?

No doubt she had by now told him about the nighttime attack on the riverbank, and his reaction was all too understandable. Probably that was also the reason for his sudden decision to no longer enjoy my hospitality. Or was there more to it than that?

In the early evening, a servant announced Alva's visit to me.

I hurried into the atrium and welcomed her. She had not come alone this time; at her side was Lons, the beautiful Britannic.

There was a triumphant smile on Alva's lips. "I have found a buyer for the Villa!" she announced, barely after I had greeted her. "The widow of the lupanarius. She came to see me this morning."

Finally, some good news. I led Alva and Lons to the peristyle garden, offered them seats in the shade of the portico, and had them served iced wine.

"Blandus' widow found a gold chest filled to bursting, after the will was opened," Alva reported. "Her husband must have hoarded these treasures for years without telling her. Now she wants to sell the lupanars and retire in the Villa. And I— that is, we—will invest the proceeds of the sale in a small estate on the south road." She looked at Lons and a tender expression stole into her face.

The young Britannic returned her gaze, beaming.

"The farm is right next to a roadside station," she continued. "We can entertain travelers, offer them a hot meal, a bed for the night. But no love services!" She smiled shyly. "The house is big enough that I can take in anyone from the old familia who wants to stay with me. And a good piece of land comes with it, too!"

Lons grabbed her hand, and the two of them now beamed at me together.

I briefly considered telling Alva about the attack on her daughter, or about the fact that she was about to set off with Orodes on the journey to Parthia, but I let it go. Suavis could tell her about it herself if she saw fit. Instead, I invited Alva and Lons to stay for dinner, to which Marcellus had once again announced himself.

Perhaps everything would end well after all. The former slaves of the Villa had a new home, and Orodes and Suavis would marry and with the blessing of the gods reach the Parthian's homeland. Chloe—well, she was left alone, but she was still so young. Beautiful as she was, she would conquer another man, one who was all hers, and surely make her fortune. And I had Layla—who would possibly, one night, drive a knife into my heart?

My hopeful thoughts came to an abrupt end. I resisted this outrageous idea as hard as I could. Layla was certainly innocent, even if she had been acting very strangely lately.

Everything would be fine!

It just had to.

Marcellus arrived shortly after sunset, bringing with him a most unusual gift. A slave had transported it in a wagon and now carried it into my atrium. It was a round table made of precious citrus wood, which must have cost a fortune.

The Roman nobility collected these pieces with great passion, almost as fanatically as rich women liked to hoard pearls. It was said that entire forests in northern Africa had already fallen victim to this luxury.

The citrus table that Marcellus gave me as a gift had a particularly beautiful grain, stood on delicate ivory legs, and looked fantastic in my atrium. "A token of my friendship," the Tribune said unctuously, then went into the dining room without another word.

I remembered that he had intended to discuss something with me during his last visit. The lupanarius' death had thwarted that conversation. But was the matter already settled—whatever it was that the Tribune had wanted from me? Or was this exceedingly generous gift related to it? Did he want to make me favorable to his cause? Or did Marcellus now really see in me such a dear friend as he claimed?

By the gods, who could understand the Romans!

I instructed a servant to call the household together for dinner, then followed the Tribune to the triclinium, my Roman dining room.

Alva and Lons were already at the table, and Layla and Chloe arrived shortly after me.

"Orodes is dining with Suavis in her room, if it's all right with you, master," Layla announced to me. "She's still a little feverish, and he doesn't want to leave her alone."

Alva raised her head. "Suavis is ill?" she asked worriedly.

"Nothing serious," Layla said quickly. Too quickly. From the looks of it, she didn't want to bring up last night's events either.

Alva nodded and put on the smile again with which she had come into my house today. The smile that did me good in my gloomy mood like a ray of sunshine in a dark night.

I beckoned a servant to begin serving the food. We had baked hazel mice, which Layla liked best, followed by a nice roast lamb and various other delicacies.

Alva and Lons praised the cuisine, Marcellus entertained us with highly piquant anecdotes about some Roman senators he knew personally, and for a few hours it almost seemed as if life and laughter had returned to my house.

I stretched out comfortably on my dining sofa and took a deep breath. The air was warm and heavy with the scent of the food.

And then it happened.

Alva and Lons had already left for home, while I was still enjoying an amphora of violet wine with Marcellus, Chloe, and Layla.

The door of the triclinium was suddenly torn open, and in rushed Suavis.

Her eyes were swimming in tears, her blond hair hung tangled from her head; her voice broke and turned into a barely intelligible shriek. "Come quickly!" she cried, "Orodes...he's dead!"

XXXVI

Suavis threw herself into Layla's arms, but my slave pushed her onto the nearest sofa in a strangely heartless manner and stormed out of the room.

Marcellus reacted faster than I did; he was the next one on his feet and followed Layla. Suavis' scream was still ringing in my ears, but finally I got going too. I sprang up and ran after the others.

Orodes, dead? That couldn't possibly be true. I felt like an actor in one of those unbearable Greek tragedies, in the course of which half the actors always met their death. My whole life seemed to have turned into such a drama. Would it never end again?

I caught up with Marcellus and Layla, and together we pushed open the door to the Parthian's chamber.

It was empty.

"In Suavis' room?" I called out—and that's where we found him.

He lay on the bed, his hands clenched into fists, his limbs contorted like in a spasm. His mouth was torn open as if frozen in a soundless scream. Any help came too late. The Parthian was dead.

"Widened pupils," I heard Layla whisper, in a voice I barely recognized as hers. "The women's beauty poison."

"Just like with Juba," I replied reflexively. Even my own voice sounded strangely foreign to my ears. I simply could not comprehend what I was seeing. None of us had left the dining room in the last few hours, not even to visit the latrine. It was simply impossible; no one could have murdered Orodes. Except...Suavis? The woman he loved?

She had followed us, appearing behind us at that moment and clinging to Layla. "Is he really—" she began, but her voice failed her.

"He was murdered," I said without consideration, "What happened here?"

At that moment, out of the corner of my eye, I perceived a movement. I whirled around.

But it was only Chloe who now also entered the chamber. She didn't say a word, remained rooted to the spot as soon as she had set foot in the room. She stared at the corpse of the Parthian. Tears welled up in her eyes, she sobbed loudly, then she turned on her heels and ran away.

Suavis let go of Layla's arm and staggered against the wall behind her back.

"Suavis?" I repeated my question. "What happened here?"

She sank to her knees against the wall. "I don't know," she breathed, "We...were asleep. I woke up because Orodes suddenly started gasping—"

Abruptly, she rushed forward, crawled to the bed on all fours, and embraced Orodes' lifeless body. "Oh, darling," she wailed, drumming her childlike hands against his chest, dousing the corpse with tears. It was a sight that would have stirred even the hardest heart.

"What happened after that?" someone asked. It was Marcellus. He, too, seemed genuinely concerned, but his voice sounded as firm as ever.

Suavis wiped her face with the back of her hand. But new

tears immediately followed. "I...thought something was tormenting him, in his dream. I wanted to wake him up, but then I realized he wasn't asleep at all. He was staring at me so strangely, gasping for breath, but he couldn't speak. And suddenly he began to tremble and twitch, as if an evil spirit had taken possession of him. He curled up, and then—" She broke off, shaken again by a crying fit.

Marcellus didn't probe any further. It was clear to see what had happened next. Orodes had breathed his last, and Suavis had rushed out of the room in panic to get help. But no one could save the Parthian anymore.

I looked around the room. On the floor next to the bed was a large food tray with two empty cups and two plates with leftovers.

"Who served you?" I asked Suavis.

She didn't react, had slumped in front of the bed and was now crouching on the floor like an injured animal. Her eyes were staring blankly into space.

I went to her, carefully pulled her up, and led her to a chair. She sank down on it like a broken doll.

"Who brought you the food, Suavis?" I repeated my question. "And the wine?"

She stared at me uncomprehendingly. "Orodes got it himself," she finally whispered. "Right out of the kitchen. At least that's what he said."

"You have to tell me everything in detail. When was that?"

"I...don't know. A few hours ago." She looked out the window, where night had long since fallen. "Orodes said you had gone to dinner, and that he was going to eat here with me because I wasn't supposed to be up yet after all. I must take it easy, he said, I—" She lowered her head again and buried her face in her hands.

The sight of her hurt me. I would have liked to take her in my arms and dry her tears—but first I had to know the truth. The whole truth.

So, I asked further, "Orodes came with the tray; you ate together, I suppose? And after that?"

"After that...he wanted...he took me," Suavis whispered. "And he acted so strange about it. Not like usual at all."

"Strange in what way?"

"Like he...almost like he knew it was going to be the last time."

"And then, after the sex? What happened then?"

"I must have fallen asleep...I think he did, too. I was lying on top of him when all of a sudden he started gasping like that. When I thought he was having bad dreams."

"Did either of you leave the room at any point during the evening?"

She shook her head.

"Did anyone come in to see you?"

"No."

"Did you two eat the same food?" interjected Marcellus. "Think, girl. Your lover was clearly poisoned with food or drink."

"Yes, we did," Suavis replied, but then her eyes suddenly grew wide. Her mouth opened, but no words came out.

For a moment, I thought she was suddenly suffering from respiratory problems herself. That the poison had also been administered to her and she only reacted to it later.

"What's the matter with you?" the Tribune asked in alarm.

Suavis' slender fingers curled around the arms of her chair. "I switched our two plates," she whispered, so softly I could barely hear her. "Mine and Orodes'."

"What are you saying?" asked Marcellus. "Why did you do that?"

Suavis was now as pale as a dead woman. "I...he brought the tray of food. Put it in front of me so I could eat on the bed while he put his plate here—" She sniffled, pointing to the chair where she sat. "He was going to eat here. But then...I asked him to get me some garum sauce from the kitchen. I never used to like it, but here in the house—" She gave an anguished sob, "here it tastes so delicious. But when Orodes left the room, I noticed that he had given me the plate with the fattier piece of meat. He always does that, always wants me to have the better piece. But I...I wanted him to have it, he likes roast so much, and so...so I—"

"So you switched the plates," Marcellus said in her place. "And told him nothing about it when he returned?"

"N-no, otherwise I'm sure he would have insisted on swapping back. I was just hoping he wouldn't notice. I had already started eating when he came back with the sauce. He just smiled at me and then started attacking his plate. Well, actually *my* plate."

"He didn't notice the exchange," Marcellus said.

Suavis shook her head. "Was...was it I who was supposed to die?" she asked tonelessly. "Was someone trying to poison me?"

"Not *someone*," I said. "Orodes himself did it."

Suavis uttered a scream. "What, no! He would never do that. He loves me, he wanted to marry me!"

"Thanar speaks the truth," Marcellus said. "Isn't it obvious? No one but Orodes could have known which of the two plates you were supposed to eat from."

Suavis stared at the Tribune as if he had punched her in the face. One could literally watch how Marcellus' words made their way into her head. How she slowly understood what he was saying, even though she couldn't grasp it. *Didn't want* to grasp it.

The last bit of color drained from her cheeks. A tremor ran over her delicate body, then she sank down sobbing.

The Tribune gave me a meaningful look.

I nodded. It made sense that way. The supper had been prepared for all of us in the kitchen. If a poisoner had tampered there, he would not have been able to foresee who would end up eating the deadly food. It had been Orodes who had picked up the plates for Suavis and himself in the kitchen. Only he could have mixed the poison into his bride's food on the way to her chamber. All the other guests had been gathered in the dining room throughout the evening, and Suavis had confirmed that no one but Orodes had entered her room.

But why on earth had Orodes wanted to kill Suavis, the woman he supposedly loved? I would have trusted the Parthian with any other murder. But not Suavis. The woman he wanted to marry, with whom he planned a new life in his homeland? Had it all been just lies?

XXXVII

I asked the Tribune to take Suavis and Layla back to the dining room. I told a lad to fetch a strong herb wine from the cellar and serve it to my guests. Then I made my way to the kitchen and started questioning the cook.

It was as Orodes had claimed. The Parthian had fetched the meals for himself and Suavis directly from the cook and poured two cups of wine from an already opened amphora.

I grabbed two of the house servants and turned Orodes' room upside down.

We did not have to search for long. At the very bottom of his clothes chest, we found a dark glass bottle that had no business being there. It was half empty and emanated the bitter aroma that I had smelled before. It had made me nauseous the first time, in the Greek's villa, in the slave quarters. It was atropa, no doubt about it. The poison of the goddess of fate that women used to make their eyes look big and shiny.

Orodes hardly needed it as a beauty product, and if he did, he would not have had to hide it. He must have slipped into his room here briefly on his way from the kitchen to Suavis' chamber to poison the food on the plate he had intended for his bride. And he had got rid of the flask here—no doubt only temporarily. Surely, he would have taken it out of his room entirely before he 'found' the dead Suavis and alerted us.

Would the vial have finally shown up in Chloe's room to

blame her? Or would it even have found its way into my chambers? Well, it didn't matter anymore. The gods had foiled the Parthian's treacherous plan. Orodes had fallen victim to his own poisonous concoction.

I took the flask and returned to the triclinium to join the others. "Atropa," I announced as I placed the small bottle on the table in front of the Tribune, "the deadly poison used by beautiful women."

Marcellus had not been there when Layla and I discovered the poison in the mansion, yet now he nodded knowingly. He seemed to be familiar with it.

Suavis, who sat to the left of the Tribune and clung to his arm, stared at the vial. Her eyes widened as if the atropa juice itself had just been dripped into them. Then she burst into tears again. "So Orodes really wanted—"

That was as far as she got. Her voice was lost in sobs. She buried her face against the Tribune's shoulder.

Layla, on the other hand, who was sitting across from Suavis, looked transfixed. Something very strange seemed to be going on inside her. For the life of me, I couldn't guess what it was.

Chloe, in turn, had disappeared. The fact that she had now lost for all time the man she loved—even if hopelessly—had probably been too much for her. It would not be easy to let her know, too, that he had died of his own poison. But that would have to wait. First, I needed answers. From Suavis.

Marcellus seemed to feel the same way. No sooner had I settled at the table than he gently disengaged Suavis from his sleeve, lifted her chin with his hand, and started drilling her with questions. "Why in all the gods' name did Orodes want to kill you?" he began.

Suavis started to cry again, and the Tribune's patience wore thin. "Calm down, girl," he said, but his tone was now commanding, not comforting. "Tell us what you know."

To my amazement, it worked. Suavis wiped the tears from her face with the back of her hand, sniffled once more, but then she had composed herself enough to speak. "Orodes was going to take me away, to his homeland. Where I was to become his wife, and never again...never again—" She gasped.

"Never again what?" asked Marcellus.

"I didn't want to lose my freedom again!" cried Suavis with fervor. "To be imprisoned like a slave for the rest of my life and at his will, whatever he commanded me to do. Ever since I can remember, I have begged the gods to give me freedom, and now it was so close! I—"

"Wait," I interrupted her. "I don't understand. Orodes wanted to marry you, not enslave you. You loved each other, you and he."

She shook her head violently, her blue eyes wide. "I loved him, that's true. But he always wanted more, especially since we were set free. I was to belong only to him, body and soul, forever! Until it felt like...like it used to be at the Villa. He was so good to me, at first. At times, when the old master was still alive. That's when he cared about me, and I felt safe when he was around me. Orodes was the chief guard in the Villa, he could come and go as he pleased, do whatever he wanted to. He always came for me at night, after the last guest had left, and took me to his chamber. I hardly got to sleep and lived in constant fear that the master might notice something. But he never did. He trusted Orodes, while in me he only saw—" She sniffled again. "I was nothing, just a commodity to him. When I met the master in the house, he didn't even see me."

"And after that? When you were released?" I asked. "You didn't have to agree to marry Orodes then if you didn't really want to."

Suavis was silent, then she looked first at me and then at Layla—who did not return her gaze.

I, however, understood all at once. "You were afraid of him?" I asked.

Suavis nodded, barely noticeable. "He murdered all those people, didn't he? I resisted believing it for so long, telling myself that he was a good man who would never do such a thing. But when the lupanarius died, I couldn't stand it any longer. That's why I decided to escape. Last night."

I was speechless in the face of what Suavis was saying—and Marcellus didn't seem to fare any better. His mouth was open, and he looked over at me with a questioning look. "You were going to run away?" he repeated incredulously. "Alone, in the middle of the night? Are you tired of life, girl? How far do you think you would have gotten?"

Suavis shrugged her delicate shoulders. "I don't know. Anything was better than...than setting out for Parthia with Orodes. I would rather die than spend the rest of my life—" She broke off, swallowing, but her eyes remained dry now.

There was a point where no more tears came, I knew that all too well. And Suavis had now reached it. Her eyes were just empty. All the brightness, the liveliness that was usually in them, was now gone.

"He would have killed me last night," she said tonelessly and as matter-of-factly as if she were just relaying some old story, "if you hadn't come to my rescue, Thanar. I see that now. I heard your footsteps, was about to call for help...then Orodes let go of me, pushed me into the water, and fled back to the house."

"You should have confided in me," I said. "I would have dealt with this villain already!"

How sure this scoundrel had been of himself, with what impudence he had returned to his bed! He had pretended to be asleep and probably had not feared for a moment that Suavis might betray him.

I shook my head but had to admit to myself in silence that the girl had probably assessed the true balance of power more realistically than I had. I would never have stood a chance against the Parthian in a man-to-man fight.

"And the lupanarius?" I heard Marcellus ask. "Your Parthian killed him too, then? But what on earth drove him to this murder?"

Suavis was silent, slumping even further in her chair. "Not just the lupanarius," she said, so quietly that I could hardly hear her.

Marcellus looked at her uncomprehendingly. But I understood all at once. "All the men before, the Primus Pilus, Rufus, Belius—it was Orodes who killed them, wasn't it?" I said. "And he also sought my life with a well-aimed arrow."

"Nonsense," interjected the Tribune. "Philippos and Juba were the ones who committed these atrocities. And they judged themselves for their deeds. They—" He broke off.

His dark eyes came out of their sockets as he suddenly realized. When the truth revealed itself to him, as it had just revealed itself to me.

"They didn't judge themselves at all?" he said slowly, as if stunned. "Tell me that's not true!"

But Suavis said nothing. She just sat there and stared down at her hands. Only when Marcellus grabbed her chin rather roughly with his hand and lifted it did she nod. "Orodes killed them all. Philippos and Juba, too. I didn't know it! I only suspected it after the lupanarius died. When he ordered me to lie for him. I had to say that we had been together, the whole evening. I knew it then, even though I still didn't—"

She slapped her hands in front of her face. "I didn't want to believe it!" she moaned, "it was too terrible! And yet I loved him in spite of everything!"

"But why, by Jupiter?" Marcellus cried incredulously. "What drove him to these mad deeds? What had all these men done to him?"

As far as that was concerned, I was as clueless as Marcellus. No human could have a reason to kill Belius. Or me. I was simply sure of that.

I saw that Suavis was trembling all over. But she was brave enough to reveal the terrible truth to us. "He killed them because of me," she whispered. "Tonight, he told me everything. Now that my hour had also come. When he decided that I should be his last victim. Oh, why didn't I understand? After he almost killed me last night by the river, I should have known that he would not spare my life. That I would never be able to escape him. But the idea that he might poison me—"

"The men," Marcellus interrupted her. "Why did he murder them? What drove him to it?"

Suavis swallowed. Then she said, "He wanted to avenge me. He swore to kill every man who ever harmed me. *Every single one who ever violated me*. Those were his words."

"Violated you?"

"Rented me, in the Villa of Lycortas. Orodes swore deadly vengeance on each of them."

"And you named these men to him," Marcellus said.

"No!" cried Suavis, startled. "He knew who took me and when in the Villa, didn't he? He watched over the house, after all. But I—" Again, she put her hands to her face and fell silent.

Marcellus could no longer hold on to himself. He behaved as if he were interrogating one of his legionaries, let his fist thunder on the table, and uttered a curse.

"Tribune," I said, "may I ask the questions? You frighten her."

Marcellus made an unwilling hand gesture. "You have harbored a murderer under your roof, Thanar," he cried. "And I myself thought him a good man! I fool! We fools! How blind we have been!"

I turned to Suavis and addressed her in a gentle voice, "What were you going to say? You can speak freely, no one is accusing you of anything."

Suavis tried something that was probably meant to be a grateful smile. She failed. "I...have complained occasionally," she whispered, "to Orodes. When the old master was particularly cruel again, or one of the guests...but we all did! If we talked about it among ourselves, shared our grief, then it was easier to bear. I couldn't have known that Orodes would kill all those men because of it! You have to believe me!"

"It's all right," I said, "of course we believe you. And I understand the fear Orodes must have instilled in you."

Suavis continued, "Earlier, when we were eating in my room, he revealed to me all his deeds. He boasted about all he had done for me. What immeasurable proof of his love he has given me. He called me an ungrateful woman because I did not appreciate it. I should have been eternally grateful to him for setting me free. For loving and protecting me. He scolded me for thinking, in all seriousness, that I could run away from him."

"He revealed everything to you because he believed he had already sealed your fate," said Marcellus, who seemed to have regained some control of himself. "With the poison."

Suavis nodded, barely noticeable. "Yes...I can see that now."

"Tell us everything, all the way from the beginning," I said. "Every word, every deed that Orodes confessed to you."

XXXVIII

"Everyone in the Villa suffered from the old man's cruelty—even Philippos, his own son," Suavis began. "But no one found the courage to rebel against him. We all feared becoming the next victim for his bear arena. Orodes must have harbored a plan to rid us of the tyrant for some time, but he would not lay down his own life to do so. But then, when Lycortas found out that my mother, his body slave, was cheating on him with his own son, and he threatened to give her to the legion as a camp whore—"

"That's when Orodes saw the opportunity," I completed the sentence for Suavis.

She nodded. She seemed calm and in control now, as if she were just telling a story that had happened to a stranger. "Orodes suggested to Philippos that he throw his father to his own beast and then dump the dead body on the forest path—to make it look like an accident. And Juba was to be a witness to make it believable, for the old master never left the house alone. So the three of them conspired. Philippos vowed to release all the slaves as soon as he would receive his father's inheritance, and Orodes did not hesitate long. He did not tell me how exactly he went about it. I think he administered a sleeping potion to the old master, dragged him into the arena, and let the beast loose on him."

"A truly infamous plan," said Marcellus, "though one must admire its cunning. But Philippos broke his word as soon as he got rid of the hated father, didn't he?"

Suavis sucked in an audible breath. "He did. He had promised Orodes to release all of us, but now he suddenly said he couldn't do it right away and was only giving freedom to Juba. He claimed that the father had died practically destitute and that he had to find a way to earn his own living before giving up the Villa. Of course, Orodes didn't believe him."

"And yet Philippos spoke the truth," I said. "His father's money chest was almost empty; I saw it myself. His cruel arena games must have cost him his fortune."

Suavis closed her eyes. She opened them again, but still her gaze was cold and empty.

Marcellus took the floor. "Orodes thought that the new master had broken his word—that's why he also killed Philippos. Again, in such a sly way that no suspicion fell on himself. He made it look like suicide, but then something must have gone wrong? Did Juba not want to keep quiet any longer, or why did he have to die as well?"

Suavis nodded. "Juba said it would be wrong to kill the young master. He thought him a good man, and he himself, after all, had already gained his freedom. So Orodes poisoned him that very evening."

"Under the eyes of my soldiers," said Marcellus. "What impudence!"

"He used atropa, the women's beauty poison. It was freely available in the house."

"And he didn't tell you about any of this back then?" I asked.

"No, sir!" affirmed Suavis. "I believed what we were all told. First that the old master had fallen victim to a beast in the forest, and then later that Philippos and Juba were behind it all. Never would I have dreamed that Orodes was a murderer!"

"And it was not enough for him to kill the pater familias—twice in a row?" Marcellus said. "All the other murders, Falco, Rufus, Belius, the lupanarius—I just can't wrap my head around that. Why did those men have to die? Just because they had lain with you? That's madness! What was Orodes up to? Taking the lives of dozens of men all over Vindobona just because they wanted to have a little fun? "

Suavis gave him a look I couldn't interpret. "Well, it wasn't fun for me, believe me, Tribune," she said coldly.

Marcellus puckered his face. "Yes, all right. I didn't mean it that way!"

"Orodes wanted to avenge me," Suavis repeated. "Every man who ever violated me, who ever harmed me, had to die. At least, that was his plan—until he caught me on the run."

"...and finally realized you didn't want to be his wife," Marcellus said.

"Yes, Tribune. I guess that's how it was. This morning he announced to me that we would leave immediately for his home. Where I would be all his. And when I dared to contradict him, when I said I would rather stay here in Vindobona, with my friends—"

"That's when he decided you had to die, too," Marcellus said. "If he couldn't have you all to himself, neither could anyone else. Something like that, probably."

"He could have me, after all. He already had me—but he just wanted more and more. He called me an ungrateful woman and that I wasn't worthy of his love...I think that's why he wanted to kill me in the end."

"Well, he didn't succeed," Marcellus said. "The gods have watched over you and judged him."

"But Rufus, the Cattle Prince—he wasn't a regular at the Villa at all," I interjected. "He had his girls at home and was supposedly pursuing some dark inclinations on the grave road—at least that's what I heard." I glanced over at Layla out of the corner of my eye, but she was still sitting there transfixed, staring at Suavis.

Suavis swallowed hard a few times. "Rufus only took me once, but that—" She faltered.

Then she continued in a toneless voice, "Rufus was the first man Lycortas rented me to. It was a while ago, I was ten or eleven years old at the time. Ordinary sex didn't interest Rufus, he was looking for something special. That's how he put it when he was lying with me then. He said he had paid a fortune for my virginity and that he would do anything to make that night memorable for the rest of my life. Which he succeeded in doing."

With a jerky movement, she wiped a strand of hair from her forehead. "I can't remember everything, I tried to forget—yet that night still haunts me in my darkest dreams. When Rufus left me at dawn, all I wanted to do was die."

Marcellus lowered his head wordlessly, and it also took me a while to regain my speech. "Why did Orodes want to pin his deeds on me, of all people?" I then asked. "I never even touched you!"

Suavis looked at me. Her eyes were still blank. "You couldn't have known, sir, but in a way you did worse to me than all those other men."

"What?" I cried angrily. "What do you mean?"

"You took from me the most precious I ever had—and

Orodes saw how much I suffered. So, I guess he chose you as the one to be executed in his place—for his murder of the Roman officer. And when that didn't work, he ambushed you with his bow."

"And finally threw you to the bear," Marcellus added. "After he had also tried to frame you for the murder of Belius."

"I don't understand," I persisted. "What am I supposed to have taken from you, Suavis? Your most precious?"

"Layla," Suavis said, looking tenderly at my slave. "She was the only mother I ever had. No, she was more than that. Mother, sister, friend. All in one person. In the few months she lived with us, she took care of me like no one ever had before. She cared for me, comforted me, was always there for me. All of a sudden, life in the Villa was bearable—and then you came and bought her. I thought I would never see her again."

I fell silent. How could I have known that? Of course, I had not asked Layla if she wanted to leave the Villa—who would think of such an idea when buying a slave? No, I was not to blame for Suavis' suffering, according to any law of gods or men. And yet, at that moment, I felt shameful.

"Orodes also said you made a good culprit," Suavis continued. "He called you an outsider, a freak, a *barbarian who doesn't want to be one*. He thought the Romans would execute you on the spot for the death of the Primus Pilus. That was the only one of his deeds that he called difficult. To murder a Roman officer, it would take a particularly bold man! He boasted about that—at the same time he must have given him some kind of sleeping potion. Falco was with me the night he died, and I remember that he complained of great fatigue. After he took me, he just fell asleep. I left him in the guest room. All Orodes had to do was drag him out of the house. I guess he then took him across the river to your harbor, and there he struck him in the chest with the axe."

"Truly not a heroic deed," Marcellus said. "Only a coward kills an enemy in his sleep!"

I agreed with the Tribune, then gave in to my own thoughts. What a fool I had been! I had harbored a nefarious murderer under my roof and even considered him a good man. It should have been obvious at the latest after the death of the lupanarius! Among two young women, almost still children, and a Parthian warrior, who were staying as guests in my house—how difficult had it been to find the culprit? How could I ever forgive myself for this blindness? I had nothing left but making a generous sacrifice to the gods for at least sparing Suavis' life and bringing the murderer to justice.

XXXIX

After all the horrors Suavis had revealed to us, we lay silent and motionless around the table. Each of us was probably pursuing his own dark thoughts, trying in his own way to come to terms with all the horrible things we had learned. Suavis was staring into nowhere with an expressionless look.

"We should go to bed, try to get some sleep," I began, but at that moment Layla sat up and straightened her shoulders. Throughout Suavis' report she had remained so silent and motionless that I had almost forgotten her presence.

Now, however, she rose and said, "I'm going to get us some honey wine. I think it will do us good after all we have just heard." She did not wait for an answer but prepared to leave the room.

I did not hold her back. A nightcap was a good idea. Our cups had long been empty, but I had instructed the servants not to disturb us while we listened to Suavis' revelations, and so we had not been entertained.

Layla stayed away so long that I was about to get up to check on her. Just at that moment, however, she returned— an amphora of honey wine in one hand, a small dark glass bottle in the other.

She poured some of the honey wine first to the Tribune, then to me, after which she wordlessly tipped the contents of the small flask into Suavis' cup and poured honey wine on it as well.

Suavis jerked back, startled. "What is it?" she asked in a toneless voice, eyeing Layla with a most peculiar look.

"Just a strengthening potion, my dear. You are white as snow."

Suavis did not touch the cup.

Layla let out a laugh. "Don't you trust me? Drink—it will do you good!" And when Suavis still remained motionless, she added, "The murderer who sought your life is dead, isn't he? So why so anxious? What have you to fear from me?"

"Nothing," said Suavis, "and if you wanted to poison me, you certainly wouldn't do it here in front of everyone!" She smiled with effort, then put the cup to her lips and drank with thirsty gulps.

"That's it," Layla said. Her voice sounded so strange, even deeper than usual, but now there was none of the warmth in it that usually made my heart beat faster. And her features were so hard that she seemed years older.

"What I don't understand, Suavis," she began when the latter had set down the cup, "is why didn't you at least confide in Thanar last night? After Orodes attacked you on the riverbank, as you say. I mean, what did you have to lose then? And today, you had dinner with him as if nothing had happened, and you still wanted him to have the fattier piece of meat? Can you explain that to me?"

Suavis said nothing in reply, just silently gazed at Layla out of her vacant eyes.

"The poor thing was scared to death!" interjected Marcellus. "One doesn't act rationally under such pressure. It's all too understandable." The Tribune was apparently as puzzled by Layla's behavior as I was. What had gotten into my Nubian, who usually behaved so lovingly and compassionately?

Was it really necessary to torture Suavis with these strange questions now? The girl finally needed rest—and a good night's sleep. All of our curiosity about further details could truly wait until tomorrow.

"Of course," Layla said, smiling thinly and falling silent. But immediately she began again, "I wonder who the second figure in the arena who watched the bear attack Thanar was? If we now assume that the former was Orodes." She tilted her head and looked Suavis straight in the eye.

Suavis did not reply to this either. Surely, Layla's continuing curiosity was as incomprehensible to her as it was to Marcellus and me.

"What I also don't understand," Layla continued unperturbed, "is the murder of Rufus, the Cattle Prince. Orodes was a masterful archer, as he proved in the attack on Thanar. And with Rufus, who was not even on horseback, it took him five arrows to strike the man down?" Again, she looked questioningly at Suavis, but again she received no answer.

Suavis looked like she was going to fall asleep at any moment, right there at the table. Her eyelids fluttered, and she had trouble keeping her head upright.

"Besides, it seems rather strange to me that the lupanarius should have followed a fearsome Parthian into the cellar," Layla said. "On the other hand, if a seductive, young girl had invited him to a secret tryst, his behavior would have been only natural. After all, he was so hungry for sensual pleasures, wasn't he, Suavis?"

"Looked like it," said the latter, now visibly irritated. "You're the one he wanted, anyway."

Layla straightened her shoulders and leaned forward. As she did so, she didn't take her eyes off Suavis. "Besides, I could have sworn it wasn't Orodes I saw sneaking out of the house last night. The figure I followed was much smaller and more delicate. And when I approached her and confronted her about what was driving her so stealthily out of the house at night, she came at me with a knife. She was well armed, the figure. Undoubtedly, she wanted to make her way to Vindobona and lie in wait for her next victim there. The choice was still great, after all, even if so many of the hated men had already met their deaths."

"Layla, what's the matter with you?" Marcellus interrupted her, "what are you talking about?"

"You too were at the river last night?" I exclaimed. "What on earth were you doing there? And why didn't you tell me?"

"What I was doing there, master? I will tell you. I crept into the guest quarters at night because I was afraid the murderer might strike again. I lay in wait because I could not believe what Orodes had revealed to me that afternoon. I wanted to see if someone would sneak out of the house at night to get their next victim in Vindobona—and who it would be. I wanted to make the murderer give up, I wanted to prevent yet another former guest of the Villa from meeting his death. I was able to catch the assassin on the riverbank, but she did not think of giving up. Instead, she came at me with a sax she had concealed in her robe. A fight broke out between us, I managed to knock the knife out of her hand, and when she tried to push me into the water, she fell herself. The water is only shallow near the shore, and the current weak. I knew she wouldn't drown."

Layla paused, looked over at me for a moment, then turned back to Suavis: "It wasn't a powerful Parthian I was wrestling with, because I wouldn't have had the slightest chance against him. Besides, the hood slipped off the figure's head, and there I saw—well, you know all too well what I saw, Suavis. You! That's why Orodes decided this morning to take you away from here, as quickly as possible. It was I who forced him to do it. That, or I would no longer be silent. No longer would I watch as one man after another was executed. In Orodes' homeland, you would finally give up killing, he was sure of it. You would leave your hatred behind, forget all the men who had seen in you nothing but an object of their desire. Who had fun with you, while you nurtured a deadly hatred for them in your breast."

Suavis wanted to spring to her feet but staggered and sank back onto her sofa. "What are you talking about!" she cried, "Are you completely insane?" Her head tilted to one side, as if her delicate body was now demanding much-needed sleep by any means necessary.

"Are you feeling tired, Suavis?" Layla asked in a cold voice.

"Yes, I—oh, you cursed witch, what did you put in my cup?"

"The same thing you put in Orodes' food. Atropa. Your lover was your last victim, Suavis. I warned him, but he wouldn't listen to me. He believed till the end that you loved him. That you would never hurt *him*. How blind he was. How blind we all were!"

Suavis jerked her head up, staring first at me, then at Marcellus. "Help me!" she cried, "Layla has lost her mind. She's lying—oh, by the gods, she must be Orodes' accomplice! It was he who tried to kill me! And now she wants to complete his work!"

Marcellus sat there paralyzed, and I didn't fare any better.

Suavis tried to get to her feet on her own. She had to prop herself up on the back of the sofa, but this time she managed.

"Somebody help me!" she cried again. "Layla put poison in my cup! I'm going to die!"

"Yes, you will," Layla said unapologetically. "And no one can help you, you know that all too well. There is no salvation against the atropa poison."

"You viper," Suavis hissed. She spat in Layla's face, suddenly seeming to shake all daze, lunged at her, and tried to claw out her eyes.

XL

That was enough to rouse me and Marcellus at last. Almost simultaneously, we jumped up, grabbed Suavis, and yanked her away from Layla.

She staggered and fell to the ground. "You murderer!" she screamed at the top of her lungs. On all fours, she crawled into the corner of the room and settled there, moaning.

She pressed her fists against her temples and shook herself, probably trying to clear her head again. "Somebody help me!" she howled, "I'm innocent!"

Layla's fingers moved to her own face. Blood oozed from a scratch, but she didn't seem to notice. "No one can help you anymore, Suavis," she said, "It's over. Over at last! All this senseless killing, the whims of a vicious, stupid child, nothing more!"

At these words, a change occurred in Suavis. She pulled herself up, even if she had to lean on the wall behind her, straightened her shoulders, and jutted her chin out. Like a fury, she stared at us from her blue eyes, which no longer reminded me of the summer sky. Rather, they made me think of a glacier, frozen for all eternity.

"A stupid child?" she repeated. Her voice was now just a hiss. "*A stupid child*?! I was the only one in the whole cursed Villa who possessed wit. And courage! If it hadn't been for me, everyone there would still be terrorized by the old monster! You think Orodes was so brave and clever? An oh-so-great warrior? You have no idea!"

She wanted to lunge at Layla again, but her legs wouldn't support her. She almost fell down when she took her hands off the supporting wall. So, she remained where she was and limited herself to shooting Layla a look full of deadly hatred.

It was as if a complete stranger suddenly stood before me. She had absolutely nothing in common with the sweet, somewhat shy Suavis I had thought I knew.

"It was me," she exclaimed proudly. "Yes, it was me! I had to instigate Orodes first, the oh-so-great fighter. He did not revolt. He submitted to his fate just like all the other sheep. He let himself be oppressed, although he had it better than most of us. At least he wasn't violated night after night by some disgusting, old lecher. I alone had to devise the plan to murder the old man and suggest it to Philippos. Without me, he would have just watched the woman he supposedly loved die as a camp whore. That's how they are, the oh so brave and witty men! They think they rule the world and that they can just take us women as they please. We are just a toy for them, to satisfy their lusts—but not me! I fought back! And I would do it again! Oh, I would have avenged every woman in Vindobona who had been made a whore! Every girl whose body and soul those abominations destroyed. Holy revenge, not only for me, but for all of us!"

I just couldn't wrap my head around what I was hearing. But Suavis did not give me time to think. She was now talking like a woman possessed, boasting about her cunning, her fearlessness, how she had incited both Orodes and Philippos to kill Lycortas. How she had whispered the idea of the bear attack to them. In the face of death, she seemed to want only one thing: glory and recognition for her deeds.

"How cowardly Orodes and Philippos were!" she cried again, her mouth twisting in disgust. "And Juba, too! How they feared death on the cross if the plan should fail. Or the wild beasts that would tear us apart in the sands of the arena. They did not see that our life was worse than any arena. For there at least it's quick, the beasts tear you to pieces, and then it's over. While we pleasure slaves are thrown to the wild beasts all our lives. Every night anew! How they trembled, all three equally, these so-called men. They feared the wrath of the gods would strike them if they so much as touched a hair of the pater familias. The old tyrant had power over them as if he were Jupiter himself! But no lightning flashed from the sky to strike us down after the deed was done. I freed the inhabitants of the Villa, all of us, from the tyrant! And it was I who made Orodes avenge me. At first, that is, just until I could do it myself! I let myself be instructed by him, in martial arts. At least he was good for that. He had desired me for a long time, always panting after me— until I gave him what he wanted. At my price!"

"Then *you* put him up to murdering all those men?" I muttered. I felt as if I heard my own voice from far away.

"Orodes killed the old tyrant," Suavis replied. "And the Primus Pilus. Falco, that sadistic pig. I poured poppy juice into his cup, and then Orodes finished him off! But I wanted more, I wanted revenge by my own hand. I wanted to feel the power, I wanted to see them die, that scum, at my own feet! Oh, how Rufus writhed, in agony, begging for his life! How I enjoyed letting him bleed to death, in the brush between the graves. Just as he had made me bleed, that night he threw himself on me. I was eleven, by all the gods, and he took me so hard I couldn't even walk for days after!"

She struggled for breath. Once again, fatigue seemed to overtake her, but she held herself upright. Her ice-blue eyes sparkled at us as if she wanted to kill us with her gaze. She muttered a vile curse.

"Then it was also you yourself who killed Belius?" I cried. "And the lupanarius? Only because they had lain with you?"

"Only? *Only?*" Suavis snapped at me. "Do you have any idea what it's like to be violated every night? Sometimes multiple times? By those vile guys who throw themselves upon you like wild animals? Can you even imagine how that feels? And when the paying guests are finally done with you, then comes another one like Juba, who thinks he is the god among the slaves, and you have to do his bidding as well. Oh, they deserved to die! Every single one of them. Even Orodes, who supposedly loved me so much, wanted nothing but my body. He called it marriage, but what would it have been but new slavery? The gods were on my side, and they still are! I curse you all!"

"And Philippos? Juba? Why did they have to die?" Marcellus thundered.

Suavis gave him a contemptuous look. "Philippos had vowed to release us all, after the death of the hated father. And what did he do? Acted like the new master. Continued to treat us like cattle."

"You were the second figure on the gallery of the bear arena, weren't you?" I interjected. "You pretended to help me escape that night, but in truth, Orodes was already lying in wait for me in the garden. You two dragged me into the arena, and you were going to watch the bear tear me to pieces."

"What a vile, bloodthirsty witch," Marcellus cried in disgust.

"And then you would have framed Philippos for the murder of me, too," I continued. The words came out of my mouth, and yet I still couldn't believe them myself. "The arrival of the Roman soldiers only forced you to put the plan into action immediately. You snuck out of the arena, you and Orodes, while we were fighting the bear. Orodes murdered Philippos, and you forged the suicide note meanwhile, I suppose?"

I received no reply, only a proud, hateful look.

"And Juba?" asked Marcellus.

Suavis furrowed her brow. "He confronted us after Philippos had died. Said we had gone too far. That he wanted to reveal the truth to the legionaries."

"So you poisoned him that same night," I said.

Suavis suddenly stumbled, gasping for breath with a quivering chest. She turned away from me and toward Layla. "I would have thought that you at least would stand by me," she hissed at my slave. "I loved you, you viper! You could have let me escape last night. You would never have seen me again, you and your oh so dear master—and the other one, your Roman." She made the word *Roman* sound as if it meant leprosy or plague. "And Chloe could have finally nabbed her adored Orodes. Oh, she would have made a perfect little marital slave, I'm sure!"

Suavis leaned against the wall, breathing heavily, and it seemed as if all the life spirits were now draining out of her. She had spent the last of her strength with her proud hate speech, but with that she seemed satisfied.

Layla wiped what looked like a tear from the corner of her eye. "I think we can let Suavis sleep now," she said. Her voice was no longer cold, but heavy with suppressed emotion.

"Sleep?" repeated Suavis, as if in a trance.

Layla nodded. "I'm not a murderer. I merely emptied a strong dose of poppy juice into your cup to make you believe it. I hoped you would want to boast of your deeds in the face of death. Because I couldn't prove anything to you. You're the best liar I've ever met, I'll give you that much. You fooled us all."

Suavis made one last attempt to pounce on Layla. But the sleeping draught was now too far advanced in its effect. She staggered a step, but before she could even get near Layla, Marcellus was with her and grabbed her by the arm. He yanked her away from Layla, pushing her down onto one of the couches, where she remained sitting motionless. "Viper," I heard her whisper, then she fell silent.

Somewhere in the room, someone moaned. It took me a long moment to realize that it was myself.

Layla looked questioningly at Marcellus. "What will happen to her now, Tribune?"

Marcellus began to walk up and down the room. As he did so, he clasped his hands behind his back as if he were an old man. "She will be tried—and undoubtedly sentenced to death. Since we're not exactly spoiled with public spectacles in Vindobona, it will probably come down to an execution in the amphitheater. They will have Suavis torn apart by wild animals in the arena, to the amusement of the entire population. If she is lucky, she will only be violated by a handful of guards in the few days or weeks she spends in the dungeon until then. Men who have never laid eyes on such a beauty in their entire lives. They will know how to make good use of the time Suavis belongs to them. And the citizens of Vindobona will be gossiping about the murders for weeks after the execution. Suavis' misdeeds will be the talk of the town, and many a man will wonder if he can really trust his slaves. Whether he doesn't give them too many liberties or privileges, whether he does make them work hard enough, so they don't have time for any stupid ideas. Whether they might not see in Suavis an example to rebel themselves."

Marcellus stopped. He looked down at Suavis, who could barely keep her eyes open. "That's how it will happen," he continued, and his voice sounded changed all at once. "Unless, at the last moment, Suavis succeeds in taking advantage of a brief inattention on the part of her guards to seize her poison flask—and spare herself and the slaves of Vindobona all this."

While the words of the Tribune were still making their way into my head, my eyes searched for the small glass vial that I had placed on the table earlier. It was still half filled with the atropa poison. I bent down, reached for it, and, with a swift movement of my hand, pushed it in front of Suavis.

She blinked under heavy eyelids, looked over at Layla once more, then her hand shot forward with a speed I wouldn't have thought her capable of in her condition. Her fingers enclosed around the bottle, and she pulled it towards her and unplugged it. Then she drank until there was nothing left.

She looked at us as if she wanted to say something else, but then her head sank to her chest, and she fell asleep. For the last time in her life.

"Thank you," Layla whispered.

XLI

"Thank you for showing mercy," Layla repeated, now in a slightly stronger voice.

"Suavis probably didn't get to experience much grace in her life," I replied.

"But she herself has shown no mercy either," Marcellus said. He shook his head. "She was blessed with such beauty, yet her heart was full of hatred."

"Her beauty never brought her anything but agony," Layla said. She walked over and stroked Suavis' silky blond hair, staring down with moist eyes at the delicate body, now completely limp.

I stepped behind Layla, clasping her shoulders. "Why didn't you tell me? That you suspected her?"

Layla turned around and looked me in the eye. "I wasn't sure myself after all, master. And I couldn't prove anything. She was just smarter than me. She was playing us all, casting suspicion on everyone but herself."

She broke off, lowering her head. "I didn't miss your gazes, master. You suspected even me, who was always loyal to you."

"That's not true, dear!" I cried, but in my heart I had to admit to myself that Layla was right. I pressed her against me. Kissed her forehead.

"I just couldn't believe it, didn't want to believe it," she continued. "That sweet little Suavis was capable of such acts, had such hatred in her. She was just a child after all." Layla escaped my arms and shook her head.

"What made you suspect her?" asked Marcellus.

Layla turned to the Tribune. Her eyes sought his and took on a tender expression when they found them. "I felt no differently than Thanar after the deaths of Philippos and Juba," she said. "It just didn't make sense that those two should have committed all those murders. Killing Lycortas, yes—I believed that immediately, but Falco, Rufus, Belius, the attacks on my master? Philippos had no reason to do that. And Thanar pointed out to me that a whole lot of questions remained unanswered." She looked over at me with the same tenderness with which she had just looked at Marcellus.

My heart reacted promptly, did a flip, but Layla already went on: "Of course that was nothing more than a vague suspicion—until the murdering started again. The lupanarius. I explained to you my reasons for thinking that a woman had done the deed. How she could stab him in the back with a hug. And the lupanarius would have followed a woman only too willingly into the cellar. After all, he desired nothing more than an erotic tryst."

Both Marcellus and I remained silent, ashamed. We had both laughed when Layla had explained this theory to us after Blandus' murder.

"And then the testimonies of your guests, master," she continued. "The night the lupanarius died. One of them had to be the murderer, that much was clear to me. But that meant that *two* of them were lying. For Chloe wanted to have been with Alva, and Suavis with Orodes. One of these couples was speaking the truth, only which one? I wondered why Alva would lie for Chloe or vice versa. The two didn't know each other closely, weren't friends as far as I knew. But Orodes and Suavis? She would lie for him and he for her. After all, they were lovers. And although I had actually assumed that a woman had killed the lupanarius, I now believed that Orodes must be the murderer. He was a clever and strong man. Perhaps he had found a way to lure Blandus into the cellar and kill him there. A pretext I couldn't even fathom. I just didn't want to believe that Suavis could be a nefarious murderer. Such a sweet, innocent girl. She spoke the truth, earlier; I was indeed like a mother to her, even though I'm not old enough to be. I loved her like my own child. She was so alive, so passionate, so smart."

"You should have let me in on your thoughts by then at the latest!" I said reproachfully. "After the death of the lupanarius."

"And cast suspicion where I wasn't sure myself? Possibly putting an innocent on the cross?" Layla shook her head. "These people had truly experienced enough injustice in their lives. But I decided to confront Orodes. I told him to his face that he had lied, that he and Suavis had not been indulging in the pleasures of Venus at the time the lupanarius was murdered. At first he denied everything, but then he broke down. He confided in me, said that everything had gotten out of hand, that Suavis was behind all the murders, and that he had helped her at first. But she had killed the lupanarius herself, and it didn't look like it was going to be her last murder. He loved Suavis more than anything, I believed him. But I wasn't sure if he wasn't lying and in truth was the murderer himself."

"So that's what you were arguing about, yesterday afternoon in the peristyle garden," I said.

Layla nodded. "Orodes promised me that there would be no more deaths. That he would stop Suavis. Oh, how I underestimated her. That very night she administered a sleeping potion to him and slipped out of the house. Fortunately, I had been keeping watch, outside the guest quarters. I just had to see if Orodes had lied and possibly wanted to commit the next murder himself that night. But it was Suavis who stole out of the house. I followed her and confronted her on the riverbank."

"That was irresponsible of you!" exclaimed Marcellus. "You should have woken Thanar!"

"He's right!" I agreed with him.

Layla puckered up her face. "Even then, I didn't have any certainty. Suavis could have all kinds of reasons for stealing out of the house. And then she told me that she wanted to flee from Orodes. That he was behind all the murders and ruled her like a slave. That she did not love him, but on the contrary was terribly afraid of him. She had allegedly stolen the knife she was carrying only for her safety during the escape. When I did not let her go, she wanted to push me into the water and thus escape me. But as we wrestled, she herself fell. At that point I didn't know what to do, I just quickly slipped back into the house through the cellar door. I knew that she would not drown near the shore."

"And you believed her story?" I asked. "The one about escaping from Orodes?"

"I didn't know who to believe anymore, master. After all the lies we had already heard in the matter? And Orodes as the culprit—that just seemed much more likely. A grown man, a warrior, full of hatred for his enemies who were destroying his life, his country. I could imagine him as a murderer, even though I had always thought of him as a good man, full of honor and character. I needed certainty, master! And finally, proof. But that seemed impossible. The very next morning—that is, today—I spoke to Orodes again. It was I who suggested that he return to his homeland, no, I forced him to do so. He and Suavis had to get out of the house, then the killing would finally stop, of that I was sure. Whoever of the two was actually guilty now. Orodes agreed at once, but then—" Layla's voice failed.

"Then Suavis proved to be smarter again," I said. "Not only did she poison Orodes, but she also effortlessly managed to make him look like the murderer. That ingenious story about the switched plates..." I shook my head. "I must confess, I did not doubt her words in any way."

"Neither did I," Marcellus grumbled, visibly indignant at having been thus fooled by a slave of pleasure. "In fact, she probably just sent Orodes to the kitchen again for the sake of the sauce, poisoned the food on his plate, and then—before she showed up crying at our dinner table—packed the poison bottle in his chest. What a snake."

"My hesitation cost Orodes his life," Layla said bitterly. "My doubts. I will never forgive myself for that."

"Don't talk nonsense," said Marcellus, "Suavis was the one who murdered him—and you successfully avenged him. That business about the poison cup you made her believe! How you provoked her to brag about her deeds in the face of death! That must have been the only way to get her to confess. Very clever of you."

A smile spread across the Tribune's handsome features. "You are simply amazing, *rosa mea*!" With an abrupt movement of his hand, he pulled Layla to him and embraced her.

I could not understand what I was seeing. Layla in the arms of the Tribune? And it didn't seem like he was holding her for the first time.

Marcellus caught my dismayed look. He burst out laughing. "By all the gods, Thanar, I can't wait any longer! Let me buy Layla off you before we all end up dropping dead! I love her, I just have to have her for myself. Name any price, I will pay it!"

I stood there as if struck by lightning.

Marcellus loved Layla?

The scales fell from my eyes. All the Tribune's visits to my house, the strange friendship he suddenly seemed to feel for me, the expensive guest gift—all of that had not the slightest thing to do with me! It was Layla he wanted. He had wanted to talk to me about that all along. How clueless I had been!

He looked at me expectantly, his youthful face reddened with passion. At the same time, he still held Layla tightly against him.

I didn't know what to say. All I knew was that it hurt immensely to see her in his arms. Layla did not tear herself away, did not protest loudly that she did not want to be sold. Nothing of the sort.

"I will sleep on your offer, Tribune," I said wanly. It felt as if I had just been handed the poisoned chalice as well.

XLII

Of course, I didn't even look for sleep that night. I wandered through my house, finally finding myself in front of the guest rooms, which now lay silent and empty. I had to think of the laughter, of the joy of life that had come here, with Chloe, Suavis, and Orodes.

What an illusion! For it was not life that had moved into my house, but death.

The door of the room Chloe had occupied was open, and when I entered to check on her, I found a letter addressed to me. Chloe seemed to have scribbled it in great haste—and in even greater excitement. Some of the letters were barely discernible in the wax of the writing tablet, others had dug in almost to the wooden backing.

Thanar, I thank you for your hospitality, I read. I wanted to tell you that among all the guests of the Villa, you were always the dearest to me. May the gods watch over you and grant you all the happiness in life.

The wax tablet slipped from my hands. I looked around the room. The few belongings Chloe had called her own were no longer there.

Chloe was gone, but where to? Her letter did not say a word about it. And also, in the following days I heard or saw nothing more of the beautiful Greek woman to whom I had once been so devoted. The man she had loved was no longer alive—had she gone into the woods to find her own death there? To be united at last with him who had not returned her love in life?

I was never to know.

Nevertheless, whenever I thought of Chloe later, I always imagined that she had not found death in a lonely and desperate way, but that she had simply gone abroad. That she had found a new home in another place, a more beautiful place. As well as new friends and a wonderful husband who gave her all his love.

I took the letter with me and left Chloe's room. I longed to go over to Layla, to embrace her as I had so often done when I couldn't find sleep.

But I did not. I had to think. I returned to my own chamber, stepped out onto the terrace, and looked across the river. The walls and towers of the legionary camp on the south bank loomed menacingly in the darkness. Not a sight I could bear tonight. I turned away, went back to my room, and lay down on the bed. Where I stared at the ceiling with sleepless eyes.

Part of me was waiting for Layla to come to my room, hoping against all odds that she would ask me not to sell her to the Tribune. Because she preferred to stay with me.

But she did not come.

Well, she hadn't explicitly asked me to leave her to Marcellus either, saying she preferred him to me. But I couldn't expect that from her. Layla was not like that, she never took a stand for her own advantage. Only for others did she ever raise her voice.

I owed my life to Layla, I had not the slightest doubt about that. How much I had been in the dark, all this time. I had thought myself to be like Oedipus, the riddle master, imagining that I could solve the murders. I had asked questions that seemed clever to me, had followed tracks like a hound dog—and had been fooled the whole time. By a pleasure girl who had hardly blossomed into a woman. An evil demon in the form of a seductive nymph. She had been trained in the highest art of Eros, but she had become a master of intrigue.

Suavis would not have rested until she had completed her bloody work—until every man who had ever lain with her paid for it with his life. And I was to pay for taking Layla, her mother, sister, and friend. I made a good culprit—*a barbarian who didn't want to be one.*

What an easy game she had had with me! I had believed her every word, all the lies—and while I gently patted her cheek and pitied her for her cruel fate, she would also have mixed poison into my cup at some point. Or rammed a knife into my back, as she had done with the lupanarius. And she would still have felt in the right.

Never before had I questioned my place in the world. Some people were born slaves, others kings. Some were granted joy in life, others nothing but agony and sorrow. It was the gods who assigned people their destiny. In all my travels, I had never come to a place where this was not true.

Suavis, however, had not wanted to submit to the way of the world.

When the morning dawned, I had made a decision. I went to the kitchen, had the cook prepare a tray with all the goodies Layla liked best, and then went to her room.

She was lying on the bed with her eyes open and sat up when I entered. I wonder if she had found sleep that night.

I put the tray down and sat with her.

"Thanar," she began, stroking my cheek with her hand, but then she didn't really know what to say either.

How beautiful she was, how full of life her night-black eyes, how gentle the curve of her lips. How could I ever hope to find happiness without her?

I swallowed. Then I announced to her what I had come to say before I weakened and changed my mind.

"I will not accept the Tribune's offer," I said. "I will not sell you to him. I am giving you freedom, Layla, and you can decide for yourself what you want to do. You shall be mistress of your own destiny, and may the gods grant you a long, happy life in freedom."

I couldn't help it, I had to pull her into my arms one last time. I kissed her with all the tenderness and longing that my heart felt for her.

"I am sure you are aware that a Roman nobleman cannot marry you," I said then, "but I believe that Marcellus loves you sincerely. I am sure he will give you a fine life as his concubine. First here in Vindobona, the few years he will be here, then wherever his political career may take him. And a great career surely awaits him, he's a good man."

I took a deep breath. Those were all the words I had thought to say. Now they were spoken, and Layla looked at me with one of her strange looks. One that I didn't even try to interpret.

My beloved black sphinx. "It is true," she finally said. "Marcellus is a good man. But I love you, too, Thanar."

My heart leapt.

"Like a father. In all my life, no one has ever been as good to me as you."

Like a father? The leap of my heart went nowhere, became a fall, into an abyss without a bottom. I was just old enough to be Layla's father—but I had never looked at her other than through the eyes of a lover.

"I thank you from the bottom of my heart for releasing me," I heard her say. Her warm, dark voice seemed to come from very far away, penetrating my ear as if through a thick fog. "But I have one more request of you."

"What is it?" I managed to say.

"May I remain part of your familia, as is customary for freed slaves? I can make myself useful in whatever way you wish. If you allow it, I could assist you in your business dealings. Travel with you. I have always dreamed of this." Her black eyes shone.

"What?" it escaped me. "And Marcellus?"

"He is dear to me. But I don't want to live under his roof, where he can dispose of me as he pleases. I never want to lose the freedom you give me."

For a moment, I felt as if Suavis had spoken those words. They were like an eerie echo. Quickly, I shook off the thought. "You will be welcome in my house as long as I live," I said to Layla.

Dramatis personae

Thanar: Germanic merchant
Layla: Thanar's favorite slave, Nubian

Titus Granius Marcellus: Tribune of the Roman Legion
Lucius Pompeius Falco: Primus Pilus of the Roman Legion

Septimus Moltinus Belius: Thanar's friend, brickmaker

Lycortas: the old Greek, founder of the Villa
Philippos: the young Greek, Lycortas' son
Orodes: chief guardian of the villa, Parthian
Juba: Lycortas' body servant, African
Alva: body slave of Lycortas, Northern Germanic
Suavis: pleasure slave in the villa, daughter of Alva
Chloe: pleasure slave in the villa, Greek

Bricius Iodocus Rufus: the Cattle Prince, large landowner

Servius Asinius Blandus: the lupanarius, brothel operator

Enjoyed the book?

Please consider leaving a star rating or a short review on Amazon. Thank you!

More from Thanar and Layla:

DEATH OF A PREACHER MAN
Murder in Antiquity, Book 2

A new calamity is brewing in the Roman provincial city of Vindobona. In the midst of a devastating snowstorm, the followers of two outlawed cults—Druids and Christians—gather in the house of the Germanic merchant Thanar. They hope for hospitality and a safe roof over their heads. But it is death that awaits them.
Have the gods themselves conspired against the inhabitants of Vindobona? Or is there a demon in human form hiding among Thanar's guests, an insidious murderer who seems to kill indiscriminately?

More from Alex Wagner:

If you enjoyed *Murder at the Limes*, why not try my contemporary mystery series too: *Penny Küfer Investigates* – cozy crime novels full of old-world charm.

About the author

Alex Wagner lives with her husband and 'partner in crime' near Vienna, Austria. From her writing chair she has a view of an old, ruined castle, which helps her to dream up the most devious murder plots.

Alex writes historical as well as contemporary murder mysteries, always trying to give you sleepless nights. ;)

You can learn more about her and her books on the internet and on Facebook:

www.alexwagner.at
www.facebook.com/AlexWagnerMysteryWriter

Made in the USA
Las Vegas, NV
01 March 2024